A Tail of Woah:

A Reverse Harem Tail

THE FOX AND THE HOUNDS

Book 1

Jacquelyn Faye

A TAIL OF WOAH
A Reverse Harem Tail

Fox and the Hounds, book 1

All Rights Reserved
Copyright © 2019 by Jacquelyn Faye
Cover Design © 2019 by Carol Marques

ISBN: 978-1-945893-07-0

First Untold Publication June 2019

Published by Untold Press LLC
114 NE Estia Lane
Port St Lucie, FL 34983
www.untoldpress.com

PRODUCED IN THE UNITED STATES OF AMERICA

10 9 8 7 6 5 4 3 2 1

Dedication

This book is dedicated to Dick Sweeney

American businessman and co-founder of the K-Cup single coffee brewing system.

Yes. I just dedicated this book to the man who invented the Keurig. You got a problem with that?

THE MAN IS A GENIUS

Without him, none of my books would EVER have been published. Or written. Probably even thought of. Hell, I'd probably still be in bed if it wasn't for him.

Glossary

Kaede: (KAI-uh-de) Maple. Just putting this in here because everybody keeps calling her Kaydee and wanted to know how to say her name.

Kitsune: (Kit-SOO-nay) Japanese fox spirit. Tails range from one to nine. It is also the Japanese word for fox.

Nogitsune: (No-git-SOO-nay) Japanese fox spirit related to Kitsune. Field fox.

Kami: (KA-mee) God.

Sake: (SAH-kay) Rice Wine.

Ojo: (OH-jo) Princess.

Inari-kami: (e-NAR-e) Japanese god of agriculture, rice, harvest, and blacksmiths.

Inari fox: Celestial messengers of the Inari-kami. Usually depicted as ghostly white foxes surrounded by foxfire.

Yokai: (yo-KAI) Spirits and sometimes demons. Ghosts may also fall under this term.

Hai: (HI) Yes.

Tabi: (TAH-bee) Traditional socks worn with sandals. Seam between big toe and remaining toes.

Yukata: (YOU-kuh-tuh) Traditionally worn outfit, not as ornate as a kimono.

Tawagato: (tah-wah-GAH-to) Shit.

Engawa: (en-GAH-wa) Porch usually constructed of wood that runs length of house.

Arigato: (ah-ri-GAH-to) Thank you.

Funazushi: (foo-NAH-zoo-shee) Japanese dish of fermented Carp

Sama: (SAH-ma) Honorific used with gods and royalty

San: (SAHN) Honorific for men or women. Translates to Mr. or Ms.

Chan: (CHAHN) Endearing honorific for women.

Kun: (KOON) Endearing honorific for men.

Ragnarok: (RAG-nuh-rok): Norse mythology. End of the world as Fenrir swallows everything. End of times.

Aesir: (ICE-ear) Clan of gods living in Asgard.

Fylgjur: (feel-JUR) Spirit animal. Spirit totem.

La Ancella: Italian for handmaiden.

Chapter 1

"It werz a derk and stermy night!"

"Huh?" Hiroki managed to stammer as he held me upright while we walked down the wet, dark, smelling of piss (not mine, I went before we left the club, although it was in the men's room because the women's had a line forty-three people deep and I wasn't waiting another *kami*-forsaken minute), garbage-strewn alley.

"I serd, it werz a derk and stermy night!" I swung the three-quarters empty bottle of *sake* at the clouds drizzling rain just as a clash of thunder shook the heavens.

"Oh! It was a dark and stormy night. You are drunk."

"So is you!" I poked Hiroki in the chest and gave him a shit-eating grin.

"Want to know how I know you are drunk?"

"Because I barfed in the dumpster?"

"No."

"Because I slipped my phone number into the front of that bouncer's pants?"

"No."

"Because I'm drunk?"

"Well, yes. But I can *tell* you are drunk, because your tails are sticking out."

I turned around, spinning in three little circles. "Yep. Onetwothreefourfivesixseveneight. They're all there."

"You have nine and you know it, bitch," he said with a small chuckle, running his fingers through his straight black hair. "You might want to put those away before someone sees you. Again."

"I not a bitch! You a bitch."

Hiroki gave me a hurt look.

"Want to know how I know you're a bitch?"

He looked behind him. "My tails are not out."

"No. You're a bitch because you put *your* phone number down the front of the same bouncer's pants." I poked him in the chest. "You got to give me a shot before you get all dazzling with the boys. It's not fair that you're prettier than I am."

"I am not. You just have horrible self-esteem and an inferiority complex."

"Meh. Who can blame me?"

"Princess…"

"Told ya not to call me that."

"*Ojo-sama–*"

"Nope. Saying it in Japanese still counts. Say it with me now. Kaede. Kae. De. You can do it. You called me a bitch, you can call me by my name." I booped his nose. You'd think after twenty-years of being my bodyguard, he would have gotten over the whole princess thingy. Plus, we lived in America. I wasn't princess of shit. Maybe the rice farms my parents owned, but little else.

"Kaede-*sama*…"

"Close 'nuff." I tripped over a black trash bag in the middle of the alley, my foot getting soaked from the rain water that had collected on the top of it. "Ewww." I shook my foot and the smell from the bag wafted up and punched me in the nose. "Oh, *kami*… I'm gonna puke again." I pulled out of Hiroki's grip and ran to the side of the alley, unleashing a torrent of *sake* and Taco Bell on the concrete, ignoring the splash-backs on my ankles and feet. If I hadn't, I probably would have just puked some more.

Is she going to be okay?

I lifted my hand and sniffed really hard, wincing as the remnants of hurl burned my nose and throat. "Who said dat?"

There was a ghost sitting atop a bashed green dumpster to our left, legs crossed, and a *disdainful* look on his face. Ever the mature nine-tailed *kitsune*...I stuck my tongue out at him.

"She shall be fine," Hiroki said and pulled the *sake* out of my hand, offering it to the ghost, who gladly accepted.

"Hey! That was mine!"

"Was. You have had enough."

I pouted as the ghost nodded his thanks for the offering. "It has been so many years..." He tilted the bottle back and I watched in horror as the liquid splashed over the dumpster he was sitting on. It had been an offering, so at least he could *taste* the *sake*, but still... What a waste.

"Thank you," the ghost moaned pitifully.

"You are welcome," Hiroki answered with a bow, elbowing me painfully in the side.

"What he said," I grumbled and did the same, paying my respects to the deceased.

With a smile, he faded from view.

"You must respect the spirits, *Ojo-sama*."

"I will when they quit drinking my damn *sake*."

"You are an Inari fox. It is your *duty* to guide the spirits. Plus, you can always make more."

"Half. I'm *half* Inari fox. The *kitsune* side of me wants to have more fun!"

"It is nearly three in the morning. *Tomorrow* we shall have more fun."

"You're a friggin' *nogitsune*! It's in your blood to have fun. Why are you being all responsible and shit?"

11

"Because I fear your parents."

"True story, bro." I nodded emphatically. My father was a full-blown Inari fox, a spirit messenger and shrine guardian for the Inari kami. Sure, he hadn't lived in Japan since 1869...but he still took his duties *very* seriously. If he had his way, I'd be a shrine maiden. Even though there was absolutely *nothing* maidenly about me.

My *mother* on the other hand, was a *kitsune*. She wore her nine tails with pride and grace and was a *real* queen among the *kitsune*. With Inari's blessing, the two of them had fled Japan and were some of the first eastern settlers in California. Everyone thought they were just Japanese immigrants, come to build a rice farm. Which they did. But they expanded their lands quickly, growing tea and raising silkworms. After a few decades, their farm had practically turned into a self-contained, thriving city with shrines, restaurants, and pretty much everything you could imagine. Yoshida it was named, and it was home.

Who knew California would be perfect for growing rice? In fact, ninety-five percent of all of California's rice was grown in the Sacramento area, and a good portion of that on my parents' farms. Life was perfect for them. Until I was born.

"I think they hate me."

"Who hates you?"

"My parents."

"Why would they hate you?"

"Because I'm utterly American. And a disappointment. Kinda slutty, smart-mouthed, disrespectful, totally not reverent in any way, shape, or form. Oh, and I might be a little bit of an alcoholic." I scrunched one of my eyes closed and peered at Hiroki through my pinched finger tips.

"They do not hate you," Hiroki answered. "They are too disappointed in you to hate you."

"Gee, thanks."

"Just trying to make you smile."

He always was. Technically, he was my bodyguard. That's just fancy-talk for babysitter. But, more importantly, he was my best friend. It was an easy title to take, since he was my *only* friend. There were a *ton* of kids my age in Yoshida, and by *my* age, I meant late teens, not mid-twenties. *Kitsune* didn't really age. Once I hit puberty in my twenties, it crawled to a sudden and abrupt stop. I looked too young to drink, but thankfully my driver's license, which had my actual age of twenty-three, was still believable. But I was going to need a new one very soon. Nobody would buy that I was much older than that. Ever.

That was the nice thing about owning your own city. You got to control all the public records…

We weren't the only supernatural creatures in Yoshida, either. There were other families of foxes, *yokai* (spirits), demons (the good kind), ghosts, vampires, you name it. We all got along just peachy, thanks to my father. He was scary enough that *nobody* wanted to get on his bad side. Except me.

Hiroki, on the other hand, was a *nogitsune*, or field-fox. Tough. Badass. *Loved* to play tricks. Smart. Witty. Funny. Sexy. He was the whole damn package. So, of course he was gay. Bisexual actually, but very feminine and preferred men to women. Secretly, I think he was pretty sweet on me, but fear of my mother kept it in his pants. We'd fooled around a few times, heavy petting, making out, and one time I actually had my hand around Hiroki Jr. before he pushed me away. How the hell he had said no after getting that hot and heavy, I'll never know. I think my mother may have threatened the safety of one of his five tails. Or his junk. Either way, I was *not* a risk he was willing to take.

His name was actually Hasashi, but I'd always called him Hiroki. It was Japanese for large sparkle. It kind of stuck and even my parental units started calling him Hiroki. As did everybody else. He was mad at first, but I think it kind of grew on him after two decades of hearing it from first thing in the morning until I passed out at night.

"Come on. Let us get you home."

"Meanie."

"It is not you that your parents will reprimand. It is I."

"S'not like you haven't heard it all a bajillion times."

"You are more right than you know, *Ojo-sama*. Might I suggest a bit of caution? Your mother and father...seem to be getting exasperated by your behavior."

"What are they going to do, kick me out?" I scoffed and kicked an empty soda can out onto the sidewalk as we emerged onto the brightly lit street.

"Your tails are still exposed. So are your undergarments."

I sighed and closed my eyes. Controlling my tails in my human form was hard enough. Being drunk made it a challenge of epic proportions. Picturing my behind without them, they shifted away in a curl of mist and I felt my already short skirt fall back down over my ass. "Happy?"

"Mostly. I was enjoying the view," he hissed in laughter, still sounding like a fox.

"Puh-leez. You've seen my ass more than I have."

"Quit showing it off and you might have a chance of evening the score."

Grabbing the closest lamppost with one hand, I spun myself around it, stopping in front of Hiroki with a grin. "Really want me to?"

He sighed. "Sometimes I do."

"Why?" I frowned at him.

"You. You are clueless at how tempting you are, Kaede-*sama*."

"Would you *please* drop the honorifics? You've been my best friend foreverrr."

"I cannot."

"But you think I'm pretty?"

"No. A flower is pretty. The sunrise is pretty. *You* are beautiful."

I blushed. It wasn't the first time he had told me I was pretty, but I kind of had my suspicions that my parents paid him to do it. My mother was a gold *kitsune*. My father an *Inari* fox. His spiritual essence bleached me, denying me my mother's golden hue and beauty. My hair was stark white, almost silver, and my tails matched it perfectly. In my fox form, I could easily be mistaken for a giant arctic fox. Even my eyes were ice blue. I'd never thought I was pretty, let alone beautiful. "Thank you."

"You are welcome, Kaede."

"You did it!"

"I tried. To at least get you to stop speaking."

"As a reward... I'll let you take me home and take me to bed."

"You mean *put* you to bed."

"Do I?" I gave him a sultry grin.

Hiroki tilted his head, listening in the distance. I heard it a moment after he did. Sirens. They were heading in our direction. "We should go."

"Hang on. I wanna see what's going on." I was a fox. Curiosity was my middle name. Little known fact, foxes are ten times worse than cats when it came to curiosity. We were just smart enough not to get killed by it. Usually.

"It may not be safe..."

"Safe? Shmafe. Here they come." I turned and watched the parade of blue lights from the police and the red lights from the two fire trucks that rounded the corner and sped past us. "Let's go!"

I could hear Hiroki sigh as I took off running after the procession. "No. Don't. Stop," he called sarcastically, knowing the futility of his words as he took off after me.

15

The sirens stopped up ahead beneath one of the taller buildings on the street. I figured it was a robbery or something until the fire trucks turned their floodlights upward. I skidded to a stop.

"It's a jumper," Hiroki said as he stopped next to me, not even winded. I was breathing a little heavier and it kind of pissed me off, even though I knew Hiroki worked out from dawn until I dragged my ass out of bed. That was like five hours of uninterrupted gym time, *every* day.

"He's going to commit suicide?"

"*Hai.*"

"What a wuss."

Hiroki frowned at me. "Do not judge, youngling. You do not know his situation."

"Still. Does he want to end up a ghost wandering the shit world he was trying to get away from for all eternity? He's not going to get to the heavens, or be reborn, with that kind of attitude. You saw that poor bastard back there," I hooked my thumb over my shoulder in the direction of the sake-thieving spirit in the alleyway, "you think he *likes* being a ghost?"

"He," he pointed up at the figure standing at the edge of the building, "probably does not know the fate in store for him." He gave the guy a thoughtful look before continuing. "Or the pain is too much for him to bear and any release would be welcome."

I hated it when Hiroki got all philosophical. He made too much damn sense. "Fine. Wait here."

"Kaede! No!"

His words fell on deaf ears. Mostly because I had my hands over them as I leaped away.

The firemen were setting up a giant air mattress in case they couldn't talk him down. The police were yelling about sending someone up just to talk, and a news van skidded to a stop behind the line of emergency vehicles. I slipped into the alleyway beside the building and let out a little power.

I'm sure, if anybody had been standing in the alley with me, they would have shit a litter of kittens with mittens if they saw me. My tails were back, but so were my paws and ears. *Kitsune* and most spirit creatures had three forms. Full spirit (I looked like an arctic fox), human (I looked like an albino Japanese girl), and a demi-form (I looked like a damn cosplayer with fox tails, ears, paws, eyes, snoot, or any combination thereof). But, with the combination came more power. I used it to leap from building to building, parkouring my way up between them until my final leap brought me over the ledge of the building.

The jumper didn't even hear me land. He was staring down over the side of the building at the people below. "I don't want to talk!" He was screaming over the side of the building. It would be a miracle if they could hear him from twenty-stories up. I used his distraction to shift back into a more human appearance.

"Hey."

He spun in a panic, putting his back to the street and losing his balance. Not the brightest thing I'd ever done, scaring a jumper standing on the ledge of a rooftop. He started to fall and without thinking, I popped from where I stood to right in front of him, my hand snagging a fistful of T-shirt and yanking him from the edge. Popping, was one of the greatest advantages of being a *kitsune*. It was kind of like teleportation without a teleporter. And it was instantaneous. The only problem was, I had to be able to see where I was going.

"What are you doing?" He snarled in anger.

"Um… Saving you?"

"I don't want you to! Stay away from me you fox freak." He let his eyes trail over me from nose to toes and gave me a disgusted look. I felt the top of my head and my ass. I was still in my human seeming.

"Huh? What are you talking about?" I played dumb. I was like expert-level at that shit. I had yet to meet my equal. But when I did, our battle would be glorious!

"Shut up. I can see you. I can see everything. I can't stand it anymore!"

His rant spoke volumes. The plain-looking, blond guy had spirit sense. He could see spirits and he didn't know how to deal with it. I sighed. There wasn't anything I could do for him. He could either learn to live with it or let it drive him insane. "I won't beat around the bush then."

He stopped staring and rubbed his eyes frantically, trying to focus on me again. "What are you?"

"A *kitsune*. Japanese fox spirit."

"Are you here to kill me?"

"Would I have saved you if I were?"

"Why did you?"

Not wanting to seem imposing, I sat down on the rooftop, ignoring the dirt, grime, and bits of roof tar that stuck to the back of my legs and my butt. "Because I don't want to see you end up a spirit."

"Like a ghost?" He took a step back, a little closer to the edge than I liked, but I could always pop in next to him if I needed to.

"Not like a ghost, an actual ghost. If you kill yourself, that's exactly what happens to you. The regret keeps you from passing on."

"It would be better than this," he answered sadly, sitting on the edge of the roof.

"No. It wouldn't. If you can see them, you can hear them. Ask them if they like being an apparition."

"I try to ignore them. They just won't go away."

"I know. What if I told you we could help you?"

"Who?"

"Other spirits...like me. We could teach you how to control your gift."

"Gift? This isn't a fucking gift. It's a joke. A nightmare. A mental condition."

"No. It's not. You can do wondrous things just by being able to see the other side."

He stood up and gave me a doubtful look. "No offense. You seem like a nice girl...spirit...whatever. But I *really* just can't do this anymore," he said and then fell backward over the edge of the rooftop.

"Fuck!" I popped to the edge of the building, looking over the edge. "Sorry, Hiroki," I said and popped again, coming out next to the jumper and wrapping myself around him. We fell for a moment until I could right myself and look where we were going.

Pop. We were on the ground in the middle of the police and firefighters, who were too stunned to do anything but stare. I looked over their shoulders at a very angry looking Hiroki. *Pop.* I appeared next to him, grabbed his hand and ran. I spared a moment to glance over my shoulder at the jumper. Two of the quicker cops already had him in their arms and were cuffing him as he stood there, staring after me. I wanted to think I had done him a favor, but the look of pure hatred he was giving me told me I probably hadn't. At least he would live long enough to learn to deal with it.

Chapter 2

A *tabi* covered toe poked me in the nose. I brushed my fingers across my face, blinked, and started snoring again. The covered toe poked me again and this time I snarled in outrage, sitting up and glaring at Hiroki. He was dressed in a plain gray *yukata* and was wearing *tabi* socks, but the expression on his face let me know I was in trouble. He only woke me up when my parents wanted to yell at us.

"What we do now?"

"I really wish you would not use the word we when asking what *you* did this time. Get dressed. Your mother and father *both* wish to speak to you."

"Berate, you mean."

"This time… This time they are well within their right."

"What?"

"I will let them explain," he said and turned around, letting me slip from beneath my covers, knowing full well I wasn't wearing anything beneath them.

I rolled off my futon and stood up, making faces behind his back, even an obscene gesture toward his butt.

"Kaede-*sama*, now is not the time. Please dress quickly."

"You're no fun."

"I am when the situation dictates. I have never seen your parents so…angry before."

"What the hell happened? This isn't the first time I've come home drunk off my ass. Hell, I was mostly sober after the rooftop bullshit."

"That is precisely why they are so upset."

"You *told* them about it?" I stared at him in disbelief, pulling on my T-shirt and sweatpants.

"No. Action Five News did."

A hazy image of a news van skidding to a stop beside emergency vehicles popped into my head. So did a replay of me popping through a hundred feet of open air to rescue a suicidal spiritually sensitive guy. If they had filmed me using my supernatural powers… I was in deep *tawagoto*. "Fuck."

"Precisely. Are you ready?"

"Yeah. We might as well get this over with."

"I wish you luck," he said and stepped aside, letting me lead the way.

The only thing we were missing was ominous music as I opened the sliding door from my bedroom and marched down the hall. "Where are they?" I asked over my shoulder.

"In the dining room. They felt it best to discuss your indiscretion over breakfast."

"What time is it?"

"Nearly nine."

That was later than I expected for a fuck up of my magnitude. They must have been plotting something special. The door was closed, and with a soft sigh, I slid it open and entered.

My parents were seated around the low table, sipping tea. Next to my mother was an *ancient* man in a black business suit. I stared in shock. "Uncle Tatsuo?"

"Kaede! My…how you haven't grown."

I squealed and ran over to him, dropping to my knees and giving him a hug. "Why are you here?"

He coughed and nodded toward my mother.

I looked up to see amber fire flare in her eyes, threatening to scorch me where I knelt. "Good morning, Mother," I said to her, giving her a weak smile. She huffed and elbowed my father.

"You are a disgrace." He shook his head. I'd heard many, many, many times over the years that I had brought disgrace to my family, my parents, my races, and even my ancestors. It was the *first* time he had skipped the recipients and just flat out called *me* a disgrace.

"I love you, too?" Blue fire flared in *his* eyes.

Uncle Tatsuo calmly put a hand over my arm. I gave him a worried look. My parents had been pissed at me countless times. There were seven days in a week, I might go one or two, never consecutive, without incurring their wrath, but this was the angriest I had ever seen them. My father reached down beside him, grabbed a newspaper, and tossed it on the table in front of me.

SUPERHERO IN SACRAMENTO?

I giggled at the headline. If they knew me, they wouldn't have asked such a stupid question. I just didn't want to see the mortal go splat. He might have ended up stealing my *sake*.

The picture beneath it wasn't a source of mirth, though. Whoever had been pointing the camera up, took a superb photo of the two of us falling, getting a clear shot of our faces. I was looking a little to the left and the suicidal guy was staring at me with a look of intense shock and anger. It would have looked like two people falling to their deaths except for my ears and tails, which were quite predominately displayed in the black and white photograph.

I squirmed as I read the caption. Whoever wrote the article had done their research and actually called me a *kitsune* with a question mark. *A man, apparently attempting suicide, was miraculously saved by some sort of creature. Police stated he was falling when the girl appeared out of*

23

thin air and then reappeared with the jumper on the ground next to them before disappearing again. She appeared to have fox ears as well as multiple tails. Could this possibly be a kitsune? Investigations continue.

"Well, at least they got what I was right."

"Daughter..." My mother's voice sent chills up and down my spine. "You have exposed us to the world."

"Oh, please. They don't know who I am. They probably had to google what I even am. I was in the right place at the wrong time. I couldn't let the guy die."

"Why?" my father chimed in solemnly. "If it is as the newspaper says, he wished to end his life. You have exposed us all by denying him that right?'

Okay. Now I'm *getting pissed.* "Denying him that right? He could see us. He sees ghosts and spirits. It was driving him insane. He didn't understand that if he killed himself, he'd become what he hated! Now he has a chance. I won't apologize for that."

"No. You *will* apologize for being seen. For putting us all at risk. For your ways, your slovenly drunkenness, your utter lack of respect, your...ways!" Father stood up and the fire in his eyes spread to his hands and swirled around him. He was officially pissed.

"No. I won't."

"Then you leave us little choice. Since you cannot seem to keep yourself from the world of the mortals...maybe you should learn how to *blend* in a little more."

I stopped and stared at him. Then shifted my gaze to my mother, who flashed me a wicked smile over the edge of her cup of tea. It was at that moment I realized why my Uncle Tatsuo was seated next to me.

Uncle Tatsuo wasn't. My uncle that is. He was one of those *really* old friends of the family who you ended up calling "Uncle" from the time you could talk. It was a little difficult to be related directly to a fox when you have scales and horns. Uncle Tatsuo was a dragon.

He was also the director of an academy for supernatural children. A boarding school whose focus was primarily controlling one's powers and blending in with the world of humans.

I turned and scowled at my mother. "You are *not* shipping me off to some fucking boarding school in the middle of the mountains of Iceland because I screwed up!"

Her nine tails flared behind her, writhing like snakes as her eyes narrowed. Even my father reached a hand over to calm her. I guess I shouldn't have dropped the F-bomb while speaking to her.

"Akane, calm," he whispered, giving me a sidelong glance of unadulterated disdain.

"Calm? Our reckless child would expose us to the world and then would tell me what I can and cannot do? The time for calm has long passed, Yasahiro."

"May I speak to her alone?" Uncle Tatsuo's calm voice broke through the moment, calming both my parents and giving me a sigh of reprieve. Talking to him would be infinitely better than being reduced to a quivering five-tailed lump of flesh any day of the week.

And there was no doubt about it. I could and would lose tails over this. When *kitsune* are born, it is usually with one tail, *maybe* two if their parents were extraordinarily gifted. As we aged, we received more for every lifetime we lived. Sometimes it was fifty-years, sometimes a century. My nine-tailed mother had married an *Inari* fox. Their combined power had blessed me with *nine* at my birth. It was, as far as I knew, completely unheard of. But as the saying goes, they who giveth, can taketh away. I'm sure it would involve a cleaver or sharp knife, but they could do it. Then I'd have to earn them back. At the rate I was going, it would probably take a couple thousand years just to replace one.

They nodded at Tatsuo, done with my antics and at the end of their ropes. "Please," they said in unison.

"Come, Child," he said and stood, offering me his hand. I wasn't stubborn enough not to take it, either. I could tell it was better to tread lightly in present company.

I should have listened to Hiroki last night when he warned me of their temperament.

I flashed the *nogitsune* a helpless look as Tatsuo led the way out of the room, out onto the *engawa*, and into the central garden. He motioned me to sit on the stone bench beside the fountain.

"I screwed up pretty bad," I said aloud, though not particularly at the dragon.

He chuckled, and it rumbled from his chest soothingly. As a child I would often sit on his lap, ear pressed to his chest, just to hear it. "Yes, Niece. You have."

"I'm going to end up stuck at boarding school for the next three years, aren't I."

He sighed and looked at the fountain. "It might not be as bad as you think."

"It's a boarding school. In the middle of nowhere. Surrounded by nothing. I don't see how it could be much better."

"Why are you so troublesome?"

"Excuse me?"

"Your mother is a queen. Your father serves the *Inari-kami*. You lead a life of luxury, wanting for nothing. Why are you so hard on those who have given you everything?"

I sighed. I wanted to deny that they did, but I couldn't. Even love, they had poured on me until I started pushing it away. "I don't know."

"I think it is because you are bored. You can only go out every night, drinking yourself into a stupor for so long before even that begins to grow old."

"True. It was fun for the first five years or so."

"You do not have many friends?"

"You mispronounced any. Hiroki is my only friend."

"Why have you not made friends in town? There are other fox families here. Other supernaturals, *yokai*."

"Because they treat me like the fucking princess that I'm not. I hate it. They practically kowtow whenever I walk by. It's fucking annoying!" I growled for emphasis.

Uncle Tatsuo chuckled again. "Then come to my school."

"Why? Would things be any different there?"

"You have no idea."

"Enlighten me."

"The only thing you have at Aesir Academy is a name, and nobody who would know it. The entire goal of the school is to train you to be more human, hide what you are. In fact, there are consequences if anybody should discover exactly what you are."

"Consequences, that sounds kinky."

"You are an incorrigible child."

"Oh, I know. My parents remind me of that fact every day."

"As well they should. Come. Do not fight them. Let them believe they are doing some good toward your life."

"Do I have to go to classes?"

"That is the point of school, yes," he said with a draconic grin.

"Can I bring Hiroki? I don't think I could do this without him."

He sighed heavily. "That depends on your parents and him. If he survives the next few minutes, he might not wish to spend any more time as your guardian."

I gulped in fear for him, his tails, and his manhood. But more importantly, I was deathly afraid of losing the one thing in my life that mattered to me. Him.

"At least you have the decency to feel sorry for him after what you have subjected him to."

"They can't punish him. He tried to stop me."

"But he didn't."

"Can we go back inside? Yes. I'll go to your school."

He nodded and stood. "This is a commitment. There will be no showing up to appease your parents and then leaving. You will be in attendance for all three years."

He saw through my little ploy. "I know," I lied through my little foxy teeth.

"Should you not fare well in your classes, you might also be subjected to repeating a year or term."

This just kept getting better and better. "I understand."

"Very well. Let us rejoin your parents and what is left of your guardian."

"Uncle Tatsuo…"

"Headmaster. There is no more Uncle for the next three years. In fact, you might be better off pretending you do not know me. I am not exactly…popular." He grinned again, forked tongue making him look positively evil.

"I find that hard to believe…"

"Eloquent. Just like your mother."

He held out his hand again and I took it, lifting myself from the stone bench and vaguely wondering what the hell I had just gotten myself into.

Hiroki was on the floor in front of my parents as they stood over him, orange and blue flames dancing around them, foxfire lashing out at him.

"Stop it!" I threw myself in front of him.

Hiroki's hand grabbed my ankle. "No. It is what I deserve."

"Shut up. It was my fault I got photographed–"

"Recorded. Although I have yet to see the video," my father interjected. I shot him an apologetic look.

"Hiroki tried to stop me, but I didn't listen. It isn't his fault, it's mine. Leave him alone and punish me."

"Oh, we shall."

"No, you won't," Uncle Tatsuo interjected. "She is now a student of Aesir Academy. All punishments shall be meted out by the disciplinary committee of said establishment," he said with a grin.

Both of my parents stared at him in shock. "You got her to agree?" My father tried to keep the excitement from his voice but failed miserably.

"On the condition that her attendant," he motioned at the still prone Hiroki, "would also be able to attend."

"That is acceptable," my mother answered. She didn't even ask him. He was my attendant, my bodyguard, my babysitter. She didn't give him a choice.

"Then all that is left is the binding contract," Tatsuo said, and reached into his jacket pocket, pulling out a scroll that was ten times too large to fit inside any suit coat pocket. When he unfurled it, he pulled it apart into two exact copies and with a flick of his wrist, provided a golden quill. "Ladies first," he said to me and put a copy down on the table.

I took the quill from him and touched it to the paper before scratching a ragged line across the parchment. "Uh... Your pen. It has no ink."

"I said it was a *binding* contract. You must sign it in your blood."

"My blood?"

"Yes. For it to be binding."

"Can I use Hiroki's? I don't like blood. Especially mine."

"Unfortunately, no."

"I have a red ink Bic pen in my room..."

"Kaede," my mother's tone left little room for argument.

I sighed and held out the quill, bringing the index finger of my left hand to the extraordinarily sharp tip and pricking it against the nib. My blood welled up, instantly soaking into

29

the tip. Before it had a chance to dry, I hastily scribbled the name Donald the Duck across the bottom. It flared. I smiled. And then the signature rearranged itself across the line into my name and instantly dried to a ruddy brown. A wax seal welled up from the parchment into the image of nine fox tails in a circular pattern.

I was officially fucked. And a student of Aesir Academy.

At least I get the satisfaction of watching Hiroki fuck himself, too. I grinned as he plucked his finger, signed, and the contract flared. *Misery loves company.*

Chapter 3

When you have a school situated deep in the mountains in the middle of fucking nothing, transportation becomes a huge issue. It's not like they can send a giant flying cheese-wagon to pick up your delinquent ass and drop you off at the front gate. When I stepped out of my front door, the last thing I expected to find was a cab.

"They sent a cab?" I looked over at Hiroki who just shrugged.

"Maybe it will take us to the train station."

"Yeah. Don't think the train runs to Iceland," I answered and headed for the cab.

"I know. I thought... I do not know what I was thinking. Sorry, *Ojo-sama*."

"No. It's just Kaede and you have no excuse for calling me anything else for the next three years. We're fellow students, not anything else. Except friends."

"*Hai*." He followed behind me. Neither of us had more than a backpack slung over our shoulder. We were told not to bring anything but toiletries, as everything we would possibly need would be provided for us upon our arrival.

"Two passengers to Aesir?"

"Uh. Yes. That's us," I said to the cabby as he opened the back door for us.

"Hop on in."

I slid in first, Hiroki right behind me. The cab was impeccably clean and looked like a normal cab without the gum stuck to the seats and horrible smelling air-freshener dangling from the mirror. How the hell it was going to get us to school was a mystery. I guessed we would find out soon enough.

He shut the door and got in the front, starting the meter and pulling away from the front gate of my parents' house. They had said their formal goodbyes before we walked out the door, but I was surprised to see them still standing outside, my father holding my mother in a tender moment.

"I guess they're glad to see me finally get out of the house for longer than a night."

"I do not think so. Your mother is crying."

I shut up after that.

"Where are we heading?" I got my face as close to the plexiglass divider as I could, to make sure the driver knew I was talking to him.

"Uh… Aesir Academy? You're not going to do very well with a piss-poor memory like that."

"No shit, Shizlock. It's not like we can drive there. Are you taking us to the airport?"

"What kind of cabbie would I be if I didn't take you where you wanted to go?"

We hit the edge of the city and he gunned the engine on the open highway. Mysteriously, there was an utter lack of other vehicles on the road. Or people. Animals, birds, reptiles, or *anything*…

"Kaede-sama, look at the road…"

I looked out the window and down at the asphalt beneath us. Waves splashed against our tires with tumultuous black water beneath it. We were driving on the River Styx. "You're a Charon," I said through the plexiglass.

The once-normal looking cabbie turned around and a skeletal face peered back at us. "Yep. Five points to Griffinpuff!"

"Huh?"

"Never mind. Sit back and hold on. Things are going to get a little bumpy!" He cackled and began swinging the steering wheel right to left. The car didn't move and floated gently down the river, slowly picking up speed. We waited for the bumpy part that never came.

Twenty minutes later, we floated around the outside of the peak of a snowcapped mountain and then dipped down into a valley of green. "When do we get to the ride, Johnny?"

"This is the ride," Hiroki answered automatically.

"This ride blows. They should have totally made that last part a water flume or something."

"After eight-hundred-years of kids puking in the back of my cab, I turned it into a kiddie ride."

"Ew. I don't blame you. Puke is gross."

"Especially *sake*-scented," Hiroki said with a grin.

"Shut up. You're supposed to be on my side."

"Always, *Ojo-sama*."

I elbowed him in the ribs and decided to keep doing so until he stopped with the princess and the honorifics. "Think they'll have *sake*?"

"I highly doubt it," he answered, rubbing the spot I had hit him.

"It's not fair."

"What?"

"My dependence on *sake*."

"You are not truly an alcoholic."

"Not what I meant. Mom gets to drink whatever she wants, but because of Dad and his service to *Inari*, I'm stuck drinking rice wine for the rest of my life." I wasn't kidding. Anything else made my stomach horribly upset. Like,

33

projectile vomiting like a flame spewing dragon, upset. It wasn't pretty.

"Yes, well... Maybe it would be a good idea to avoid liquor while at school."

"What fun would that be?"

"You might want to consider limiting your intake of fun for the next three years. Get through this, then worry about it."

"What fun would that be?" I grinned at him, let my face change in a partial shift, and flashed him my rows of sharp teeth.

"Spoken like a true fox," the cabbie said with a chuckle. "You might want to tone it down on the conversations that give away what you are. I'm not a student, nor do I give a mortal shit what you are. But we are almost to the school. Anybody who can overhear you *there* will be very interested."

"The headmaster mentioned something about that. What do they get if they figure it out? A plaque? Trophy?"

"Extra credit. If they guess correctly. And you lose points. Three correct guesses and you have to repeat the year."

"You better take extra care controlling your tails, *Ojo-sama*."

"And you better start calling her by her name. You're both obviously Japanese, that will be a big clue right there and not one you can hide. Calling her princess might start giving them clues."

I elbowed Hiroki in the ribs again and shot him a reproving look.

"My apologies, Kaede-*sama*."

"Just Kaede. *Chan*, if you must. I know twenty-three years of conditioning is hard to break. But do it anyway."

"*Hai*."

"There it is," the cabbie called out, pointing a bony finger in the direction of Aesir Academy. "Your home for the next three years."

"Joy," I said with just a hint of snark to flavor my sarcasm, but if I were being honest, the place was pretty fucking impressive looking. Gray stone spires and buttresses seemed to grow from the massive walls, while walkways and bridges connected everything. Dragons flew overhead and a myriad of busses, cabs, carriages, trains, planes, and automobiles drifted down lazy rivers, landing strips, and highways that touched the front of the castle in different tiers. Ours was the lowest and the sun disappeared as we floated beneath the highway above us. I breathed a sigh of relief when the cab floated to a stop.

"Two gold," the driver said and held out his hand.

I started to panic when Hiroki slapped two glinting coins into his bony palm. "Your mother," he said by way of explanation when he saw my confused look.

"She gave us fare for the ride home, right?" He ignored me and got out of the cab. "Right?"

I growled and slid over the seat, my legs sticking to the pleather seat. I shouldn't have worn a skirt, but I wore little else. Iceland in the fall wasn't conducive to exposed bare skin. Gooseflesh covered my skin the moment I got out of the car. I was about to let loose with a coat of fur when Hiroki grabbed my arm, slowly shaking his head. "Giving away what you are the moment you get out of the cab would probably break some sort of record."

"Well then, shut up and run. It's probably warm inside and they probably have cocoa or something."

"That would be Switzerland, not Iceland."

"Fucking Icicle-land."

"It is not that cold."

"Yeah…sure. Let's go with that."

"First years?" A tall blonde woman wielding a clipboard and a pen asked as we stepped toward the walkway leading to the school.

"*Hai.*"

"Names?"

Hiroki started answering her questions while I looked around. The loading tiers above us didn't have walkways into the school. Giant spiral staircases wound down to ours and students were literally pouring from them, heading directly for the giant double doors.

"Okay, I have both of you on my list. You may go inside," the woman walked away, flagging down the kid getting out of the cab behind us.

"Thanks," I said, trying to be polite, but she ignored me.

"Come, Kaede. Let us go."

"Okey dokey, Hiroki," I said and gave him a grin. He hated it when I said that and flashed me a disgusted look. He headed for the door, and just as I started walking, two-hundred pounds of jock slammed into my side.

We both stopped dead in our tracks and stared at each other. His jaw clenched in annoyance and I could see the heat dancing in his blue eyes. "Watch where you're going, scrub," he said with a low growl and a huff. Just as he started to walk away, he stopped and sniffed the air around him, his eyes resting again on me. Nostrils flaring, he continued sampling the air around him, eyes narrowing and kind of a scary look on his face. "What are you?"

"Um, hi. I'm the girl you just *ran* into. I don't think we're supposed to tell each other what we are, but if *I* had to guess right this minute... I'd bet that you were an asshole," I said with a smile, and skipped off to catch up to Hiroki, who had stopped halfway to the double doors to watch our exchange. He wasn't looking at me, either. He was staring at the douche bucket who had ran into me.

"You okay?" He asked as I passed him.

"Yep. Just the local jock strap trying to mark his territory by being a dick."

Hiroki chuckled and followed me inside.

∞ ∞ ∞

"This has to be the way," I pointed down the long corridor toward the open double doors. "Everybody else is going that way."

"Judging by the sign over the doors that says it is the great hall, I am inclined to agree with you."

"Oh. I missed that part."

"The obvious? You usually do."

"*Somebody's* in a mood."

He sighed. "My apologies, Kaede-*chan*." I covered my lips and stifled a giggle at his use of *chan*. I could see him struggling with it, but he finally got it out. After twenty-fucking-years, my little Hiroki had finally done it. "There are many predators among the students. My nerves are on edge."

"Yeah. Ignore it. They don't know who is who, and what is what. We're safe. Not like we're going to get eaten on the first day."

"I do not know. The gentleman out front looked like he wished to feast upon you."

"I know right? I musta smelled like a big old juicy steak. He couldn't stop sniffing the air around me."

"Be careful around him. And the two who were with him."

"Huh. I didn't even notice them."

"They looked as if they were cut from the same cloth."

"Or haunch of ass meat."

Hiroki snickered. "Yes. Or that."

We entered the great hall. I don't know why, but I had been expecting some sort of dining area with long tables running the length. It looked more like an auditorium filled with church pews. My excitement level dropped considerably while the growling in my tummy increased in pitch. I was starving and looking forward to some food. Even school food.

"When are they going to feed us?"

"Probably at lunch which is," he paused to look at his watch, "two-hours away. Will you survive?"

"Maybe. But if I start chewing on your arm, you know why."

We sat at the edge of the row of seats in the back, planning on staying there until one of the teachers wrecked our plans of an early escape. "Scoot in until you're next to the other students. Make room for everyone."

Sighing, I got up and headed for the middle of the row, stopping in my tracks when I saw who was the last one in the row. Mr. Jockstrap. Smiling, I waved as I sat down next to him and crossed my legs in front of me. Feeling the growl in his chest, more than hearing it, I turned to him.

I almost shut up because he was so damn good looking. Shaggy blond hair pulled back in a short ponytail. Chiseled jaw. Blue eyes. But then I came to my senses. "You're awfully grumbly over there, did you get some bad chicken? I think I have some antacids in my bag. You want one?"

He ignored me. *Me.*

He scooted over as much as he could, away from me and closer to his other buddies. I leaned forward to check them out. They must have had the same idea and were making no qualms about it. They both were leaning forward, too.

"Hi!" I gave them a little wave, too. One of them looked just like Jacques Strahp. Same chiseled jaw and stylish blond hair. The other, though, had long, brown hair in a ponytail that disappeared down somewhere around his ass. He was thinner than the other two, as well. Not nearly as muscular, but even sitting down, I could tell he was the tallest of the three. "I'm Kaede."

Jacques' twin was another man of few words and leaned back against the bench without so much as batting an eye.

Tall dark and sexy gave me a small smile. "David," he said softly before leaning back. At least one of them wasn't stuck up.

The other two gave him a look and he faced forward, the smile never leaving his lips. I liked him already. "So, what did you fellers do to get sent to Camp Pretendtobehuman?"

"Do you ever shut up?"

"When I'm sleeping."

Jacques shook his head and continued to *try* to ignore me.

"At least tell me your name, because I'm going to be honest with you, the one I have in my head for you is *pretty* unflattering."

His head turned so fast I could almost hear it. His scowl was kind of frightening, as were his nostrils flaring a mile a minute. "It couldn't be any worse than what I call you in *my* head."

"Mine's probably funnier, though. You don't seem like you have much of a sense of humor."

David must have been listening. He snorted.

"'Annoying bitch' is funny."

"You think it is? Have you ever laughed when someone called you that? I mean, it's *fitting*, but not really chuckle or chortle worthy." I nodded in emphasis, lifting my lips a tad.

Jacques was turning red. Never a good sign. "You...you...you–"

"Light up my life? Make me whole? Lift you up?"

He stood up and growled. His twin stood up and wrapped his arms around him, keeping him from taking a swing at me, but the way his muscles were bulging, I gave him fifty-fifty odds of containing his rage. My work there was done.

"Ugh. I can't believe you farted," I shouted and stood up, ushering Hiroki to exit the pews. There was a solid wall of students all the way to the end, a factor I hadn't taken into consideration. Our escape route was blocked. "Ooopsie. Guess I'll just have to deal with the smell," I said and nervously sat back down.

"Trade seats with me," Hiroki said exasperatedly.

I crawled over his lap and plopped down on his left, grateful to be away from Jacques. Hiroki simply crossed his arms and stared straight ahead, ignoring everyone and everything around him. Including me.

"*Arigato*," I whispered as I leaned a little closer.

"Restraint," was all he said.

Jacques' twin finally wrangled him down beside Hiroki just as Uncle Tatsuo walked out onto the stage. "Greetings students of Aesir Academy," he said without the aid of a microphone, his voice booming to the farthest reaches of the great hall. There was a smattering of applause, nobody truly seeming to be happy to be there. It looked like I wasn't the only one sent there as a punishment. That didn't stop Uncle Tatsuo. He chuckled merrily at everyone's lack of enthusiasm. "Tough crowd."

One person giggled.

"Let's get right to it then, shall we? You are here for a very specific reason. To learn to blend into the human world. Some, if not all of you, have showed an utter lack of restraint in your attempts to do so as of yet. By the end of your stay at our fine establishment, you will be able to balance checkbooks, discuss finance options for retirement with your neighbor Paul, attend pot-luck dinners, order from a menu at fast-food establishments, and not end up on the evening news!"

"He's looking at me," I hissed at Hiroki.

"Yes. He is."

"Very subtle."

40

"Not in the slightest."

"That was sarcasm."

"It was lost on me."

"I see that."

The teacher standing behind us coughed and shot me a menacing stare when I looked at her over my shoulder. *Where the hell were you when I was about to get accosted by the troll?*

I looked around Hiroki. Jacques wasn't paying attention to Tatsuo. He was staring at me, looking like he was wondering if I would taste better braised or fricasseed. I gave him a grin and turned my attention back on my uncle.

"You all were warned before your arrival that it is of the utmost importance that you do not divulge your specific nature to your fellow students. This is part of your grade. If you can go an entire year without anyone learning what you are, you pass. This is dependent on your test scores and whatnot, of course. Now the fun part. At the entrance to the great hall, you might have noticed a box upon the wall. Above said box are entrance forms. Should you think you know the truth of someone's nature…you may guess. Simply fill out the provided form. A word of caution before you do. Should you guess *correctly,* bonus points will be added to your final grade and deducted from the person you have correctly identified."

The round of applause was much louder this time. Extra-credit always got everybody's attention. A few people even whistled while others began studying those around them.

"Now for the bad news," Tatsuo continued. "Should your guess be off the mark, incorrect or only partially correct… Points will be deducted from *your* final score and added to the person or persons you guessed incorrectly."

The silence in the room was almost deafening. Even the crickets were afraid to chime in.

"And for the *piece de resistance*, should three people correctly guess what you are in any given year... The student must *repeat* the year as they have utterly failed in hiding their nature."

This time his speech was met with outright groans and objections.

"*Silence!*" His voice left little room for argument and might have cracked the foundation a little. Don't piss off a dragon. Everybody fell silent. "This is not up for negotiation. There are no do overs, no begging, no pleading, and most of all...no mercy. These rules have been in place since the founding of the school and it is something we take very seriously. Do your best to appear human. Also, keep in mind that some of your instructors are, or were, human. You will be polite and courteous at all times. There are far greater punishments than repeating a year. Do you understand?"

Everybody nodded. Even me.

"Magic, supernatural powers... I urge you to use them with discretion. There isn't a ban, but this might lead to someone discovering your nature as all powers and magics have a certain flavor. Be careful. And be careful who you trust." He gave the audience a smile that seemed to land on me.

"There is one last thing I wish to discuss. Once you have guessed, be it correct or incorrect, as to a fellow student's nature, a gag spell shall be immediately placed upon you as soon as the slip touches the box. You will not be able to share your guess with any of the other students. Any attempt at doing so, will trigger the spell. The results will vary from species to species, but they are *all* unpleasant. I suggest you heed my warning and maintain your silence. There will be one or two of you who will doubt my sincerity. Let me offer you my condolences now, as I might not be able to keep a straight face after the spell has gone into effect."

I clapped, ignoring the fact that I was the only one. Uncle Tatsuo gave me a small bow.

"Now, you will be shown to your rooms. All of our dorms are co-educational. Trysts, relationships, and whatnot are not forbidden. We will leave you to your best judgement. If you do not like your rooming assignment, I suggest you get over it quickly. There will be no changes made. I will see all of you for lunch. Enjoy your time at Aesir Academy. I'm sure, years from now when you are quite old and feeble, should you age, you will look back on these years with utter distaste and disdain. Our job is to teach you. Not entertain you," he said and strode from the stage. An angry looking woman strode forward to take up his place.

"I am Assistant Headmistress Lateran. First Years will follow me. Second Years will follow Dean Cobb." She pointed to the gentleman at the end of the stage, he motioned to the floor below him. "And Third years will follow Coach Genevieve," she said and pointed to the opposite end of the stage. "First years gather outside the great hall. I shall join you momentarily.

Chapter 4

"Let us go," Hiroki said almost worriedly.

Standing up, I waited for everyone else in our row to filter out the other end. I could almost feel the heat of anger from behind us as Jacque and his cohorts followed us out.

Kitsune, by nature, were not large, and I had no trouble sneaking my way through the crowd that had gathered outside the double doors where we were to wait for the Assistant Headmistress. Leaning against the wall, I made myself unobtrusively seem even shorter, hiding from the much taller trio and feigning disinterest in everyone and everything around me.

"You went too far, Kaede-*chan*."

"I know. He was just such a jerk I couldn't help myself."

"He is also three times your size and you do not know what his nature is. You might have made an unnecessarily formidable enemy."

"I know. I'll ignore him from now on."

"If you can."

"I will."

Hiroki nodded, satisfied for the moment. There was a blustering by the door as Lateran gathered everyone behind her as she wove through the throng of people.

"Follow me, people. We will get you to your dormitories. There, the floor residents will have your room assignments. I just want to reiterate what the Headmaster said, there will be no switching of rooms. Get to know your roommate before you judge them. Also, something he left out. You may *not* guess as to your roommate's nature. Everyone needs a place to unwind, and your rooms are a safe haven. The gag spell he *did* mention also includes tattling on your roomie, so to speak. So, mum's the word. Also, should you run into anyone you might have met *before* you entered Aesir Academy…you will find the results of trying to guess *their* nature the same. When you stepped upon the platform outside the school, the spell went into effect. It knows who you know."

There was another groan that rose up from the ranks of the first-year students. They must have spotted easy prey and then had it yanked from their maws. I chuckled softly to myself.

She led the way out of the building, pointing at various things as we passed. I didn't pay attention because Hiroki ate that shit up like sushi. By the time we reached the dorms, he'd probably be able to draw me a detailed map of the entire campus.

It took almost thirty minutes to reach the dorm building. It was like being on a guided tour of Hollywood. Every piece of broken stone, statue, and building had a long history at Aesir Academy, and she knew it all. She also felt the need to share it with everyone around her and then ask questions after. Luckily, I was too short to get called on.

"And this will be your home for the next year. Well, except when you go home for two weeks over the summer. When you come back, you will be taken to the second-year dorms. Welcome to Breckenridge Hall!"

She seemed kind of disappointed when nobody seemed to give a crap.

"Well, right this way," she said and opened the door.

The front room was gigantic. Couches, a fireplace, televisions, gaming consoles were set up everywhere into little alcoves. It wouldn't be a bad place to hang out. To the left, was a countered area with a matronly looking woman standing behind it.

"This is Helga Swenson, your dorm mother," Lateran said and turned the mic over to her. Except there was no mic and she just kind of pointed at the amused looking woman.

"Greetings, children," she said in a sing-song voice. I gave her a smile and a wave. It was never too early to start kissing ass. I wasn't sure what the rules were, but there was a damn good chance I was going to break them. It is always wise to butter your bread before it ends up in the frying pan.

"Well, I will leave you to get settled in your rooms. Classes will start tomorrow, so get plenty of rest. I'll see you in the morning," Headmistress Lateran said as she positively beamed at us.

"That woman needs to be medicated," I whispered to Hiroki, scowling at Lateran

"Oh, no I don't, Dear! I just love my job." She turned and looked right at me. "Did I mention I have excellent hearing? I must have forgotten that, which is strange because I have an impeccable memory. Especially for faces. I never forget them. Or names." Lateran narrowed her eyes at me, and her smile turned into a wolfish grin.

My ass was toast. No amount of butter was going to save it, either. "I said dedicated! Did you think I said *medicated*? Wow. That would have been rude! See you in the morning. Have a great day!"

"Oh, I will. Sleep well, Kaede."

Fuck. She knows my name. I grinned and waved.

"Guess I'm not the only one who thinks you're a pain in the ass."

I looked over my shoulder. Jacques and his buddies were standing behind me. My day just couldn't possibly get any better. "Oh, hey. No. Most people think I'm a pain in something. Asses. Necks. You name it. So…are the three of you rooming together? Who's on top? Which one gets to be

47

the creamy center of the three musketeers bar? Which one–" Hiroki's hand, completely covering my mouth, kept me from talking. I licked his palm, but he was used to it.

"Forgive her. I forgot to administer her afternoon medications." Hiroki started to pull me away. Instead of fighting him, I went limp in his arms and let him drag me to safety. We called this maneuver Seventeen-D. It worked wonders, but was even more effective if I had the opportunity to put an Alka-Seltzer tablet in my mouth before he covered it. But that was Seventeen-E. They weren't armed, so that would have been overkill.

"Keep your pet on a leash," Jacques snarled.

"Oh, you are mistaken. I am *her* pet."

At least the other two were laughing. Jacques looked like he had an aneurysm in his immediate future. David even winked at me. I liked David. He didn't hate me.

He turned us around a group of people milling about waiting for their room numbers, and the tri-sexual trio was finally out of sight. I was half-relieved and half-disappointed. So many more jokes were milling about my little fox-brain to tease them with.

Hiroki removed his hand from my mouth, wiped my saliva off on the front of my T-shirt, and started laughing. "Creamy center of a three musketeers bar," he said between chuckles.

"Right? I had a million more, but thanks for pulling my fat out of the fryer."

"I am less worried about those three than the headmistress."

"Headmistress." I laughed. "How do you think she earned *that* title?"

His eyes widened. "I am sure through hard work and perseverance. Dedication, and honesty."

"She's come back and is standing right behind me, isn't she?"

48

Hiroki nodded, not taking his eyes off Lateran.

"Seventeen-E?"

He shook his head. Time to go for the classic One-A. I popped out of existence, leaving Hiroki to deal with Lateran. I popped back into existence by the front door and quietly slipped outside. Leaning back against the entrance to Breckenridge Hall, I chuckled. As soon as the *head*mistress left, I would be free to go back inside, find my room, and hide under the bed like a smart little fox.

The door opened against me and I immediately saw the flaw on my plan. Lateran couldn't exactly leave if I was blocking the door. I squeaked, ran around the stone column beside the entrance, and peeked around the corner. Luckily it wasn't her, it was David.

"Oh, it's you," I said and stood back up.

"You were expecting Rome?"

"Who's Rome?"

"My friend, whom you have been so elegantly tormenting since our arrival?"

"You mean Jacques?"

"Jacques?"

"Oh, that's what I've been calling him in my head."

"Are there many voices inside there?"

"It's like a choir sometimes, but as I harnessed my power for good, I learned to drown out the ones who tell me to do naughty things."

"I think they're still singing."

"Like canaries."

He laughed and leaned against the column. "I don't think I've ever met anybody like you."

"Well, I had a twin sister, but she's in prison so the odds of you meeting her are slim to none."

His eyes widened. "Truly?"

"Nah, but it sounded cool. So, what brings you to my neck of the woods?"

"Well, I was waiting for an opportune moment to introduce myself."

"You already did. You're David. Jacques' friend." I sat down on the concrete base of the column but gave up and stood again. David was too tall to sit and talk to. I was going to get a crick in my neck.

"You are very fidgety. Why do you call him Jacques?"

"Well, I didn't know his name was Rome and he kind of was acting like a Jacques Strahp."

"Jacque Strahp?"

"It's French for athletic supporter?"

"I'm confused…"

Cute but stupid. My favorite flavors. Like "Athletic supporter… I was calling him a jock strap."

"Ahh. I see."

"You know what those are, right? Under the butt nut huts?"

"Yes." He chuckled. "I am intimately familiar with their usage."

"Intimately?" I wiggled my eyebrows.

"Yes. I played sports in school."

"Oh. That's much less fun. You ever launch water balloons from them?"

He tilted his head, scrunched his eyes, and stared at me like I had lost my damn mind.

"Sorry. I'm not usually this hyper. In awkward situations, I tend to get a little…"

"Crazy?"

"I was going to go with distracted and whimsical, but I'm sure those are in the definition of crazy somewhere."

"You…"

"No. Not psycho. Just hyper."

"No. I was going to say you are very unique."

"Yerp."

"Yerp?" He scrunched his eyebrows, looking even cuter.

"Means yes."

"In which language?"

"Ermagerdian."

"Erma?"

"Gerdian."

"And this is the national language of?"

"Ermagerd. Its capital is Memeville."

"You are making all of this up." He was catching on and dazzled me with a quirky little smile. When I said dazzle, I meant, *Daaaaamn he's cute.*

"Yerp."

"Would you care to have dinner with me some time?"

"Won't your boyfriend get jealous?"

"We are not mutually exclusive," he said straight-faced.

"Woah. You guys really..." I made dirty gestures with my fingers.

"Nerp. Just wanted to see your reaction."

"Ermagerd! You speak Ermagerdian like a native!"

"Once you learn the phonetics, the rest comes naturally."

It was official. I was in love with David. *He gets me. I should probably let his therapist know.*

"I'd like that. Don't bring your friends. Wait... Are they brothers, because they look an awful lot alike."

"Twins in fact. Identical."

"Huh. I figured they just both belonged to the same fraternity. But then their names would have been Todd and Chad. What's the other one's name?"

"Remy."

"Rome and Remy? Really? Ridiculous." I fake scoffed.

"Do not let them hear you say that..."

"What? I'll piss them off? Been there, done that, got the tattoo."

"Dinner tonight?"

"Woah, Mr. Pushy. I already said yes, but don't you think we should wait at least twenty-four hours? Give a girl a chance to primp and preen."

"Tomorrow then?"

"It's a date. Cafeteria?"

"Since our restaurant selection is very limited, I think that is a wonderful idea. Pick you up at seven?"

I gave him an earnest smile. David of the dimples and sweet smile was okay in my book. Much better than the testosterone twins any day. "Perfect."

He held out his hand for a shake. I took it and gasped at the heat coming from it. "You okay? Running a fever? Or do I just make you hot?"

He pulled his hand from my grip and gave me a worried look.

"If you think I give two rats' asses about extra credit and am trying to figure out what you are, you are *sorely* mistaken."

His eyes narrowed for a moment, but he must have trusted his gut instinct and the curvy smile returned to his lips. *The fool! Bwahahaha. Just kidding, I really don't care. Besides, I'd take that smile over extra credit any day.*

"I am just very warm."

"Can I borrow you when it starts snowing?"

"Cuddle buddy?"

"I was thinking area rug, but sure. Cuddle buddies work, too."

"So strange and yet so interesting."

"That's me."

"We should probably find out where our rooms are, no?" He motioned toward the door.

"Uh… Yeah. Could you let me know if the coast is clear?"

"Rome and Remy are probably already in their rooms."
"I'm more worried about Headmistress Morticia."
"Lateran?"
"Her, too."

Chapter 5

"Seriously?"

"Seriously," Hiroki answered, seemingly as shocked as I was.

"I mean, I understand the whole co-ed dorm idea. We're all mostly grown-ups here, but they put us in the same room?"

"*Hai*."

"Did you use your magic on that nice lady who looks like somebody's granny?"

"No."

"Did you give her exorbitant amounts of money?"

"No."

"Sweet. You saved me the trouble then. I *really* didn't want to get stuck bunking with somebody named Karen."

"I suspect your uncle had much to do with it," he said as we headed up the wooden staircase to the second floor of Breckenridge Hall. "I am your attendant. He probably put us together for your safety. Or that of your roommate."

"Hmmm. Yeah. That I can believe. We're on the second floor. People have a tendency to jump from high places when forced to spend large amounts of time with me."

"I have yet to jump."

"That's cuz you're my widdle Roki." I pinched his cheek.

"A shame they do not have a third floor. The end might come quicker."

"Har har. What's our room number?"

"201."

"Look at that. First one. That will be handy for quick getaways." I paused a moment to commit the stair landing to memory. I couldn't pop to someplace I hadn't been or couldn't see, but if I memorized it, I could get from my room to the stairs in literally the blink of an eye, but only if I was close enough. I could probably make it to the stairs from my room without looking, but any farther was pushing it.

Hiroki sighed and grabbed my arm before I could turn the key to our new love-nest. "Kaede-*sama*... May I urge *caution*? You are already treading upon a barely frozen body of water. Especially with the headmistress, who's berating skills rival that of your mother's, for your information. Thank you for leaving me with that. But, *please*, let us just get through our time here with a minimal of...trouble?"

"What fun would that be? Plus, you keep using this caution word like I know what it means. Hiroki! Relax! This is like college without frat houses, beer bongs, and grades! Pass or fail buddy. There is no honor roll or GPAs to worry about."

"You did not even finish high school. You were expelled, remember?"

"I'm telling you that fire was *not* my fault. The chemistry teacher hated me and left the propane valve open on purpose. I was framed...framed I tell you!"

"I was there when you turned the knob."

"Oh yeah. Well, I didn't put the lit Bunsen burner in the room."

"Yes, you did."

"I thought that was you?"

"No. You asked me to hand it to you. I should have said no."

"See? I knew it was your fault."

He sighed again. He made that noise a lot. If he kept losing air like that, I was going to have to keep a can of fix-a-flat and an air compressor around for emergencies. Nobody wanted a flat Hiroki.

I turned the key in the knob and opened the door to our new home. And was utterly disappointed. Seriously. There were two beds, two dressers, two desks and chairs, and *nothing* else. I mean, it was pretty, completely made of wood, and seriously depressing. The utter lack of entertainment was appalling. How was a girl supposed to live without a television? Or even a mini-fridge? "Wait a minute... Where the fuck am I supposed to keep my alcohol?"

"That was one of the dorm rules you missed while you were outside flirting."

"I wasn't flirting. I was hiding. And if I didn't hear it, it's not a real rule, right?"

"Kaede-*sama*..."

"*Chan*."

"At least wait a month before you start abandoning all sense of propriety."

"You're a *kami*-damned *nogitsune*! I'm *supposed* to be calming you down. What the hell happened to your noble heritage?"

"It met you and wanted, with all my might, to protect you."

"I hate it when you get all sweet and shit. Knock it off."

"*Hai*."

I hugged him anyway. "I wish you liked girls."

He laughed and pushed me away. "You know I do. It is you I cannot stand."

"Uh, huh," I said with a smile and sat down on the bed, the one I had claimed as my own. "So, you're telling me that if it wasn't for the fear of my parents...you would have been all over this?" I motioned at my body in a dorky erotic way.

57

"No. I prefer my girls with a little less penis on them."

"I don't have a ding-ding."

"Kaede-*sama*, some days, I think yours is bigger than mine."

"That's not saying much. I've seen you naked."

He made a hurt expression, but I knew he was full of shit. I *had* seen Hiroki naked on occasion... Calling his cock tiny would be like calling an aircraft carrier a dinghy.

Now, I just need to figure out how to get my hands on it...

"Is that the bed you wish to occupy?"

"No. Just warming yours up with my butt."

"My apologies, I had assumed you wished to be closest to the bathroom."

"Kidding. Yes. This is my bed. No touchy."

He rolled his eyes and shook his head. "A simple yes would have sufficed," he mumbled under his breath.

"Well, I'm going to take a bath before dinner." I stood up and started to lift my shirt over my head before stopping cold. "Uh... Hiroki? Why am I not seeing a door to the bathroom in our room?"

"Because there is not one? There are community bathrooms on each floor. Had you not been outside flirt–"

"I wasn't fucking flirting! Seriously? I have to *share* a bathroom? How the hell am I supposed to get my fur clean?"

"Shave it off?"

"Gah! I hate this fucking place. Let's go home. I need a drink."

"Feel free. I shall wait here. It should not take that long for your mother to remove your tails and kick you halfway across the planet."

I dropped back down to the bed and fell over sideways, burying my face in the strange smelling pillows. They weren't my pillows. It wasn't my bed. It wasn't my home.

Finally, a little something inside me broke, and the tears started falling down my face.

It only took Hiroki a moment to notice, even though he couldn't see me. How he knew, I didn't have a clue, nor did I care. He crawled up the bed and lay down behind me, putting his arms around me and pulling me into him. At least *he* smelled like home.

Hiroki's arms were warm and comforting. I rolled over and buried my face in his chest. Gently, he kissed the top of my head. "Do not give up before it begins, Kaede. You can do this."

"I don't want to."

"Here, there, it does not matter. You are you and always make the best of any situation. You must look for the bright side in all things."

"What's the bright side?"

"You have me." His response was so uncharacteristic, I had no choice but to smile.

"Forever?"

"I have loved you since the day you were born, Kaede. It is my plan to continue doing so until the end of time."

"Wait. Like love love…or just like a kid sister kind of love?" I was expecting him to sigh and he didn't disappoint. It just took longer than I was expecting.

"Which would you prefer?"

"You already know that answer."

"Why me? There are literally hundreds of men at this school."

"Because, you are you," I said, throwing his words back at him.

"Even if we became lovers…you know nothing could *ever* come of it. We are not in the stars, Kaede. Your parents would never allow it."

As much as I hated to admit when he was right, he was. "Who's looking for a relationship? Not this fox, let me tell you. But who says we cannot have a little fun every once in a while?"

I probably said the wrong thing. He instantly stiffened, and not in the good way. "Go have your bath. It will be time for dinner soon."

I almost started crying again when he kissed me on top of my head and let go of me. I'd never felt so utterly alone in my life.

∞ ∞ ∞

The awesome thing about showers is, nobody can see you crying. The tears just sort of blend in and you can stand there crying for an hour without a single person asking you what the hell is wrong with you. Not that the snotty ass bitches in the stalls beside me cared anyway. Their conversations ranged from boys, to boys, to boys. Apparently, one of the first years had already blown someone and *everybody* knew about it. I wouldn't tell anybody, not that I had anybody to tell, but I wasn't that experienced. I talked a mean game, but I could count the number of guys I had slept with on one hand. Human guys just had a tendency to shy away from the supernatural. Unless you were some sort of succubus, getting laid wasn't always easy.

The few guys I *had* fooled around with lived in the town my parents had built. Foxes mostly, but there were a few *yokai* as well. My longest running relationship had lasted a lengthy six hours. Standing under the shower, in the girls' washroom of my new school, I came to the realization that I *might* be high maintenance.

Reaching out and gripping the shower knob, I turned it until the flow of water stopped. I stood there for a moment, letting the water cascade from me and fall to the white-tiled floor beneath me. I had just wrapped myself in one of the towels left in our room when the door to my stall was pulled open.

"Oops. Sorry. Didn't realize this one was taken. Aren't you a little *old* to be a student here?" She paused to stare at my white hair. "Or are you another one of those dorm nannies spying on us teenage girls?"

I cocked my eyebrow at the extraordinarily tall Scandinavian Amazonian standing in front of me with her hand on her hip. "If I were to spy on a teenage girl, it would be on one with breasts. I almost didn't notice you standing in front of all the flat white tiles." I chuckled and motioned for her to get the hell out of my way.

"You little–"

"Really? This is how you want to play this? You're going to try and bully me on the first day of fucking school? Couldn't you at least wait a week? Pretty sure that was in the bully handbook I took off that last dead body."

The two girls standing behind her sneering at me gave a little chuckle at my attempt to defuse the situation. One look over her shoulder was enough to paint the smirks back on their lips. She turned her head back to me, and just that one look at her cohorts must have topped off her tank of bully juice.

"You have no idea who you're dealing with, do you?"

"How did I know you were going to say that? Does a free book of clichés come with the bully book? Or did you have to pay extra for it?"

She sputtered and motioned for her friends to back her up. They took a step forward, but the shower stall didn't allow for three abreast thugs. "You know what? You can keep your little shower stall. I don't think I want to use it after you, you disease infested *rodent*."

"Bully books, clichés, *and* insults? Somebody blew a wad of cash at Barnes & Noble. But then again, you look like you're used to blowing things. And I'm sure you have a lot of experience with wads... Oh! It must have been you that was giving out welcome to the academy blowjobs! Shit, if I had known that, I woulda borrowed somebody's dick and lined up. Can I borrow yours?"

Know that exact moment when you just *know* you took things a little too far? Yeah. That was one of those times. Her fist locked on target and went straight for my exhaust port. I popped into existence behind them and turned to watch the show.

Elsa's fist, without anything to stop it, such as my face, hyper extended her arm. I giggled and clapped when she lost her balance and fell into the shower head first. The other two screamed and lurched forward to catch her and save her a large bill from the dentist. Luckily, one of them got their hand in the towel she had wrapped around herself, yanking back just as her face was about to connect with the floor.

I walked over and grabbed my shampoo and conditioner from the stall, and headed for the exit, not even bothering to cover up. "Remember, ladies... You mess with the bull, you get the shit," I called over my shoulder and waved. As soon as I was back, naked, in the corridor leading to my room, I popped back in front of my door. Unfortunately, I couldn't teleport through doors or walls, otherwise I would already be hiding under my covers. I wasn't a brave fox, nor apparently was I a smart fox. I had gone to take a shower without my room key, trusting that Hiroki would be there to open the door upon my return.

I started pounding on the door as soon as I appeared, fumbling to get the towel around me while holding two bottles of hair care products. Unfortunately, my door wasn't the first to open. Slowly I turned... Jacques had opened *his* door, which by the grace of *kami*, was directly across the hall from ours, to see what the commotion was.

His eyes weren't focused anywhere near my face. In fact, I could almost feel the heat from his gaze on my still wet, very exposed ass...

"Howdy, neighbor. Enjoying the view?" I wiggled my butt for emphasis

He stared for a moment longer. I stopped fumbling with the towel and just stood there, ass to the wind, so to speak. His hungry gaze traveled up my back, caressed my shoulder, and stared at my face. He scowled, walked back into his room, and slammed the door behind him.

Totally worth it.

Screams of rage erupted from the bathroom at the end of the hall, I pounded frantically on the door again. By the time my fist connected with the wood for the fifty-third time, Hiroki opened it and I fell into the room atop of him. "Thank fuck. Took you long enough," I said and kicked the door closed behind me.

Chapter 6

"Seriously? Home economics?" I was staring at the list of classes while Hiroki and I tried to *find* the first one on the list.

"Yes. And if we do not hurry, it will be over before we get there."

"I'm good with that."

"Physical Education? What the ever-loving fuck?"

"You could stand to shed a few pounds. Loose some of that *sake*-gut."

"You wanna die?"

"Eventually. Yes. If it is at your hand, I shall pass on happy."

"That's kind of morbid."

"I was joking. Like you could kill me. Who would fold your underpants?"

"At least I wouldn't have to worry about you wearing them."

"That was one time, and the lack of circulation to my extremities was painful."

"Shouldn't have popped a chubby."

"I was referring to my legs."

"Uh huh. Suuure you were."

He stopped walking and it took me a moment to notice he wasn't beside me anymore. I turned around and he was pointing at a set of double doors. "I believe this is the place."

I shoved the class schedule into the pocket of my newly issued blazer and scratched the back of my neck. The blue wool with red trim was itchier than a pile of hay after a skinny dip, but it was classy. It even had a fancy crest embroidered on the pocket. The pleated skirt was actually kind of cute, too. But still itchy. I was going to have self-inflicted claw marks on my ass by the end of the day. "You sure?"

His nostrils flared as he scented the air. "Quite."

"Oooh. Too much garlic," I made a face and waited for him to enter first. He wasn't very tall, but tall enough for my scrawny ass to hide behind.

He turned the handle and pulled it open, gave me a smile, and stepped back for me to enter first. He did it on purpose, knowing full well I hated going anywhere first. "Some bodyguard you are."

"I think you are safe at school."

"Bull shit. Somebody tried to murder me in the shower!"

"Were you talking at the time?"

"Yes," I answered, failing to see the relevance.

"At least the mystery has been solved, Kaede-*sama*."

"You're a big meanie."

"*Hai*." He made a sweeping gesture toward the door.

I closed my eyes and took that fateful first step into the home economics room. Nobody was cooking, but the walls, floor, and ceiling had been saturated with enough cooking oils for the smell to linger like a heavy cloud. At least to somebody with the nose of a fox. I could also tell more than one student had failed horribly at their assignment, the smell of carbon remained strong in the air.

"Thank you for gracing us with your presence," a shrill voice called from the corner of the room.

"Yeah… Big school, got lost, sorry about that."

66

"Find an open work station and we'll begin our introductions," the short, gnarly looking tree stump of a woman said as she waddled toward the front of the class.

I glanced around the room. Unfortunately, all of the stations in the *rear* of the room were the first ones to fill up, leaving only two of the front three stations opened. Sighing, I headed for the one closest to the window in case I felt the need to jump. Dread filled me as I sat on one of the two tallish stools. I could cook, for the simple fact that I fucking loved to eat. I'd been doing it since I was a little girl. *Hiroki* could get a job at a Japanese restaurant if he wanted to. He was exponentially better than I was. Why the hell we had to take home economics was beyond me.

"I am Professor Welheim," she said and wrote her name out on the ancient green chalkboard. Unfortunately, the W sound in her name came out as a V sound and the heim sounded like she was trying to speak Klingon or launch a hunk of lung pudding across the room. Of course, I immediately started giggling.

"You find my name humorous, Miss…"

"Take."

"Your last name is Take?"

"Yes."

"Miss Take."

"Yes."

She narrowed her eyes and grabbed a clipboard off her desk. "I don't seem to have a Miss Take on my Roster."

"There must be some kind of mistake!" I slapped my knee. I was expecting at least a chuckle or two from the rest of the class, but nothing. "Just kidding. I'm Kaede Tanaka."

"See me after class, Miss Tanaka."

Of course, the whole fucking class erupted in a unified, "Oooh." Bastards. They were supposed to be my people and left me hanging to side with Miss Velkhhhhhhheim. "Sure thing," I said and gave her an innocent smile.

"Since we have that introduction out of the way, let's continue getting to know one another, shall we?" She pointed at Hiroki.

"Hiroki Nishimura."

She waited for him to say a little more, maybe mention a hobby or two, possibly a blood type. He didn't. He stared at her until she called on the table behind us.

"She's fun," I whispered out of the side of my mouth.

"Two-minutes into class. I think that might be a new record."

"Nope. Remember when I got suspended walking into class that one time?"

"The flaming gerbil or the moose antlers?"

"The gerbil. It took the teacher almost three whole minutes to notice the antlers."

"Ah yes. Both admirable."

"You get me."

"You get me. In trouble mostly."

Sometime during our discussion, we had stopped whispering. Professor Velheim was staring at the two of us, aghast. The rest of the class was staring at us like we were insane.

"Sorry," I whispered.

"Mr. Nishimura, please join Miss Tanaka in seeing me after class."

"*Hai.*"

Instead of oohing, the class just full out erupted into laughter. They needed to seriously work on their timing. It sucked.

I pretended to be a good student while the remainder of the class introduced themselves. My eyes narrowed when Elsa stood up. "Hi, I'm Sabine."

"Of course she is."

"Sabine Lateran."

"Why do I know that name?"

"Because it is the same as the headmistress," Hiroki answered."

"I'm dead."

"I am to assume she is the one you had an altercation with in the shower?"

Professor Guggenheim coughed in our general direction. I waved, reached into my pocket, and offered her a cough drop I had found on the floor in the hallway. I knew I'd find a purpose for it later. She just shook her head and continued with the introductions.

Finally, they were over. I applauded in an attempt to unify the class in a feeling of comradery, but they weren't having it. They did like to stare, though. I shrugged and turned back around.

"Well, the best place to start is always at the beginning."

"A very good place to start," I sang. She ignored me for once.

"To *get* to the beginning, I need to know what you are capable of. In the back of the class, you will find a store room and cooler full of ingredients. You and your partner have forty minutes to flabbergast me with your best dish." She paused to cast a dire look at me and Hiroki. "After I have seen you taste it."

"What should we make?"

"We should decide *after* we see the ingredients available, no?"

"You're a fart smeller."

"Pardon?"

"Smart feller. My bad." The rest of the class was already heading into the store room. "Come on. Everything will be gone by the time we get in there."

Surprisingly enough, there was no line, there was enough staples to make *anything* we wanted, and the chances of them running out of *anything* were about the same as me winning a Nobel Peace Prize.

"A traditional Japanese meal?"

"We should probably go for simple. Maybe a nice curry."

"I will see if they have curry roux."

"I will find the rice," I answered and gave him a sweet smile. He narrowed his eyes but nodded.

All the dry ingredients were on storage shelves toward the back of the room. "Why the hell do they have so much stock for a home economics class?"

"Because the doors on the other side of the room are accessible from the cafeteria. This is their storage facility, but the home economics class uses a portion of the goods."

I screeched, jumped in the air, and landed facing Professor Welheim. She might have the body of a bull dog, but she had the stealth of a cat. "*Kami*. Make some noise or something."

"Just keeping an eye on my new favorite pupil."

"Me? I'm your favorite?"

"Let's just say I love a good challenge. That's you." She chuckled evilly.

"Sweet! It's a challenge!" I held out my hand to shake on it.

She looked down but didn't take it. "Since I have you here, let me be frank. You will tone it down in my class. You will be on time. You will try your hardest to complete the assignments. And you will stop being so disruptive."

"Um. I think you're totally missing some of the finer points of the word challenge. That means I don't get to make it *that* easy! May the best...um...person win!" I stepped around her, grabbed a large bag of rice, and started hauling it to where Hiroki had left me. He could carry it. It wasn't exactly light, but I needed every grain in the bag. And a jar. "Hey, Professor! Any jugs lying around?"

She hadn't taken her eyes off me. "Utensils, pots, pans, and anything else you may need is back in the classroom."

"Sweet. Thanks." I gave her one last grin and headed for our work station. Hiroki could handle dinner, I had something else in mind.

I gave up waiting on Hiroki. Slinging the sack of rice over my shoulder, I practically ran back into the classroom and dropped it on the counter. Before Hiroki got back, I had commandeered a rice cooker, and a plain clay jug that would work perfectly for my plan. I filled the jar with rice and then proceeded to measure out scoops into the cooker, adding a touch of salt and oil. The jar I filled with water and covered.

I looked around the room, and the few people who were back were busy chopping vegetables or prepping the meat for their dishes. Hiroki was either still looking for the ingredients or me, but either way, I had precious little time left. All *Inari* fox were granted the powers to be a messenger for their god, *Inari. Inari* was the *kami* of rice and craftsmen. Blacksmiths as well. But being an agricultural god of rice blessed us with one awesome ability...

I put my hands against the outside of the clay jar and called a little bit of foxfire, standing in front of it to block the view of everyone behind me. The lid rattled and a puff of sake scented steam wafted upward and caressed my nose like a long-lost lover. Why long-lost lovers caressed peoples' noses was beyond me, but it didn't really matter. I had a jar of *sake*.

I grinned and grabbed the small teacup I had found by the jug.

"Yeah, buddy." I lifted the lid, dipped in the cup, and sat at my desk happily sipping and waiting on Hiroki. Actually, using a bit of caution, I opened the cabinet by my knee and set the jar inside. Pulling out a maple leaf from the inside of my blazer, I pressed it against the side of the jar. There was a brief sizzle of power, and when I pulled my hand away, the jar was completely invisible. Out of sight, out of possibility of detection from troll-like professors with culinary utensils lodged in their rectum. Unfortunately, the spell wouldn't last that long, just about until the end of class. I could turn myself invisible, too, but only for a few moments.

I grinned like a…fox and sipped my sake.

Hiroki returned a few moments after I had dipped my teacup in for a refill. "I believe I have everything."

"I got the rice." I pointed at the cooker, that I had forgotten to plug in and turn on. "Want me to start it?"

"*Hai*, the curry will not take long. I thought prawns would be a nice change with a white curry. There was no roux, I shall have to improvise my own."

"Carry on."

"Chop the vegetables?"

"Of course. Glad to be of assistance."

I should have shut up. He knew something was up and noticed the teacup in my hand. His nostrils flared. "You made *sake*?" He whispered and hissed, even though the teacher was still in the storeroom.

"Yep. Wanna sip?"

He looked around and pulled the cup from my hand, taking a healthy swig of it. "That might be your best yet."

"It's because I *really* wanted it. I poured a lot of love into its making."

"Please, do not get caught."

"Do I ever?"

"Do you wish me to lie to you?"

"Yes. Tell me I'm pretty."

"That would not be a lie."

I smiled at the carrot I was chopping, my heart warming a little. Maybe it was the *sake*. Stopping my chopping, I downed the rest of my cup and set it aside, vowing to refill it as soon as I had finished dismembering the vegetables.

It only took a few minutes to have everything bubbling away nicely in the pot. Except for the shrimp, they got added just a few minutes before the curry was ready. My mouth was watering from the aroma. I ducked down and dipped my cup one last time. Class would be over soon. As I sat there, sipping happily, the professor stopped in front of our table. "No beverages in class, Miss Tanaka." She held out her hand for my cup. I downed the last of it and handed it to her with a smile.

"Sorry. Cooking is thirsty work."

She narrowed her eyes at me and brought the cup to her bulbous nose, inhaling it briefly. Her eyes widened in surprise. "Cooking wine?"

"Nope. Just water," I lied.

She let it go but gave a good look over the top of our work station. "Is there wine in your dish?" She ignored me and asked Hiroki.

"No, ma'am."

"What is your dish?"

"We made a white curry with prawns."

She reached over and pulled the lid off the pot just as the rice dinged. She fanned some of the steam over to her face and inhaled deeply. "That smells exquisite. Are dishes from Japan all you can cook?" This time she looked at the two of us.

"Oh, hell no. We're from California. We can cooks just about anythings."

"Hopefully *you* cook better than you speak."

"I does." I nodded emphatically.

She just shook her head and moved on. I waited until she was out of earshot, then waited a minute more after learning my lesson the hard way with Headmistress Lateran. "I don't think she likes you very much," I said to Hiroki.

"Be that as it may, she likes you even less."

"Really? Cuz I was picking up a whole 'I dig your wittiness' vibe from her."

"I believe that was nausea."

"Oh. I don't think your curry smells that bad. Maybe it's the shrimps?' I picked up the pound of raw shellfish and gave it a sniff. "Nope. It's your curry. Quite possibly your cologne. Maybe your face."

"Kaede-sama. Shush." He pulled the testing fork out of the soft flesh of one of the larger slices of carrot, tested a potato, and took the shrimp from my hands, dumping it into the bubbling pot.

"Know what would be good with that curry?"

"Please do not say *sake*."

"Rice wine!" I grabbed the cup off the counter and knelt down beside Hiroki. I felt around for the lid, unable to see it. With a grin, I filled my cup.

Chapter 7

"Who the fuck puts PE right after drinking class? That's just mean," I said with my head hung over the side of the fence, the remnants of curried prawns on the other side.

Hiroki was still holding my hair. "I believe it is called home economics. Nowhere in the syllabus, course description, *or* class schedule did it use the word drinking."

"Well, I needed something to help me deal with that mean ole teacher."

"Because patience and silence are not your virtues."

I turned my head and looked at him. "You're being very judgy today."

He just sighed and patted my head. "Yes. I am. You are being very frustrating today."

"In my defense, I am very frustrating *every* day."

"And yet you do nothing about it."

"Fuck no. It's fun."

He gave a soft chuckle.

"What's the matter Tanaka? You preggers?" Sabine's inane giggle grated across the last of my already frayed nerves. I truly hated puking.

"Yep. Tell your dad I want child support!" I grinned at her as she kept running and laughed when she stumbled.

"Push that one too far and things could get ugly," Hiroki admonished.

"Puh-lease. She's already ugly."

He turned and looked at her retreating backside. "In a tall, svelte, athletic, sexy sort of way, I suppose."

"Ew. I just threw up in my mouth."

"I know. I held your hair."

"Plus, look at the girl's mother. We all turn into our mothers eventually. She's going to crash and burn."

"I look forward to the day when you adopt your mother's calm, serene beauty."

"Oh, shut up. I'm sure she was twice as wild when she was my age."

He gave me a sad look.

"What?"

"Nothing."

"Don't you fucking nothing me, spill it."

"It is not my tale to tell."

"Hiroki, I swear to *Inari*…"

"Fine. Incur his wrath, but my lips are sealed."

"Grrrr!" I stomped away from him, completely forgetting he had a fistful of my hair. "Ouch!"

"My apologies."

"Uh huh."

"We should continue running before we get singled out by the instructor."

"You mean Captain Doom? I swear that guy is a human drill sergeant, hell bent on making us poor, unathletic supernatural folk suffer for his shortcomings."

"He *is* human. As for a drill sergeant, that I do not know."

"Wait. You can tell?"

"*Hai*." He said and started jogging. I pumped my little legs to catch up to him and fell into rhythm next to him. My stomach was still lurching, and my head was still swimming, but at least the earth stopped spinning. At least from my perspective.

"How?"

He touched the side of his nose and gave me a wink. "I can tell what a good portion of the students are as well. As long as I have scented their kind before."

"Holy fucking extra credit. We're gonna pass with flying colors."

"That would be cheating."

"Last time I checked, using your abilities was *encouraged*. As long as you didn't give away what you were. What is Sabine?"

"You are actually correct. I guess a natural ability wouldn't be considered cheating."

"See? I told you!"

"I shall earn as much as I can to ensure I graduate."

"What about me?"

"What about you? Telling *you* so you can earn credit *would* be cheating."

"Sometimes I truly hate you, Roki." I sighed and gave up. He was a natural born trickster, but he held himself to a very strict moral code. Getting him to go against that was impossible and I would just be wasting my breath.

"No, you do not. You love me," he said with a very foxlike snicker, scrunching his eyes as he laughed.

I didn't deny it. Just jogged along silently. Another person came around the bend and slipped up next to me. "Still on for dinner?"

"David!" I gave him a happy little grin. "I saw Tweedle Dum and Tweedle Roid Rage, but I didn't know you were in this class." I wasn't lying, either. I'd seen Rome and Remy stretching before our twenty-six-mile run and given them a super-wide berth. Like different time zone wide.

He chuckled at my latest attempt at humor. "I saw you."

"You did?"

"Yep. Puking over the fence? Rumor is you're pregnant?"

"Hardly. Let me guess...tall blonde and bitchy?"

"Sabine? Yes."

"Figures."

"She is spreading rumors about you?"

"Yeah. She found out I was sleeping with her father."

"Um…"

"I'm kidding. Yeah. She just doesn't like me. But feel free to spread the rumor of her father's infidelity around, though."

Again, he rewarded me with his melted chocolate drizzled marshmallow chuckle. It made me feel warm and fuzzy inside and out. The fox wanted to come out and play. He nearly stumbled beside me and stopped running. I turned around and started circling around him. "Are you okay?"

"Kaede-*sama*?" Hiroki was jogging backward.

"Keep going. I'll catch up."

He raised an eyebrow but did as I asked, turning and leaving the two of us in the middle of the track.

"David?"

"Yeah. I'm fine… Let's go before Coach yells at us for stopping."

"You stopped. I'm still jogging."

"You mean walking fast?"

"You're teasing me?"

His grin was enough of an answer. He started jogging again and I fell into step beside him. "Sorry about that. Didn't mean to break your rhythm."

"Ha! I have no rhythm. You should see me dance."

"I'd like that."

"What?"

"Seeing you dance. As long as you didn't mind if I joined you."

"You want to dance with me?"

"Yes."

"Do you hate your toes?"

"I…heal quickly."

"Fine. It's a date."

"You haven't even gone out on one with me yet and you're already agreeing to a second?"

"Dinner tonight is our first? Even though it's at the school cafeteria?"

"Yep."

I blushed and smiled.

"Pick you up at six? Now that we know what time they start serving food."

"Sure."

"What's your room number?"

"201."

"You're right across the hall from Rome and Remy?"

"Yeah. That was awkward. He saw my naked butt last night." I *might* have said it to make David a little jealous. He didn't take the bait and chuckled it off. "So, you were the naked girl in the hallway last night. There were rumors of that, too."

"Not my fault. Sabine slipped in the shower and blamed me."

"Ah. So you were the bitch in the shower, too?"

"What the fuck? Is there a rumor newsletter that I should know about?"

"No. Sabine told me."

"Sabine tells you a lot of things…"

"Yeah. Clingy ex-girlfriend."

The hackles on my hackles rose up and hissed in annoyance. "Ex?"

"Yeah," he said almost apologetically.

"Completely ex, though. Right? Not in a 'still get together for dinner' or 'I'm bored and need a booty call' kind of way?"

He laughed and there was an utter lack of warm and fuzzies. He must have noticed my discomfort and reached out and put his hand on my arm on the upswing from jogging. He slowed our jog and led us into the center of the track.

"Kaede... This was several years in the past. I...did not care much for her and broke things off soon after they started. I'm not a masochist, so the odds of me *ever* courting that disaster again are non-existent."

"Oh. Okay. When you put it *that* way."

"You don't believe me?"

"Um... Don't tell her this, but she's like a fucking supermodel. How could you *not* be attracted to her?"

"While she might be pretty, her...nature makes her an unsuitable mate."

"Mate? Did you guys mate?" I winced as the words poured from my mouth like an evil curse.

He gave me a half-smile half-frown and narrowed his eyes at me. "Do you *really* want to know the answer to that question?"

"No. I didn't even *really* want to fucking ask it. Sometimes I hate my mouth."

"Why? It's beautiful."

Holy fuck, did I blush. "Uh... Um. Yeah. Wow."

"Too much?"

"No. Say it again. Slowly."

He took another step closer to me, even though I probably smelled like curried prawns, sweat, and vomit. He leaned down and inched his face closer to mine. "I said that I think you have a beautiful mouth."

"Wasn't that in *Deliverance*?"

"I think they used pretty. Pretty doesn't even begin to describe the curve of your smile. Beautiful is only moderately ample, but I didn't want to drive you away, thinking all I could think of was your lips and how soft they must be. And how much I enjoy it when they utter my name. What it would be like to kiss them, and what they would taste like..."

"Keep talking and you're going to find out. Later. You probably wouldn't be a big fan of the taste right now." I wasn't a big fan of how uncomfortable jogging was going to be right now, either. Hopefully nobody would hear me squish as I ran by.

"Then I won't have anything else to live for."

"Um… I have a lot of body parts."

He actually blushed. I slapped his arm. "I meant my eyes and stuff. Get your mind out of the gutter." *Please don't. Keep it in the gutter. Gutter is good.*

His blush got even worse. "I wouldn't! I'm…" He sighed. "I'm just kind of shy."

"How the fuck are you shy? Like, oh, my *kami*… You had me at hello and then you go on this articulate rampage of sweetness. You don't get to call yourself shy."

"Fine. I'm not shy. But I wasn't thinking of…" He looked down at my very tight gym shorts. "I would never disrespect you like that."

I leaned in closer, putting my lips next to his ear and whispered, "But, I might like that."

Leaning back, I grabbed his hand and pulled him back out onto the track, wanting nothing more than to get the rest of the classes done and have dinner with him.

"So, when you said mate. You didn't mean like soul, insta-love, bonded for all eternity type stuff, did you?"

"Of the thousands of species of supernatural creatures, I think the total that are life-bonded is around three. I can say that I am not one of them. My parents were divorced before they died."

"Ooops. My bad."

"No worries. Come on, I'll race you."

∞ ∞ ∞

"I will be close by but shall not interfere with your date."

"Thanks, wingman," I said to Hiroki and slipped into the school issued evening wear. I hated not having my own clothes, but at least the fashionistas wouldn't have anything to fight about. Basically, they were school uniforms without the blazers and a little less fancy.

"How do I look?"

"Like a school girl. Kind of creepy. Ditch the makeup, it makes you look like you're trying to look older."

"You just don't want him to think I'm attractive."

"He would have to not have eyes for that to be possible."

That deserved a hug. Since it was all he would allow. "I love you."

"I am fond of you as well, Kaede-*sama*."

"Shut up. You love me and you know it."

"Sometimes. When you are not getting me in trouble."

"What? I *never* get you in trouble. It's your own poor decision-making abilities that put you in jeopardy."

"I shall remember that next time you ask me to do something."

"What were we talking about?"

"Your tawdry makeup."

"Fine. Let me borrow one of your makeup wipes."

"You are hilarious."

"I know."

I ran into the bathroom and pulled out my pack, ripping one out and rubbing my face until it was red but clean. Hiroki was standing behind me and staring at me in the mirror. "Much better."

"Yeah, yeah. Sure it is."

"It is. You do not need makeup. You are only covering that which is perfect."

"You trying to get into my pants?"

"You are wearing a skirt."

"Oh. Did you want to wear my skirt?"

"No. It would clash with my shoes," he said and turned away.

"Roki?"

"Yes?"

"Thank you for telling me I'm beautiful."

"I simply share the truth. Be careful tonight but have fun. Not your usual levels, though. We don't want you getting expelled."

"Good advice. No *sake*."

"I do not think they serve alcohol…"

"That was a joke."

"It is hard to tell with you."

There was a soft, subtle knock on our door. "Bye, Roki. Be unobtrusive."

"*Hai.*"

I opened the door and was rewarded with one of David's warm, sultry smiles. "Hi, Kaede."

"Hi yourself. You remember Hiroki?"

David's eyes widened in surprise. "You are roommates?"

"Yes."

"That is…unexpected."

And not something I want the whole school to know. I quickly exited the room and pulled the door shut behind me. "It's okay. He's my manservant and probably finds you more attractive than me."

"You don't think I'm attractive?"

"No! I mean, yes! You're very attractive. I meant he finds *you* more attractive than *me.*"

"Oh. He likes guys."

"Yes."

"Cool. Hungry?"

"Always."

He pulled back and gave me a once over. "I find that a little hard to believe," he said, referring to my appearance.

"Nope. I do. Trust me. I drink a lot, too. Just burn energy like bridges."

"*That* I can believe."

"Whatcha mean by that?" We stepped from the bottom of the stairwell and he pulled the door open to the common area.

"Just that you look like if somebody pissed you off, you would have no problem making their life a living nightmare."

"Oh."

"Vindictive?"

"Yep." He had no idea.

"So… Where are you from?"

"California," I answered, grateful for the small talk. Small talk I could do. Big talk, not so much. It wasn't that I was stupid, although Hiroki might beg to differ, I just had the attention span of a gnat drinking Red Bull. I was pretty sure there was some squirrel mixed in with my fox ancestry. You should see me freak out when I run out in front of a moving car.

"Northern?"

"Yeah. How could you tell?"

"Spent some time there. You fit in."

"Is that a compliment?'

"Definitely. One of my favorite places."

"What about you?" We exited the dorm and stepped into the cold night air. I shivered, even through my jacket. I felt my fur bristling to be let free and keep me warm. I wasn't sure how David felt about unshaved girls, so I kept it under wraps.

"All over. My family became close with Rome and Remy's. It's how we ended up at school together. Got in a bit of trouble…"

"Oh, I know that feeling."

"I can imagine," he answered with a little smile. "You've got trouble written all over you."

"It was permanent marker. I tried to get it off, I swear."

He chuckled at my joke and suddenly the night didn't seem as cold as it had just a few minutes before. "So. Three years, huh?"

"Sadly."

"What did you do to earn such a shitty sentence?"

"Saved a human from jumping off a building. Got recorded on TV. That was the last straw. It's been a long time coming. Even my own parents were sick of my shit."

"Let me guess, endless nights of partying, drinking, and debauchery?"

"Not so much on the debauchery, but the other two... Oh, yeah."

"Same with us. We were on our way home when Rome fell asleep at the wheel. Ended up getting into a horrific car accident."

"Glad you guys are okay."

"The other car, not so much," he said guiltily. I could hear the pain in his voice.

"Did you guys get caught?"

"Not by the human authorities, but our clans..."

"They flip shit?"

"To put it mildly. Eat a human and you're just succumbing to your natural urges. Get drunk and crash into them with a stolen vehicle..."

"That sucks. I'm sorry."

He nodded and opened the door to the dining hall. Warmth and the smell of food washed over us, and I blinked in surprise. The food smelled *amazeballs* and I almost started drooling.

He reached over and wiped the corner of my mouth. "Somebody's hungry."

"Just a tad."

"Come on. Let's eat."

Chapter 8

We were one of the first ones to get to dinner and I was amazed to see that instead of long, cafeteria tables, the dining hall had been set up like a restaurant. Hundreds of tables varying in size filled the enormous room and the food was served buffet style. And it was all you could eat, and I was planning on it. My plate looked like someone had flipped a stuffed wok over on it into a perfect dome shape. It was mostly stable, but the removal of even the smallest piece of food would have threatened the structural integrity. So, I resisted the urge to pick at it while we walked to our table.

"You can make more than one trip, you know," David said as I shifted the plate in my hand as we walked, maintaining the center of gravity.

"I know. I plan on it."

"You're going to get *more*?"

"Oh, David. Sweet, sweet David. Never judge a woman by how much she eats, sweetie. Bigger men have died for less."

"Good point. I was going to offer to carry that for you, but I wasn't sure I could lift that much."

"And here I was just thinking how quickly I could fall for you..." I set my plate down on a little two-person table tucked away in the corner.

"You were?"

"Was."

"Damn. I was so close. Maybe I can make it up to you and regain your favor."

He set his food down and pulled out my chair for me. "Not by pulling out my chair. I'm pretty independent, though it was a sweet gesture."

"May I procure you a beverage, my lady?"

"Saving me a trip. That's worth at least two favor points."

"Sweet! What would you like?"

"Whatever. I'm not picky if it's not alcohol."

"I shall return." He gave me a smile and surprised me when he caressed my cheek. While I would have normally found the gesture to be completely weird and kind of creepy, with him it *wasn't*. It was sweet and oh so warm. His fingers heated my still cold flesh from the walk to the dining hall. I wasn't sure if it was from his over-active body heat or just the gentleness of his touch. Either way, I shifted in my seat, wanting nothing more than for him to touch me, again

I sat down and got a head start on my trough of food. Plate of food. Troughs would have been convenient though. Hiroki came in through the main door, briefly glanced in my direction, and headed toward the buffet while I munched on a chicken wing.

"Here you go," David said from behind me, almost causing me to choke on the bone when I jumped. "Skittery little thing, aren't you?" He set a glass of iced tea down in front of me and another by his plate of food.

"Comes with the breed," I mumbled.

"Pardon?"

I sighed. "This wouldn't be so bad if it weren't for the whole 'keep what you are hidden at all costs' thing. That's just fucking stupid."

"I agree. But they are trying to get us to blend in with the human world. Hard to do that when you're running around with fur, ears, tails, and claws."

I blinked in surprise. "Do you?"

"Do I what?"

"Run around with all that?" I wasn't sure if he was telling me about himself or fishing for what I was. He did seem a little excited when I got...excited. His nostrils were flaring, and he was looking at me like a cheeseburger.

"No. Do you?"

"When I cosplay. Sometimes."

He gave me a grin and scooped a forkful of mashed potatoes into his mouth. "You trying to figure out what I am, Kaede?"

"No. As I said. I couldn't care less."

"Tell you what. Go out with me and I'll tell you what I am."

"I am going out with you. To dinner. Right now."

"I mean all the time. Be my girlfriend and I won't keep any secrets about me from you."

I stared at him in confusion. "Girlfriend? Um... I don't know if you know this, but we just sort of met and I'm kind of annoying."

"I find you charming."

"We still just met."

"True. I guess we could give it some time. We'll just have to date a whole lot. Quickly, so you can get to know me faster."

I grinned at him, open mouth full of chicken wing and not caring in the slightest. If he wanted to be my boyfriend, he had better get used to seeing me gnawing on meat. At mealtimes. "Too bad there isn't anything to do. Like go to the movies. Clubs. Restaurants. Anything."

"There is the village."

"Excuse me?"

"The village?"

"What village?"

89

"The village at the base of the valley. We're allowed to go there on the weekends..."

"Why wasn't I made aware of this?"

"The headmistress mentioned it in orientation. Rome and Remy told me since I was outside with you. Your manservant didn't tell you?"

I sighed. "He's more like a babysitter and probably didn't tell me to keep me out of trouble."

"Are you that much trouble?"

"Hi. I'm Kaede Trouble Tanaka. Nice to meet you." I stuck out my hand.

I'd meant it as a joke, but he took it and I gasped as his hand slid into mine. Heat slid over me like a warm, wet blanket and my lungs threatened to explode as suddenly I was running through the forest, chasing the full moon overhead. I looked down at my paws, my giant paws covered in gray fur. I threw my head back and howled at the moon, my snout blocking the view of the ground beneath me. I wasn't a fox...I was a wolf.

"Kaede?"

Reality snapped back into focus as David gave me a worried glance. "Did you feel that?"

"Feel what?"

"Nothing." I sadly let go of his hand.

"Sparks? You felt the magic between us?" He was joking, but if he only knew...

"Something like that." I cut a piece of roast beef off, careful not to spill food across the table, and set it on my tongue. I frowned, grabbed the salt shaker and covered everything. The food was tasty...just kind of bland. I tried another bite and smiled in satisfaction.

"You're going to get hypertension."

"I'm already high-strung. Might as well be salty, too."

"You're a strange creature."

I gave him another smile. He wasn't even eating, simply staring. "What?"

"Strange but beautiful."

"And fun at parties. Your food is going to get cold," I said and pointed at his plate with my fork.

He nodded and cut a large piece of meat off his slab and wasn't as gentle with it as he was with his mashed potatoes. Can't always hide the carnivore. I was surprised he was eating veggies. Foxes were omnivorous. I tried to maintain a healthy balance between my protein intake and my love of fucking carbs. Especially the chocolate variety.

"What are your plans after dinner?"

"Go back to my room. Have a nice long hot shower. Lie in bed and moan at being stuck going to school for the next three years."

"Come on. We're both likely immortal. It will go just like that," he said and snapped his fingers. "How old are you?"

"Twenty-three."

He grinned at me.

"What?"

"You're twenty-three?"

"Yes? How old are you?"

"Twenty-two."

"Oh. Wow. I thought you were younger. Is that young for a wer…your race?"

He narrowed his eyes and I mentally kicked myself. I'd almost given up that I knew what he was. I wasn't ready to do that. Yet. "We age until we hit our thirties, then stop. Few of us live forever, though."

"Occupational hazards?"

"No. Other lands to hunt. We move on from this world."

"Oh. That sounds…metaphysical."

"It is."

"What about the twins. Are they the same as you?"

"No. We share many characteristics…but they are extraordinary and rare."

"You seem pretty rare to me."

"How so?"

"You're sweet and hot. The usual combination is dick and hot. Or sweet and ugly. You're a rarity."

"What about you? Friggin' beautiful and adorable."

"Those mean the same thing."

"No. The beautiful was referring to your outside. The adorable was in reference to your personality."

I blushed with a mouthful of beef. "Fanks?"

"You're welcome." He gave me one of his signature smiles and I melted a little inside. In fact, I was starting to leak… I shifted uncomfortably and tried to think of unsexy things. Like Professor Welheim in a two-piece and Lateran doing body shots of tequila off her. I gagged on my roast beef and stopped the leakage.

The damage was already done, though. My excitement had excited David. His eyes were glowing a soft amber color as he stared at me, nostrils flaring and his tongue tasting the air around him. "What are you?"

"Oh, boy." I set my fork and knife down on the edge of my plate I had actually managed to clear a bit of food away from. "You okay, Big Guy?"

"Yes. Your scent…"

I didn't really want to think about it. *Damn my leaky lady bits. Kitsune* were *very* sexual creatures by nature. I probably shouldn't have gotten turned on around a fucking werewolf. Judging from the look on his face he didn't want to fuck me as much as put me between two pieces of bread.

"Both predator and prey in nature. You need to leave?"

He growled softly, I felt it more than heard it.

"David… Can you control yourself?"

He shook his head, not in denial, but to clear it. "Yes."

I sighed in relief as his eyes stopped glowing and he continued eating his food, trying very hard not to look directly at me. "You want me to go?"

"Hell no." This time he did look up, a worried expression clouding his very masculine features. His brown eyes looking like so much chocolate.

"Okay. I won't. You're not going to eat me, are you? Little Kaede cake after dinner?"

He grinned. "Not unless you ask me nicely..."

He turned the damn faucet back on and I wasn't sure if he was going for sexual innuendo or cannibalistic kink. "Um..."

"Sorry. Too sexy for first date?'

"So, you meant it as sexy and not food?"

He shot me a worried glance. "That's what you thought?'

I nodded.

"You know. Don't you." He wasn't asking.

"What you are?"

He nodded.

"Yep. Kind of saw it when I shook your hand."

He sighed. "You gonna put my name in the box?"

"Nope." I meant it. I wasn't a dick like that.

"Thank you."

"So...just to clarify. When you went all," I paused and leaned a little closer and whispered, "wolfy, you didn't want to eat me?"

He chuckled and shook his head. "Not like that."

It was my turn to blush.

"I don't think I've ever wanted anyone more in my life... In fact, if you asked me to stand up right now, I'd be forced to politely decline."

"You're hard?"

"Got any six-inch iron spikes you need nailed through a tree trunk?"

My eyes widened in surprise. I really kind of wanted to look under the table, but that might be considered a little rude in some circles. "Glad I'm not the only one."

His eyes widened. "You have a dick?"

I stuck my tongue out at him. "I meant aroused, smart ass."

"You find me attractive?"

I gave him a sultry smile and sipped my iced tea.

"You are going to be very dangerous to hang around with, Kaede Tanaka."

"Danger is fun, David..." I realized I didn't know his last name.

"Lupescu." He filled in the blank.

"That's not Japanese."

He chuckled. "Romanian."

"David is Romanian?"

"David isn't. *Dah-veed* is how it's really pronounced."

"Oooh. I likey. Can I call you that?"

"You can call me whatever you want."

"Slumming tonight, David? Or are you helping the slow kids with their homework." Sabine's voice broke our conversation. I rolled my eyes. She really needed to get a life.

"Oh, it's you. Here I thought they were serving sushi." I sniffed the air. It was childish, I admit, but so am I.

"What do you need, Sabine?" David covered his mouth with his hand, trying very hard not to laugh at my childish joke.

"I was going to invite you to come eat with me."

"I'm already eating with Kaede."

"I can see that. Why?"

"Because I invited her to dinner?"

"Why?"

"Isn't it weird like that with little kids? It's always why, why, why," I interjected.

"What is your problem?" She put her hands on her hips and turned toward me.

"Oh, gee. I don't know, Miss Rocketscientist. What could my problem *possibly* be? Maybe you?"

I half expected her to take a swing at me. Or dump my tea. Maybe stomp her foot and go buy a Gucci purse off eBay or something. Instead, she just snarled and walked away. Her two cronies behind her giving me snide looks and following behind her. At least they left.

David just started laughing.

"How in the world of fuck did you ever date that nasty bitch?"

"Because she is the sister of my two best friends..."

I blinked in confusion. Then it dawned on me. "You're fucking kidding me. Rome and Remy, Sabine and Headmistress Lateran are all related? *And* they all hate me?"

"Well, I'd argue with you, but... Wait! I don't think Remy hates you. Rome just hates everybody."

I sighed and slumped into my seat. "Only me."

"Could rub an entire family the wrong way?"

"Well, in my defense, it didn't take much. And Sabine was a major twat waffle the minute I met her."

"She has her moments," he answered through a grin.

"They gonna give you shit for dating me?"

"Probably. But I'm not part of the family, so it doesn't matter what they think."

"So, they're not..."

"No. I told you. If you want to find out what they are you're going to have to figure it out on your own. Sorry, Kaede."

"No. Not for the stupid extra credit. I just want to know if I'm going to get my ass chewed off."

"Not by them," he said and winked at me.

I shuddered in my seat.

95

Chapter 9

"He really is attracted to you. I hope you know that. I don't care what you say about him liking guys." David's voice caressed my insides while his breath tickled my ear.

David was leaning against the arm of the couch, legs spread out, and I was leaning against his chest. It was one of the most intimate positions I could ever have imagined while having clothes on. His heat pressed against my back, warming me thoroughly. I looked up to give him a grin, but all I could see was his chin and the direction he was looking, and it was toward Hiroki. He had gotten up from the loveseat next to us to get us some drinks and snacks while we were watching a movie.

"I never said he was gay. He just prefers men to women."

"But not you. I don't think there's a man in this world he would rather have in his bed more than you."

"I've tried."

"You have?" He looked down at me and blinked in surprise.

"Hell yeah. Roki is hot. You should see him without clothes. But…"

"But?"

I sighed. I'd been dating David for two weeks, mostly dinners in the cafeteria and cuddles in the common room, but I still hadn't shared what I, and Hiroki, were. We weren't officially boyfriend and girlfriend, yet. That was the deal. I trusted him and wanted to tell him, but he wouldn't let me until I said yes. Even though I knew what he was. "Ask me again."

"But?"

"Not that. Ask me to be your girlfriend."

His grin grew from ear to ear. "Kaede Tanaka, would you do me the greatest honor of becoming my girlfriend?"

I grinned up at him and kissed his chin, since it was the only place I could reach with my lips. But, leaning back against him was the most comfortable spot in the universe, and I wasn't giving it up. "It's about damn time you asked. Slacker."

"Is that a yes?"

"Yes."

He leaned over a little farther and this time I could reach his lips with mine. When he pulled away, I whispered, "*Kitsune*. Mostly."

"Bless you?"

I rolled my eyes. I really didn't have to worry about people guessing what I was. *Kitsune*, outside of Japan and our little town in California, weren't the stuff of legend like werewolves, vampires, and dragons. There was only a smattering of them in fiction. I shouldn't have been shocked that David didn't know what the hell I was, either. "*Kitsune*. Many tailed foxes. Ever see that one anime with the kid who wanted to be a ninja but had a fox spirit trapped inside him?"

"Yes?"

"Total bullshit, but the thing inside of him was a *Kitsune*. Supposedly."

"That's what you two are?"

"Kind of. Roki is actually a *nogitsune*. They're like distant cousins. Beefier and less spiritually powerful. But I'm only half. My father is an *Inari* Fox."

"And that is?"

"A celestial fox servant of the gods."

"Holy shit."

"That's probably why I smell so good to you. I'm like a big bucket of KFC to your wolfy nose." I reached up and boinked the tip of it with my finger.

"No. You're more like a fill up box. Nothing buckety about you."

"You say the sweetest things. Wait! You want to fill up my box?" I wiggled my eyebrows at him. We hadn't done the deed yet, but it was another of those 'when you're my girlfriend' things he was so adamant about.

"Yes. And I'm not the only one."

"As I said, I've tried. He's too afraid of my parents to ever fool around with me."

"Because he's a little different? A naugahide?"

"*Nogitsune*. But that's not even the real reason. He's my guardian…"

"Ah. I see. Well, that's the *only* thing keeping him out of your panties."

"Who said I'm wearing any?"

He chuckled but then stared at the skirt covering me. My plan had worked. It was all he could think about. "You vixen." He'd started calling me that after we had our one-week anniversary of not formally dating. But who was keeping track? Little did he know I actually was a female fox. I grinned the first time he called me it.

"Yep. So, does it bother you that Roki thinks of me sexually?"

Curiously, he looked away and blushed, shaking his head. "No."

"What was that look for?"

"What look?"

"That look. You're looking out the window instead of at me. Or the TV."

"It's just kind of hot."

"What is?"

"That you two are so close and yet so far away."

"You're not jealous?"

This time he did look down at me and gave me a small smile. "Nope."

"You're weird."

"Uh… Your boyfriend. Kind of one of the prerequisites."

"True dat."

Hiroki came back carrying two bags of popcorn, and three bottles of Coke. "They did not have tea," he said stiffly.

"That's okay," I said and took one of the bottles from him. "Thanks, Roki."

"You are welcome." He handed the other bottle and bag of popcorn to David.

"Thanks."

"Welcome."

"You can sit with us, you know." David pointed at the spot currently occupied by my feet.

"That is all right. I do not mind sitting over here."

"Suit yourself."

I kind of looked up at him out of the corner of my eye. He was still looking at Hiroki with a curious expression on his face. As nonchalantly as I could a shifted against him. He wasn't as unaroused as he should have been. Not wanting to draw attention to us, I turned to the side and pulled his head toward mine, in the pretext of giving him a kiss on the cheek. "You got the hots for my bodyguard?"

David pulled away and shook his head, his eyes widening in surprise. I just chuckled at his reaction and settled back against him, watching the movie and snagging a handful of popcorn out of the bag.

He leaned over and set his Coke on the worn coffee table next to us. "Why would you think that?" His words were barely decipherable he spoke them so softly.

Instead of giving him an answer, I leaned forward, pretended to scratch my back, and slid my fingers across his semi-hardness. He shuddered beneath me.

"Oh," was all he said.

"Yeah, it was sort of a major clue."

"I'm not, though."

"Uh. Huh."

He just shook his head and focused on the television. Roki hit play and the movie started again. I had no idea what we were watching, but the two of them seemed pretty excited by it. I was there for the snuggles. Over the course of our two-week unofficial dating period, I'd realized one very important thing. I kind of liked it. I'd never had the opportunity to get close to anybody but Hiroki, and the experience was eye-opening. Physical contact without sex wasn't amazing, it was a drug. It became something I yearned for from the moment I woke up until the instant his hand slid familiarly over my back, stopping at my hip and pulling me close. Maybe I was a third *kitsune*, third *Inari*, and a third snuggle bunny. No matter the ratio, I was a hundred percent sure I didn't want to kick the habit.

I turned a little between David's legs, practically rubbing the side of my face against his shirt and breathing in his scent. He spread his legs a little more, letting me curl up however I wanted to. Tucking my legs up closer, I slid an arm behind him and sighed contentedly, and when he leaned in and kissed the top of my head, an unfamiliar warmth spread through me like wildfire. It wasn't sexual in nature, I wasn't turned on, I was happy. The sensation was better than *sake*.

Ignoring the movie completely, I closed my eyes and breathed in David's pine scent. It was a little different than usual and held a hint of musk that set my nostrils flaring. Few creatures had a better sense of smell than the cunning, always wary, fox. The change was *almost* imperceptible, but there it was.

Nonchalantly, I tilted my head from his chest and watched his face. His nostrils were flaring, and his breathing was a tad off, too. I did some mental math and added the change in scent, and his change in breathing, with the coefficient of drag of his semi-hard wolf de-nom-nom-ninator and came up with the solution. He was aroused, and I could smell it. I chuckled softly against him.

"What?"

I turned my sidelong glance into an obvious stare. "You're aroused."

"Of course, I am. You're sitting between my legs and smell yummier than a T-bone."

I pulled my shirt away from my chest and gave myself a little whiff. I smelled like orange jasmine, but I couldn't tell if I smelled aroused or not, just him. Pressing my nose against *him*, I scented him again. It was getting worse, but not in a bad way. The subtle musk smell was becoming more prevalent. So was the thing poking me in the side. "Just my smell?"

"What do you mean?"

"Is that all that's turning you on right now?"

"No. Your warmth, your scent, and the fact that you're leaning against me right now…"

"Oh. Want me to move?"

"Not even a little."

I grinned at him and put my head back down, trying very hard not to squirm until he could get back into the movie. It took a few minutes but as soon as he was preoccupied, I struck. I shifted in the seat and wrapped my arms around myself, giving the appearance of making myself more comfortable. In actuality, my hand was between my side and his rapidly stiffening cock.

His hips curled slightly, pressing himself against my fingers. As subtly as I could, I started moving the back of my index finger, up and down against him. He was standing proud and my finger was just below the tip.

"What are you doing?" I barely heard his question. His whisper was so soft. Unlike the rest of him.

"Scratching an itch on my rib."

"Uh, huh."

"There. That's better." I sat up and gave my side one last scratch and pulled my sweater off, draping it over me like a blanket and resuming my position. This time, however, I made no pretense of subtly. My hand covered him and slowly rubbed him from bottom to tip.

David reached down under the blanket and stopped my hand from gliding over him, shooting me a worried glance. It must have been a while.

"You okay?" I let innocence drip from my voice like honey.

"Yeah. Are *you*?"

"Peachy keen honkey dory." I grinned up at him before turning back to the movie I wasn't paying any attention to.

When he thought I wasn't going to continue torturing him, he finally let go of my hand and reached over for his Coke. I struck like an Eastern Green Mamba. My thumb and finger grasped the slider of his zipper and yanked it down. He fumbled his bottle and tried to set it back down on the coffee table as quickly as possible. My hand snaked its way into his pants and wrapped around him, just as his eyes widened as far as they could possibly go and he mouthed the word, "Kaede…"

I may have flashed a little bit of my toothy grin as I fished him out of the opening in his trousers and held him in my hand. I'd meant to turn him on more, just to tease him, but the warmth of him in my hand, the rigidness of his flesh almost caused *me* to gasp. Good thing I was lying about not wearing panties.

I let my hand trail slowly up as I loosened my grip on him. Smiling as he shuddered beneath me, I ran my finger over the tip.

"Kaede…"

"Yes, David?"

"You're going to be very sorry if you continue doing what you're doing," he answered levelly.

"You're going to get mad?"

"No. Not at all. How could I? But you're going to have a literal mess on your hands."

I grinned at him. "Hand. Singular."

"Semantics."

"I don't think that's what it's called." I started stroking him again and he lost all capacity for arguing. He was putty in my hand. Extraordinarily hard putty.

"Kaede…"

"David…"

I felt him start to pulse in my hand. He wasn't kidding. It must have been a while for him. It had been a while for me, too, but I had no compunction about taking matters into my own hands, so to speak. Just the night before, Hiroki had launched a pillow at me just as I was climaxing. Guys must have been a little more hesitant to rub one out in front of each other. Come to think of it, I'd yet to catch Hiroki in the twenty years that we'd spent together.

The feel of the pulsing contractions in my hand were strengthening. I was no expert, but it was fairly obvious he was ready to blow.

"*Kaede*…" Even my name was strained as he was trying to hold back.

Rubbing my cheek against his hard stomach, I dipped the lower half of my face below the collar of my sweater and took the tip of him in my mouth, letting my tongue flick against him.

That was all he could take. His hardness swelled in my hand and liquid fire literally poured from him, filling my mouth. I swallowed as fast as I could, expecting him to stop after three or four large spurts, but it kept coming. Either it *really* had been a while, or werewolves ejaculated more than normal. I was hoping for the former. While I didn't *mind* the taste, I wasn't exactly a fan, either.

"David!" An angry voice nearly caused me to bite down.

"What's up, Rome?" David's voice cracked as the pleasure centers of his brain were still firing.

You've got to be fucking kidding me. I pulled him from my mouth and tucked him back into his pants, not bothering with the zipper. I wiped my mouth, just in case, as I sat up and let the sweater fall onto David's lap.

"Let's go," Rome made a sweeping gesture toward the entrance to Breckenridge Hall.

I looked down at David, who seemed just as confused as I was. Then a look of understanding crept into his beautiful brown eyes. "Shit. I forgot."

"Forgot what?" I cocked an eyebrow.

"I told them I would help with something and I forgot. I'm sorry, Kaede." His frown told me he wasn't lying.

"Oh. No worries. I have something to take care of, too," I said with a little wink.

"You don't mind?"

"Well, the timing sucks." I paused to snicker. "But no. I'll just finish up on my own."

He glanced down at my lap.

I nodded.

The look he gave me, like I had just pulled all of his Christmas presents from under the tree and tossed them into the fireplace, made it all worth it. I'd never stop him from spending time with his friends, but I was sure going to make him regret it. Especially after I swallowed. I should have just let him go all over his pants. Watching him stand up in front of the twins would have been monumentally epic.

Giving him a little room to move, I slid over to the other side of the couch. He got up slowly, still unsure if I was okay with him leaving. "This won't take long... Want me to come find you after we're done?"

"Nope. It's getting late. I'll see you tomorrow."

"You're mad."

I shook my head and gave him a smile. "Seriously, no. I'm not at all. I'll just miss you."

"I'll miss you, too."

"Are you two done? Let's go, David."

"Coming."

"Nope. You already did that," I answered helpfully.

He blushed and leaned down to give me a soft kiss. "I'll see you tomorrow, Kaede."

"You better. And you're taking me into the village for a real date."

"Deal," he said with a smile.

One more kiss and he was trailing after Rome like a little puppy. I stared, half-hoping he'd come back, and half-happy he was spending some time with his friends, but wishing he had nicer ones.

"You okay?"

I nodded, not taking my eyes off David until they left through the door. Finally, I turned to Hiroki. "Yeah. Just all turned on and alone."

"Welcome to my world."

"Shut up. Your celibacy is self-imposed."

"Not anymore."

"Huh?"

"You have a boyfriend now."

"Oh. Yeah."

"Did you forget already?"

I shook my head. "I meant you had your chance. Several thousand of them. Can't blame me."

"No. But I can blame you for turning me on with your little spectacle."

"Spectacle?"

"Did you honestly think I wouldn't see the motion of your shoulder, hear your whispers, and the sounds of your..."

"I get the point." I held up my hand and lay back down on the couch, propping my head on the pillow David had been leaning against and smiling at his still lingering scent.

I was just focusing on the movie when I heard Sabine's voice as it passed by. "Come on. We're going to be late. Rome, Remy, and David are already there."

Assuming she was talking to her cohorts, I resisted the urge to sit up. She obviously hadn't seen me on the other side of the couch. David's something to do included his ex-girlfriend. He left that little fact out of the equation...

Chapter 10

"I'm going to suggest that you don't do this." Hiroki sounded exasperated. He did most of the time, but even more so than usual. But he was still following behind me as I trailed after Sabine.

"Shhh. She'll hear you."

One of her two lackeys slowed her pace and turned toward us. I dropped to the ground, holding myself above it as Hiroki ducked behind a tree. From my position, I could still see her squinting at us with a confused look on her face. Not wanting to take any chances, I covered my hair with my arms and rolled behind a larger tuft of tall grass. Hopefully she didn't have supernatural hearing.

It took almost a minute for her to finally turn around and rush to catch up to Sabine. Silently cursing, I did something I rarely ever did, went full fox. The night around me took on a silvery hue and everything became much clearer, sound became sharper, and the smells around me…became overwhelming. They bombarded my nose, but I could pick through them and identify them with a thought. Unfortunately, my fur glistened under the moon like a raver under a blacklight.

Hiroki's nose poked me in the butt. He had shifted too, but his muted browns and reds blended in with our natural surroundings better than I did. He looked *way* more like a normal fox than I did. Even his tails were thinner and he disappeared like a freaking ninja.

I batted him across the face with half my tails.

"They're going to see you," he said with difficulty. Fox mouths were not intended for human speech.

We were outside the school and at the bottom of a path leading up one of the multitudes of mountain trails. Casting one more glance at the direction the trio had gone, I bounded for the closest tree and plucked a leaf from the ground with my mouth, careful not to damage it. Pouring a bit of power into it, I touched it to the fur on my hindquarter. With a puff of smoke, my pure white fur became a mottled brown, and eight of my tails disappeared. To the casual observer, I looked like a normal fox.

"Better," Hiroki yipped.

In our fox forms, it was only a matter of moments until we caught up to them, just as they reached the mouth of a large cave. "What are they doing?"

"Cave party?" Hiroki seemed as curious as me.

"And they didn't invite us."

The three of them were looking around, for *kami* knows what. Finally, they entered the cave. Just as I was about to dart from the tall grass from the side of the trail, Hiroki stopped me. Getting bit on the tail wasn't the most pleasant of feelings, but he saved me from being spotted. Two dogs, of epic proportions, leapt down from a rocky ledge above the cave entrance. They weren't just epically proportioned; they were the size of small horses. Black, sleek fur rippled down their stocky forms as their muscles bunched while they walked around, sniffing the air and growling softly.

Not daring to talk, Roki began pulling on my tail, urging me to get the hell out of there. I was quick. I was nimble. But I wasn't stupid. I would hardly be an appetizer for the two beasts scenting us.

Roki let go of my tail and we belly crawled away. The two beast dog monsters didn't show any sign of pursuit, thankfully. I shuddered just thinking about how close I'd come to becoming kibbles and bits.

"That was close," Roki hissed when we were far enough away.

I just nodded, curiosity tearing my insides apart. If it were just David and the dick twins, letting it go would have been a lot easier. Knowing that his ex-girlfriend and her bitches in waiting were involved made it more than unbearable. If I didn't think the two black monster dogs would sniff me out in a New York minute, I would have slapped an invisibility spell on my ass and gone back in there.

"What do you want to do?"

"Go back for now. We'll check things out...later."

Instead of answering, he nodded his vulpine head once and stealthily started picking his way through the field way more silently than I could manage. I wasn't a very good fox. In fact, that was the first time I'd been a sober fox in a very long time.

One moment, I was staring at Roki's ass, the next it was three feet in the air and heading straight for an unsuspecting field mouse. Without a second thought he scarfed the whole thing down, turning and giving me a grin with the tail hanging out the side of his mouth. I shifted back into my human form, thankful my clothes transformed with me. I always snickered at shifters in movies and how they *always* were naked when they shifted back. That would be horrifically inconvenient. But probably a little bit of fun, too.

"That's fucking disgusting."

He swallowed his Mice Krispy Treat and shifted, too. "They are delectable."

"I'll take your word for it. No way am I eating mouse sushi. Mushi? Whatever. I feel sick."

"You need to listen to your instincts more."

"My instincts are telling me chocolate tastes way fucking better than rat guts."

"Sometimes you are *too* human."

"I thought that was the whole point of this place?"

"No. It is to *appear* human. You are two extremes. Too much of one and not enough of the other. You need to find the middle ground. Life is all about balance."

"Blah blah blah."

He sighed and rolled his eyes. "One day, many, many hundreds of years from now, most likely, you will understand the wisdom of my words."

"I understand them now. But, and you may not have noticed this, but I'm pretty unbalanced in everything I do."

"Yes. I have noticed."

"Shut up. Let's go back to the dorm."

"*Hai.*"

∞ ∞ ∞

Fumbling with the last button on my pajama top, I walked over to our room door and twisted the handle. I'd told David I would see him tomorrow, but I figured he couldn't resist seeing me before he went to bed. They were out later than I'd been expecting, or hoping, but I was glad he decided to say goodnight. Pulling the door open, I gave him a sultry grin. "Miss me?"

It wasn't David. It was one of the twins.

"No." He cocked an eyebrow at me.

"Oh. It's one of you." My grin faded into something more akin to a face I would make if Roki ate a raw mouse and fed it to me like a momma bird.

"We need to speak."

"No, we don't," I said and closed the door. On his hand.

He didn't move it, either. Or make any painful noises. He was utterly disappointing. I pulled it back an inch and

112

slammed it again to no avail. He wasn't budging. I pulled the door open all the way.

"Fine. You convinced me. What do you want?"

He looked over my shoulder and narrowed his eyes at Roki standing behind me. "Tell your girlfriend to take a walk."

"Don't trust yourself around him? I don't blame you. He's pretty damn cute and I saw you eyeing his ass earlier. But the odds of you getting him to leave me alone with you are nonexistent."

"Fine. You take a walk with me. We have something to discuss."

"I'm in my jammies already. We can talk tomorrow."

"This is not a request."

I sighed, weighing all my options in my head. There weren't that many. "Fine. Give me a minute to change."

He nodded and gave me a satisfied smirk. I was probably the last person on earth to admit it, but whichever twin he was, he was attractive. Shoulder-length blond hair, piercing blue eyes, chiseled jaw with just a hint of stubble. However, when he smirked, I kind of wanted to bash his face in with a brick. Not because it pissed me off, but because it made him look even hotter. Too bad I'd rather eat nothing but raw rodents for the rest of my life in human form than spend any time with him.

I closed the door and he didn't impede it with his tree-trunk hands. Sighing, I crossed the room, past my dresser, and straight to the one wood-trimmed window in our room.

"Kaede?"

"Tell Douche McNugget if he wants to talk to me, he has to catch me first." I grinned, opened the window, and popped to the grass twenty feet below. Looking up, I waved at Roki shaking his head and giving me a grin from the window.

Looking around, I took off across the quad between the dorms. Across the way was Davenport Hall, home of the

113

second years. I'd just have to blend in there for a while until Rome or Remy got tired of waiting and then I could pop back into my room and my nice warm bed. The important thing was I outfoxed the meathead. It wasn't that hard, but I was still proud of myself.

I was chuckling to myself when I rounded the corner and smacked face first into meathead's chest. "Nice try."

Blinking in confusion, I stared at the face of the other twin. I don't know how I knew, but I knew without a doubt it was his brother. Go me. I could tell them apart, but I didn't know which one was which. "Pretty clever. He knew I'd run."

"Yes."

Sighing, I had to ask. "So, which one are you? Romeo or Ruliet?"

"Remy."

"Oh. The nice one. My lucky day."

"Wait here. My brother is coming."

"Oh. He's still with Hiroki?"

"Pardon?"

"Joking. But I'd probably pay to watch."

"Watch what?"

"Romarokipalooza."

"You are a strange creature."

"Not so bad, yourself. So. Is this going to take long? Because I gotta thing I need to get to."

"Just a warning."

"Is this about David?"

He was kind of cute when he scrunched his eyebrows like that. Maybe it was how I could tell them apart. His expressions were softer. "No?"

"Oh. I thought you were going to tell me to stop dating him."

"He is free to date whom he wants."

"Just not your sister."

114

"I did not mind."

"I do. I won't allow it."

"As I said. You are a strange creature. Here is Rome."

I turned around to see how much trouble I was in. Judging by the snarl, I'd say pretty deep. Good thing he wasn't the boss of me. I was standing there by choice. I could have been back in bed by then, if I wanted to.

"Is he as mad as he looks?"

"You are not dead, so no."

"How come he hates me so much?"

"That is between you and him."

"You don't hate me?"

"Not as of yet. I find you mostly amusing. When I'm not having to subdue my brother from causing you bodily harm."

"He's the emotional twin. You're the intellectual one, huh?"

"No. I'm the funny one."

I turned and looked at Remy over my shoulder. He had the tiniest of smiles plastered on his face and it propelled him from the realm of hotness into supernova sexiness. They should both do it more. When they weren't picking on poor, innocent little foxes.

"Hiya, Rome. Bout time you showed up. I was getting tired of waiting for you and entertaining your brother. When you said you wanted to take a walk, I was kinda expecting you to keep up, if I'm being honest."

"I doubt you know how."

"Ouch. That hurted. What can I do for you?"

He didn't stop walking until he was inches from squishing me between him and his brother. Not that I would have minded...

Mmmm. Manwich.

He didn't touch me, luckily for him. I didn't know what I would have done to him. Bit him in the ankle, or kicked his shin, or something equally as painful. "Stay away from the cave."

"Huh?"

"You heard me. Stay away from the cave. If I catch you there again, it will not end well for you. Do you understand me?"

"Uh…what cave?"

I almost had him. For a fraction of a nanosecond, I saw the doubt cross his face. Unfortunately, he realized I was playing dumb and the doubt was replaced with seething hatred.

"Oh. That cave! Yeah, wasn't planning on going back. Me and guard dogs don't mix."

"Guard dogs?"

"Yeah. Big black ones. Look like they shoulda had three heads and would fall asleep if you played harp music."

"What?" They both asked simultaneously.

"Fluffy? Nevermind. What's in the cave?"

"Death," Remy said softly behind me.

"Scary."

"He is not joking. You have been warned. Stay far away and all will be well. Choose to ignore our warning and your fate is your own," Rome said menacingly. Don't get me wrong, pretty much every word out of his mouth spoken in my general direction had some degree of a menacing lilt to it, but this time it kind of sent a shiver down my spine. I liked it.

"Say that again, but slower. And can you curl your lip a bit?"

He ruined it by looking confused and then angrier than I had yet to see him to date. Literally, his face flushed and then began to redden like a tourist at Disney Land who thought sunblock was for women folk. He sputtered and clenched his fists. Remy grabbed my shoulders and started to turn me, putting himself between Rome's anger and my pretty little face.

"Fine, I'll stay away from your dank, dark cave. Nobody wants it anyway," I said over my shoulder.

He snarled. So help me *kami*, he fucking snarled. There might have been some globules of spittle reflected in the overhead lamps. The boy had serious anger management issues.

"He in therapy?" I asked Remy as I looked up.

"Do not joke. In fact, now might be a good time to leave. Heed his warning, please."

"Awww. You do care."

"No. I do not wish to clean up the mess."

"Message received. Cave bad. Bed good. Night, kids," I said and pulled free from Remy's grip, popping back to the other side of the quad and waving goodnight to the twins.

Hiroki stepped from the shadows and dispelled his katana. I gave a wry smile. The twins might think they're all big and bad, but they'd never seen a pissed off Roki with a sword. Had they truly intended to harm me, I wouldn't have put money on their genitals surviving the night. There was more than one reason he was my babysitter-slash-bodyguard.

"Did you hear all that?"

"*Hai.*"

"What do you think?'

"I think you are going to get yourself into more trouble."

"I think you're right."

"No. Don't," he called softly to the air in front of us, sighed, and rolled his eyes. The Hiroki Triple Play.

Chapter 11

Slipping the piece of paper into the Guess Box outside the great hall without anybody seeing me was easier said than done. But I did it. I grinned at my joke, popped back to the end of the hall, and slipped outside the double doors without even making a creak. I needed to hurry to get to the dining hall before David started to wonder where I was.

Walking as quickly as possible, I popped when I could in the shadows of the buildings, trying to remain unseen but not really caring if the odd one or two people spotted me. The number of supernatural creatures that could teleport was longer than my list of infractions. I doubted anyone would even care. We had been living under the fear of the stupid guessing game for three weeks, and to date, not one person had hazarded a guess.

Chicken shits.

Sounding brave, even to myself, I had just gotten the ball rolling. A small joke to alleviate some of the tension. I just needed to wait for the punchline to be delivered.

"Hey, beautiful."

I gasped and spun as David stepped from one of the shadows I had teleported to. "*Kami* damn it. You scared the shit out of me."

"Not as bad as having your girlfriend teleport in front of you."

"Sorry. Thought I was going to be late," I said with a grin, his girlfriend comment warming the inner fuzzy parts of my heart.

"So. What no good were you up to that you needed to teleport to dinner?"

"Uh…hello. It's called popping, not teleporting. You make me sound like a sci fi nerd when you say that."

"Oh. Popping is so much more eloquent. I stand corrected."

"Well, it has an actual Japanese name, but I won't foxsplain it to you."

"Nope. Popping is cute. So, can you pop other people or just yourself?" We started walking toward the open doors leading to the dining hall.

"That sounded dirty. But no. I can only pop myself and what I'm carrying. If it's not too heavy."

"Could you pop with a small child?"

"Nope. Too heavy. But that seems to change under duress."

"What?"

"It means stress."

"I know what it means. What does that have to do with it?"

"I can pop with people if my life depends on it. Like…say…falling from twenty stories up."

"I'd call that stressful."

He had no idea. "Can't pop through doors or walls either. And I have to be able to *see* where I'm going. Unless it's someplace I memorized every detail of. But that's not very helpful either if there's walls and doors in the way."

"Probably safer for everybody else if you couldn't. Can't imagine how much trouble you'd get into."

"True story."

My hand touched the tray when I felt, rather than heard, the bell chime throughout the entire school, valley, and possibly the rest of Iceland. I barely managed to resist covering my ears.

"What the fuck?" David didn't manage to resist. I guessed werewolves had better hearing than foxes.

"You okay?"

"Yeah. What the hell was that?"

"Attention students," Uncle Tatsuo's voice reverberated through our heads, chests, and asses. He must not have wanted anyone to miss the memo. "The very first guess has been submitted. I would like to, at this time, share with you the results of said charming deduction. We do not normally broadcast guesses, but I doubt this one was so far off the mark, it should not provide any clues. The supposition was submitted by a Mr. Ballzitch. He postulates that First Year Student Sabine Lateran is…some sort of genetic experiment gone awry by trying to mate a blue-assed fanged baboon with a mutated herpes virus. I am sorry, Mr. Ballzitch, but your guess is highly incorrect. You will have points deducted from your final grade and they shall be awarded to Ms. Lateran. In a *completely* unrelated issue, Kaede Tanaka, please report to my office."

"*Fuuuuuuuuuck.*" I was fucked. I'd expected some sort of announcement about the misuse of the Guess Box. I didn't expect Uncle Tatsuo to read the whole damn thing to the entire school. Nor did I expect him to figure out it was me. I even had Hiroki write it so it didn't look like my normal illegible scribbles. The old bastard outed me. Turning slowly, I saw Sabine sitting at one of the tables in the middle of an apoplectic fit, her cronies holding her down to her chair.

"Please tell me that wasn't you," David said slowly.

"Uh. No. No way. I would have been much more creative with her supposed lineage. Uncle Tatsuo probably just wants to catch up."

"Uncle?"

Fuuuuuuuuuuck. "Uh, not really. More like a family friend. Eat. I'll catch up with you later." *If I'm still alive.*

"Okay. Want me to wait?"

"Don't know how long I'll be, but that's sweet. Thank you," I said and kissed him quickly on the cheek. "Wish me luck."

He just chuckled.

Ignoring the laughter, ooohs, aaahs, and humming of funeral marches, I headed to see Uncle Tatsuo.

"It was completely unrelated, people!"

∞ ∞ ∞

"Sit."

I resisted the urge to bark and plopped my butt down on one of the two leather chairs in front of Uncle Tatsuo's very imposing looking desk. I say imposing because the feet and sides were carved into the likeness of dragon scales and feet, and because it was almost as tall as I was. I felt like a kindergartener sitting in front of the principal for finger painting an ass crack on Little Jimmy's face.

Ahhh. Memories.

"So. What can I do for you, Headmaster?"

"Just sitting here in shock that you actually called me Headmaster."

"Well, you told me to leave the uncle part off. Uncle Headmaster? Nah. That sounds kinda pornographic."

"Quite. Do you know why I called you here?"

"You missed me?"

"Surprisingly enough, I did."

"Awww."

"But that is not the reason. You have one more guess."

"The herpes thing?"

"That was you?" He leaned forward and gave me a shocked expression.

122

"What? No."

The crafty old bastard winked at me. "I didn't think so. No person of your intelligence, despite her love of mirth, would *ever* use one of this schools most sacred challenges to insult a rival. Would she. Because said student would understand that I would be required, as a matter of principle, to reduce her to a smoldering pile of ash, yes?"

"Definitely. If I hear anything, I will definitely let you know who the perpetrator of such a heinous crime was. They should *definitely* get their ash handed to them. See what I did there?"

"I did."

"So why am I here?"

"The cave."

"Exqueeze me?"

"I was informed that you inadvertently learned the location of a certain hole in the mountain that a little fox should stay *very* far away from."

"You know about it?"

"As has every headmaster before me. It is one of the reasons why the school is in this valley."

"Why?"

He leaned in even closer. "Because…it is none of your business. You were warned by the gua–Lateran brothers. Now I am warning you, Kaede. Stay away from the cave."

As imposing and frightening as he was, he might as well have hung a big neon sign over the entrance that read, "No Girlz Allowd." It had officially become a moral imperative that I find and identify the contents of the cave. It was a *kitsune* challenge. Do it but don't get caught. Maybe he *wanted* me to know what was in the cave. Judging by the look on his face, he definitely didn't, but he was a good actor. So, the possibility was there.

"Fox's honor, Uncle."

"You're going to have to do better than that. I've known too many foxes."

"On my honor as a student of Aesir Academy, I shall leave well enough alone and not disturb your dirty little cave."

"Kaede. It is an order. I will beg and plead with you if I must, but I can't stress enough nothing good is inside that cave."

He definitely wants me to look. "Okay, Uncle."

"There is only death."

"Gotcha."

"Get out."

"Okey dokey." I grinned at him and lifted my butt off the leather seat, saluted, and headed for the double doors. Twisting the handle, I used all my pitiful strength to push it open and slip between them, letting it fall closed behind me. Just before it clicked shut, I heard the headmistress' voice.

"You were right. That one won't listen. Not even to you."

I *really* wanted to go back in and find out what else they were going to say about me behind my back, but there was no way to get back in.

Where the hell was she hiding? Under the desk? Bow chicky wow wow. You go, Uncle. Wait. Ew. She's a mountain troll.

Shrugging, I headed back toward the dining hall. Hopefully Sabine and the Sabinettes were done with dinner and I could scarf some nom-noms before dinner was over. I hated fighting on an empty stomach.

I'd almost made it into the dining hall when one of the twins stopped me with his chest. My head slammed into his pecs when he stepped from inside the door. Luckily it was Remy. Rome probably would have swatted me in the head just to make *sure* I got a concussion.

"Sorry," I said and shook my head.

"It is all right." He made no move to walk around me.

"Are they still open?"

"For another hour, yes."

"Can I uh...go in?"

"Yes?"

"Can you uh...move?"

His chuckle held a small feeling of menace, sexiness, and some subtle overtones of chocolate harvested by virgins in the rain forests of South America. He was definitely dangerous, and Danger-Makes-Me-Wet was my Native American middle name.

David! I shook my head again to clear it for completely different reasons than being a crash test dummy.

"You need to be careful."

"I know. I said I was sorry for running into you."

He chuckled again. "That is not what I am talking about."

"The cave? Yeah. I know. Just had a meeting with the headmaster."

"That, too. But still not what I'm referring to."

"Your brother?"

He sighed, tired of the guessing game. "Come on. Let's get you some food. Maybe you'll be able to think better with a full stomach."

I blinked in surprise, staring at him as he turned and walked back into the dining hall. "You're going to eat with me?"

"No. I'm going to have some coffee and talk at you while *you* eat."

"Oh."

He pointed at one of the tables and walked over to it, settling his large frame in the wooden chair. He noticed me standing there and motioned for me to get my food.

I didn't have to be asked twice. Told twice. Whatever. I was starving. Practically running down the buffet, I shoveled food on the plain white china, grabbed some silverware and a glass of juice, and headed back to the table. I nervously glanced around as I sat the plate down, worried someone would see us together. By someone, I mean David.

"Don't worry. I'll tell him we talked."

"You could tell?"

"And smell your fear."

"Ew." I sniffed my pit.

"How does a tiny thing like you pack away so much food?"

"I store most of it in my cheeks," I answered and sat down.

"I have seen your ass. It isn't big, either."

Unrolling my silverware from the linen napkin, I stopped to cock an eyebrow at him. "You guys have a sense of humor?"

He was dangerous, and sulky, but fuck if the smile didn't light up his face like Times Square on New Year's Eve. "We've been known to crack a joke or two."

"Both of you, or just you?"

"Mostly me. Rome is…Rome."

"Mr. Angrypants."

"Most of the time, yes. Life has not been easy for the two of us. He shoulders more responsibility than I."

"I thought you were going to have some coffee." I started shoveling food in my mouth.

"Yes. I shall."

While he got a cup, I tried to put a big dent in my food. I was over halfway through when he sat back down. "Gods. Did you use a straw?"

"For what?" I stopped chewing.

"To eat with. You sucked down half your plate already."

"I was hangry."

"Hangry?"

"Like hungry but pissed off because you're hungry."

"I like that."

126

"Feel free to use it." I slowed down my culinary inhalation due to the fact that now there were witnesses involved. Picking at a chicken leg as nimbly as I could, curiosity finally got the better of me. "So, why do I need to be careful?"

"My sister."

"She don't like me."

"To put it mildly."

"Why are you warning me?"

"Because I do."

"What?"

"Like you."

"Why?"

"I've asked myself that question at least forty-two times."

I nodded. "Me, too!"

"I think that might be one of the reasons. Your self-depreciating humor. Your humor in general. Plus, I like how angry you make Rome, even if it makes my life more difficult."

"But you don't like me picking on your sister?"

He sighed. "Gods know she deserves it, but she is different from Rome."

"How so?" I took another bite of my chicken leg. Meat lollipops were my favorite. All the kinds. Wink wink.

"Rome understands the need for self-restraint. He may throttle you if you get out of hand, but he would never cause lasting harm. My sister…"

"Not so much?"

"Will kill you, cook you, and fucking eat you. Please stop pushing her buttons."

"She's safe. Not into chicks."

"Not what I meant."

"I know. Tell you what, Remy. Tell her I'll call a truce. She leaves me the hell alone and I won't get under her skin."

He nodded. "Thank you."

Chapter 12

"How much trouble are you in?"

Nearly tripping while jogging, I righted myself and adjusted my stride to match David's. Again, he had snuck up on me without me realizing it. Hiroki nodded and started running, giving us a little alone time. Physical Education was one of the very few classes David and I had together.

"I'm not. Got off with a warning."

"How did he know it was you?"

"I guess the twinsies ratted me out."

"Were they pissed you made fun of Sabine like that?"

"Huh? No? That wasn't what I got called to the office for."

There was a moment of silence while he processed the information. "What *did* you get in trouble for?"

Shit. Lie or tell the truth? I sighed. We hadn't been dating that long, I didn't want to ruin it by lying to him. "I followed you to the cave the other night."

"What? Why?" He slowed his pace.

"Well… See, I was fine with you going with the boys, but then I overheard your ex mention something about going, too, and I kinda had this little *jealous* moment and I kind of wanted to kill her, but I opted for following her and then I was chased by these two big dogs. It was a total mess. Two out of ten, would not stalk again."

"Sabine? Led you to the cave?"

His voice was chilly. Icy even. "Yes."

He just nodded and kept jogging.

"You're not mad that I followed her in a fit of jealous rage?"

He shook his head. "No. That was natural. I should have said something to you about her being there, but I really didn't think about it. I'm pissed at her for being followed."

"Oh. Why? What's in the cave?"

"Trust me, Kaede. You don't want to know."

"See, that's the thing. Everybody keeps telling me that and it just makes me want to know *more*. I mean seriously. I'm a fucking fox. We *hate* shit like this."

"I wish I could tell you, but I can't. I can only tell you it's better if you just forget the whole damn thing. We're talking dangers of epic proportions here, Kaede. Epic."

"Can you at least give me a hint?"

"End of the world type stuff."

"Oh. That is epic." I blinked in surprise. Maybe I would leave the cave alone. Maybe. Maybe not. I mean, a little peek couldn't hurt. "Yeah. I'll stay away."

"Thank you." He gave me one of his patented smiles.

"So. Full disclosure. I had dinner with Remy last night."

"I know."

"He told you?"

"Of course."

"Did it make you want to follow him to a cave in the middle of the mountains?"

"For what?"

I blinked. He couldn't be that dense. "It doesn't bother you if I spend time with your friends without you?"

"No? Why would it?"

"You trust me that much?" I felt a little guilty for trailing Sabine.

"If it weren't Remy or Rome, or even Hiroki, I might."

"Huh?"

He sighed and turned his head to look at me while we were jogging. "The twins and I..."

"Don't tell me you're into each other..."

"What? No! Well, there was that one time at Band Camp."

"Huh?"

"Kidding. No. We're...pack. Rome is the closest thing I've had to an Alpha in a very long time and they're not even werewolves. I'd share anything with them."

"Even me?"

His silence was enough of an answer. I started to slow down, and he stopped. "What the ever-loving fuck, David? Were you going to tell me this eventually?"

"If... I don't know."

"So, they walk up to you and tell you they wanna fuck me, and you're good with it?"

"If that is what you wanted." He blushed and looked away.

"What if I don't. Wait a minute. There is no what if in that statement."

"Then I would be forced to fight them, knowing without a doubt I would lose."

"What?"

"I would lose?"

"You would fight for me?"

"I'd do more than that. I'd probably go down, but I wouldn't be breathing when I did it. I'd keep going until that last breath left my lungs."

"That's pretty sweet, but morbid."

He stopped and I stood in front of him, looking up at his worried expression. "The truth usually is."

Putting my hands on my hips, I nodded. There was more truth to his words than I was comfortable admitting. "So, just so I understand... Let's just say if Remy found me attractive and wanted to be my boyfriend too, you wouldn't bat an

131

eyelash. But, if I didn't want to date him, you'd fight for me?"

"Yes. Rome, too."

"Let's not go crazy with this fantasy. He'd rather throw me off the top of a mountain than spend a second listening to my usually incoherent ramblings."

David chuckled, nodding slightly. "He was like that with me in the beginning, too. He doesn't open up to people easily. Just be prepared when, and if, he does. His friendship is worth the wait."

"Tall, dark, muscly, and broody? Yeah. Bet he's a ton of fun at parties."

David's smile got a little bigger. "Just going to have to trust me on this one."

"Whatever. Good talk. We should do this again sometime. When I'm drunk, because honestly I feel a little gross."

"Understandable. Just wanted to be honest with you."

"But why Hiroki?"

"Because he loves you. I don't think I could ever say no to you and him. I'd just have to pray that you wouldn't leave me for him."

"You just think he's hot."

"He is attractive," he admitted with a grin. I couldn't tell if he was joking or not. I was hoping for not.

"You should see him in panties."

"I'd rather see you in your panties."

"That can be arranged."

"I'd also like to see you without them."

"That can be arranged, too." I hissed a chuckle of fox laughter.

"You even laugh like a fox." He reached out and lovingly caressed my cheek. I shifted uncomfortably in my very tight gym shorts. The conversation, while surreal, had aroused me from the beginning. His touch was almost

132

enough to send me over the edge. I groaned and leaned into his caress, kissing his fingers.

"You wouldn't be kissing those if you knew where they'd been," Sabine said snidely as she and her cronies slowly jogged by.

"The same place that every finger in this school has been? Including your two friends running beside you?"

Not heeding Remy's advice when dealing with his sister, I went a little too far. But, in my defense, she did start it. I was just better at it. I was still soaking David's fingers in *sake* before I let him anywhere near my hoo-ha. I'd just have to make sure they were thoroughly dry. I already learned that lesson the hard way.

She stopped, spun on one foot, and launched herself at me. David immediately pushed me behind him and stuck out his chest, bracing for the impact that never came. Remy tackled his sister mid-air, landing in the grass of the center of the track. "Run," he snarled over his shoulder, giving me an "I told you so" look.

Using the opportunity, I literally got David back on track and heeded Remy's second piece of advice and ran as fast as my little legs could carry me.

"Sorry about that," David said, easily matching my stride.

"That you used her as a finger puppet?"

"Yeah. Not my proudest moment."

"Did you use her like...I can't think of anything witty. Did you put your dick in her?"

His blush was all the answer I needed.

"Ew. I put that in my mouth."

"I've had several hundred showers between then and now."

"So how long we talking? Last week? Cuz that's how many I would have taken between then and now."

"It was years ago."

133

"Okay. That I can live with."

"You're a jealous little thing, aren't you?"

"Yep. Mine. You might not care if you share, but Homey don't play dat. Got me, Mr. Lupescu?"

"Loud and clear, Ms. Tanaka."

∞ ∞ ∞

"Please?"

"No."

"Pretty please?" David flashed a smile as we walked into the dining hall. I cocked an eyebrow at him, honestly hoping he didn't think that just because he flashed me that sexy, sultry little smile he would get his way. I wasn't that easy.

He tilted his head down, not taking his eyes off me and giving me puppy dog eyes. Fucking puppy dog eyes! I was helpless as my insides liquified. "Fine. But if Rome gets snippy with me, I'm getting snippy back. And I use scissors."

He beamed. "Tell Hiroki to join us."

We were having dinner. Together. All of us.

Kami help me.

I held three fingers over my head. A moment later, Hiroki was by my side, giving a little bow. "Is everything okay?"

"Yes. You are invited to dinner."

"*Hai*," he said cautiously.

"That's all you had to do?" David seemed impressed by the whole ordeal.

"Yeah. It's been a while. I couldn't remember if it was three or four fingers."

"Four would have been bad." Hiroki frowned.

"What's four again?"

"Stick to the shadows, strike low, and take the head."

"Oh, yeah. Four is bad," I said to David. He turned white and led us to the buffet.

I winked conspiratorially at Hiroki. He knew damn well that was five. Or, at least I think it was. Maybe it was four. I'd have to ask him later and write it down.

David handed me a tray, plate, and roll of silverware, ushering me to go first. I think he liked to watch me fill my plate.

"I just want to go on record as saying this is a horrible idea."

"But you agreed to it." David grinned at me.

"Agreed to what?" Hiroki sounded confused.

"We're having dinner with the twins."

"Did you lose a bet?"

"No. David pouted."

"You are a sucker. Did he make puppy dog eyes?"

"Yes!"

"Is that her weakness?" David asked Hiroki.

"*Hai.*"

"I'll have to write that down."

"It only works once. After that I become immune. You wasted it. Now you'll never get to see this cool trick I can do with my tongue, three jolly ranchers, and a rubber band."

"That sounds dangerous."

"But it feels good." I felt him shudder behind me as I piled meatloaf on top of my mashed potatoes.

"Damn it!"

I filled my glass with juice and set it on my tray, turning and waiting for Roki and David to finish. "Do the twins know about this dinner date?"

"It was Remy's suggestion. Rome, I don't know."

"But no Sabine, right?"

"No. I value our relationship and my twig and berries."

"Smart man. I wouldn't say twig though. More like a thick branch."

"Thank you." He grinned like a schoolboy.

I grinned at him and let him lead the way. He seemed to instinctively know which way to go and found the twins in the back corner, already eating at a large circular table.

Rome looked up and his forkful of wound spaghetti stopped halfway to his mouth. His eyes narrowed, focused on me for a moment before shifting their icy gaze on his brother. "Now I know why you wanted the bigger table."

"I know not of which you speak, brother." His grin gave away his obvious attempt at lying.

Rome motioned us toward the three empty seats, acquiescing with a deep sigh. I sat down next to Remy, putting an entire table between Rome and me. I figured I could pop halfway across the hall before he got over the table. Not that I wanted to, or planned on, testing that theory. But sometimes, shit just happens. My mouth was the usual catalyst, but I figured it was some sort of birth defect or genetic disorder. My parents pissed me off whenever they talked, too.

Remy gave me a small smile as I shifted in my seat and unrolled my silverware from my napkin. David sat next to me, putting Roki between him and Rome.

"So...How are you, Rome?" I said to break the ice.

He paused eating again and narrowed his eyes, trying to see if I was baiting him. "Never been better. We shall see how long that lasts."

I smiled at him. At least he wanted to be at the same table as me as much as I wanted to be there with him. About the same level that I wanted to be disemboweled with the snippy side of a pair of rusted toenail clippers.

"Thanks for saving my ass this afternoon," I said to Remy softly.

"I tried to warn you."

"She said something nasty and my mouth is a licensed first responder."

He nodded. "I watched the scene unfold."

"You were guarding me?" I grinned and spooned some meatloaf, gravy, and potatoes into my mouth.

"No. You got lucky. I just happened to be running behind her."

"I'll talk to her," Rome said, giving me a little shock.

"Thank you?"

He nodded and continued eating. Feeling like we had a breakthrough moment, I smiled at him which just caused him to frown at his food.

"See?" David said softly, giving my leg a stroke with his left hand, stopping just at the hem of my skirt. The heat of his hand felt so warm, I sighed at his comforting touch.

"We wanted to thank you," Remy said, taking a sip of his drink.

"We did?" Rome couldn't help but ask.

"We did."

"For what?" I was just as confused as Rome.

"For staying away from the cave like you were asked."

"Told," I interjected.

"That as well. Sorry to involve the headmaster. For your safety, I thought you might listen to him. He is quite imposing."

"Uncle Tatsuo? Hardly. He can be scary, but I've seen him in…his…dra–" I trailed off. They were all staring at me, except for Hiroki, who was rubbing the bridge of his nose.

"Uncle?"

"Not by blood. Old family friend."

"*You're his kitsune niece!*" Rome stared at me wide-eyed and open mouthed.

"Me? No. What's a *kitsune*?"

Remy started chuckling beside me. David squeezed my knee.

Sighing in resignation, I put my spoon down. I deserved it. "Guess you guys are getting some extra credit." My last hope is that I was only half-*kitsune*. Maybe it wouldn't count if they guessed half-right.

"Since Headmaster Tatsuo has been telling us about your antics since we were children, we will not submit a guess," Remy said and then looked to his brother.

"Did you really blow up a school?" For the first time since I'd met him, Rome actually sounded impressed.

"Maybe. You a cop?"

"What?"

"Five-oh. You gonna bust me? Because there is a gag order on that case."

"No?"

"Okay. Then yes."

"The flaming hamsters?"

"Just the one."

"Confetti fire extinguishers?"

I chuckled and nodded. "I'd forgotten about that one."

"It was all true?"

Rome was starting to scare me. He was gazing at me with something akin to hero worship in his eyes. Shifting in my seat, I answered him with a simple, "And those were just the ones I got caught doing."

Remy started laughing. "You should have introduced yourself sooner. Rome might not have wanted to maul you when he first met you. He might have even asked for your autograph."

"Shut up, Remy."

I grinned at him. "See? Even annoying people can be cool."

He huffed. "I never said you were cool."

"I was talking about you." I winked to let him know I was kidding. He didn't speak sign language. His quickly reddening face was either leading to an outburst of animosity or an aneurism. "Lighten up, Francis. I was kidding."

His eyes narrowed, but he didn't flip the table. He chose wisely. I could tolerate a lot of things; threats, beatings, snide comments, but don't fuck with my meatloaf.

Then I noticed his eyes weren't focused on me. Neither were Remy's or Hiroki's. David was looking at them trying to figure out what was going on when I felt the heated presence behind me.

"What the fuck is going on here? You're *eating* with this bitch now?"

"Oh. Hi, Sabine," I said over my shoulder, not deigning to turn around. I didn't need to. If she tried anything, I would have seen it on the faces staring at her.

"Yes. We are." Rome told his sister evenly.

"You want to join us? I can scoot over," I said and slid my chair closer to David. Just in case she decided to. *Mine.*

As soon as Rome's eyes widened, before he could even utter a word of warning, I popped across the table, rematerializing beside him and watching as Sabine's swing met nothing but the empty air of my chair. She tumbled forward, stopping herself just before she faceplanted into my meatloaf.

"Get back here, you fucking bitch!" She snarled and a pure miasma of malice wafted over the table just as she squatted and launched herself at me.

There was a wall behind me, and I waited until the very last possible moment and just as I was about to slip back to my seat, Rome's hand shot out and grabbed a fistful of her blazer, stopping her dead in her attack.

"You will stop!" Shivers ran up my arms as Rome's voice echoed in my head.

I didn't have a single sibling. The relationships between brother and sister were a complete mystery to me. However, I was pretty sure that spitting in your brother's face was generally frowned upon. Especially when he threw her halfway across the alcove of the dining hall where our table was.

"Nice throw."

"Not funny. You should go. I'll calm her down."

I thought about arguing. I still had a half a plate of meatloaf… But, he was being nice to me and defending me. I'd listen. This time. "Come on, Roki."

"*Hai*."

Sabine was untangling herself from two students and the three chairs she had slid into, and picked herself up off the ground, staring at her brother incredulously. Expecting a string of obscenities, I nearly covered my ears as a primal, enraged scream erupted from her mouth.

I popped across the table, grabbed my plate of food, touched David on the shoulder, and popped the entire way across the room. Without looking back, I stepped through the doors and spooned food in my mouth as I walked.

"That went about as well as I expected," Hiroki said as he appeared beside me.

"Better. I thought it would be Rome trying to kill me tonight."

"True."

"Want some meatloaf?"

"No. I ate enough. Thank you, Kaede-*sama*."

"Let's stop by the Home Ec room. I'm out of rice."

"*Hai*."

Chapter 13

"I'm bored."

"Want to go watch a movie?" Hiroki was standing by the window in our room. With our dinner interrupted, we had gone straight back there. I'd been content for the first five minutes until I realized we didn't have a fucking thing to do.

"No. I want to go do something."

"You want to get into trouble."

I poured some *sake* into my stolen coffee mug. "You sure you don't want any?"

"With as well as you have been getting along with the indigenous life, I think I shall remain sober. It is better to keep you safe."

"Safe, shmafe." He had turned his gaze back outside our bedroom window, looking down at the ground level. "Whatcha lookin' at?"

"Keeping an eye out for danger."

"It will come through the front door, not the window."

"When it is centered on you, it will come from all directions."

"I do have that effect on people."

"*Hai.*"

"But not you," I said thoughtfully.

He turned his head and narrowed his eyes. "You know I would never hurt you."

"Yeah. But you don't do anything to make me feel good, either."

A frown touched his lips. "My apologies. But you have a boyfriend now. That falls into his realm of expertise."

"What about you?"

"What about me?"

"Why don't you have a girlfriend? Or a boyfriend?"

He laughed. "You are a fulltime job. I would have little time to devote to someone else."

My heart cracked a little. Not because he was being mean, but because he was being truthful. It hurt a little. "Yeah. I'm a big pain in the balls," I said and set my mug down. "I'm gonna go to the bathroom."

"I shall foll–"

"No. I'll be fine walking down the hall and back. Be right back," I said and nonchalantly grabbed the jar of *sake,* tucking it into the blazer jacket I had never taken off. With my arm tucked inside, I walked out the front door. When it *clicked* closed behind me, I popped to the stairs and then down to the first floor, not looking back as I strode through the double doors leading out of Breckenridge Hall.

Just to be sure, I made a series of jumps, popping across the campus and not walking until my feet touched the trails leading from the school grounds. Just wanting to be alone, I picked one at random and drank straight from the jar as I left everything and everyone behind.

The moon peeked between the overhead trees illuminating the path needlessly. But I still smiled up at the cool glow overhead and sniffed the air around me. While the temperatures were low, the jacket and the *sake* kept me warm enough. I did, however, wish I had some pants on. My ass was a little chilly and I rubbed it as I walked.

Walking for almost a half-an-hour, I realized I was quite lost and sat down on a frigid outcropping of rock to drink some more. The clearing seemed somehow familiar even to my rice wine dulled senses. Then an overhead cloud moved past the moon and a gleam of light illuminated the entrance to a *very* familiar cave.

"Huh. Looky looky. How'd that get there?"

Grinning as I stood, I downed the last of my drink and set the jar gently on the rock ledge, frowning as it fell when I let go and shattered against the ground.

"Shhh!"

Looking at the entrance to the cave, a large brownish black dog the size of a Volkswagon stepped from the entrance and looked around. It was smaller than the two black ones that had been there the other day and not nearly as frightening. That might have just been the *sake* flowing through my veins.

"Fluffy puppy," I whispered and foxed out. Not fully, just ears and tail. I popped in front of it, not the wisest thing I had ever done, I admit. But the look on its face made it totally worth it. "Hi, Puppy!"

It growled and tried to bite me, its giant head tilting as its jaws snapped around my waist. I popped ten feet to the left just as they snapped shut. "Bad puppy!"

Its fur looked totally soft and I wanted to touch it. It began bucking as I appeared on its back, straddling it like a mechanical bull and maniacally cackling as I stroked the fur on its neck. It wasn't very soft. An utter let down.

"Scruffy puppy," I said disappointedly and appeared on the ground behind it, slapping it on its ass.

It bucked again, and spun, its huge paws landing on the ground in front of me. Launching another attack, I reappeared beside it, but too close. It swiped me with a paw, and I flew across the clearing. Just before I impacted against a rock wall, I popped to the ground, but my forward momentum carried through the transition and I rolled to a stop on the dusty, dirty ground staring up at the star filled sky.

"Ouuuch." Gingerly, I sat up, my eyes widening as the giant canine tore across the clearing, intent on swallowing me whole.

I screeched and popped over to the entrance to the cave, reappearing just in time to see the six-hundred-pound canine slam into the wall that I'd narrowly missed being splatted against. It wasn't as lucky. Its head impacted with a sickening *thud* and it dropped to the ground.

"You dead, puppers?" I kind of felt bad. I didn't mean to kill it. I reappeared next to it and poked it with my toe, sighing in relief when I saw the rise and fall of its chest. Then, I screamed when it erupted in a violent pillar of black smoke. Jumping backward, I watched in fascination as the smoke twisted and dissipated in the cool breeze, leaving a prone girl lying unconscious on the dirt.

"Sabine's buddy? What the fuck are you doing here?"

My head shot up, looking around for her friend, but she was apparently alone. I slipped my foot under her shoulder, flipped her over on her back, and winced at the bright red gash across her forehead. "You're gonna have a wicked headache..."

Looking up at the entrance to the cave, I realized she'd been saddled with guard duty, and the object of my innermost desires was currently quite open for my perusal. With a grin, I let sleeping dogs lie, and practically skipped inside.

It wasn't a cave. It was a fucking temple.

And there was a god enshrined within.

The hair on the back of my neck rose as I tiptoed quietly within and looked around. The *Inari* half of my fox was roiling in the massive amount of spiritual energy, even if it wasn't the *Inari-kami's*. To it, a god was a god. I wasn't the most reverent of *Inari,* either. When I was little, I took great pride in helping my father at the temple. As I grew older... I only thanked him when I made *sake*.

The energy inside the cave was unlike anything I had ever felt before. Anger rolled through it in waves, the urge for destruction, but at the same time it felt...related. It felt like me. It was angry at the world and those who had brought it into it.

Whatever it was, it was beneath me. Every trace of energy was pounding up at me from below. I fell to my knees and put my hand on the ground, wanting nothing more than to soothe its pain. The flames in the bowls of oil perched on the stone ledge lining the inside of the temple flickered around me as a breeze swept through the square shaped room.

A soft caress of understanding grazed the edges of my consciousness. Whatever god had been enshrined, it was slumbering in a fitful nightmare. The soft touch became a pool, not of rage, just overwhelming as it completely submerged me. Old didn't even begin to describe the entity holding me in its mind. Ancient. Always. Lupine to my vulpine. It whispered words I couldn't hear and wouldn't have been able to understand if I had.

"Who are you?" My voice sounded oddly muted, even in the stone chamber. Like I was under water.

Fenrir.

I'd have to have been a fool not to know the name. Fenrir, the wolf of destruction. The Norse god who was supposed to devour the world at the end of times. I'd read the story so many times as a child, it was engrained in my memory. *Ragnarok.* In fact, it was Uncle Tatsuo who had first told me the story. The three children of the trickster god, Loki. Fenrir, Jormungandr, and Hel.

Who are you, Child?

I was in deep shit. My decision to walk into that cave suddenly didn't seem like the brightest idea I'd ever had. I wished somebody would have warned me.

"Sabine," I lied.

Trickster…just like my sire. I can see your name, though it is unusual. Kaede…

A normal person of sound mind and body would have run. I popped the fuck out of there, running when my feet touched the hard-packed dirt at the mouth of the cave, kicking up dust in my efforts to put as much space between me and the god of destruction.

"Uncle Tatsuo is gonna kill me," I chanted repeatedly as I ran the entire way back to campus.

∞ ∞ ∞

"Are you sure you're okay?"

I nodded at Hiroki, tired of him repeating the same damn question over and over again. It had started last night, when I got back to the room after my little meeting with Fenrir. I'd just nodded then, not daring to elaborate, and crawling into bed after a long shower. When he woke me up to go to class, it had started again, almost as if he could smell the trouble clinging to me like the stench of defeat. Maybe it was the stench of I fucked up.

"Yeah! Totally fine. Why do you keep asking?"

"You seem rather subdued. Experience has taught me that usually equates with you doing something you shouldn't have and are afraid to tell me. What did you do?"

"Nothing, Roki. I went for a walk, drank a little *sake*, froze my ass off. I wasn't in the mood for company is all," I said with a smile and hoped he didn't notice.

We almost made it to Home Economics when he narrowed his eyes over my shoulder. "Then why is your boyfriend and your two new friends barreling across the quad like you buried their sister in a shallow grave?"

I gulped audibly, memories of Sabine's friend lying in the dirt stabbing me in the heart. I hadn't even thought of her when I got the hell out of Dodge. Hopefully, she didn't get

146

eaten. "They must be late for class, too. C'mon, Roki. I don't want to get yelled at."

"Since when?"

I grabbed his hand and pulled him through the front door, practically dragging him down the hall and into our classroom.

"Miss Tanaka, so good of you to join us." Welheim sounded a little too pleased with herself. "Unfortunately, the headmaster would like to see the both of you in his office. Discreetly," she whispered, still loud enough for the rest of the class to hear. I knew because the first three rows started snickering.

Roki pulled his hand from my grasp. "A walk?"

"Yes. We should go for a walk. To the headmaster's office. Apparently."

He stiffly turned and headed for the door. I meekly followed, grabbing the back of his jacket in my fingers, subserviently, letting him lead the way. When he opened the door, the twins and David were already standing there.

"You are to follow us–."

"To the headmaster's office. Already got the memo."

The twins turned and started walking, Roki following without question as David gave me a sad, somewhat disgusted look. "Why? All you had to do was stay away." He turned and shook his head, staying by my side, probably to ensure I didn't run. I won't lie, I kind of wanted to. A lot.

"I was drunk and ended up there. It wasn't like I was planning on ending up at the cave." *I think.*

"You have no idea what could have happened…"

Yeah. I kind of do. In fact, I already did. "I know."

"No. You don't."

I let it go. David's anger was probably *nothing* compared to what probably awaited me at the hands, claws, whatever of Uncle Tatsuo. I bet he was regretting his decision of talking my parents into sending me to Aesir Academy. If I hadn't already doomed the world to destruction. Then I might be the last of his worries.

"Sorry," I said meekly and reached for him with my free hand. As soon as I touched his arm, he pulled away and sped up, trailing behind the twins in front of Hiroki.

"Do not run," Roki whispered. "It will only make things worse. I assume you went to the cave?"

"No. But that's where I ended up. It wasn't planned."

"It usually never is with you. I will protect you if it is in my ability."

"No. This time you take care of yourself," I whispered. He'd caught enough shit for my behavior. This was the biggest fuckup of my lifetime. Anybody's lifetime, probably. I'd take the heat.

We walked in silence until we reached the double wooden doors of Tatsuo's office. Without so much as a knock, the twins each pulled one open, motioning for us to enter. Sabine and her mother were standing off to the side and my uncle sat behind his desk, looking very unhappy.

I opened my mouth to unleash a tirade of apologies when he held up his hand for silence. "Do you know what is in that cave?"

I nodded.

"You remember the stories I told you as a child?"

I nodded again, not trusting my voice to answer.

"Do you understand what you *could* have unleashed upon this world?"

"I do." I managed to get the words past my trembling lips.

"Good. Luckily he still sleeps…"

Uh… Maybe I should tell him. I should tell him. I can't tell him. He'll kill me. "Whew. That was a close one."

He narrowed his eyes at me. "Yes. Too close. How did you realize who slumbered in the temple? Was it the engravings that gave it away?"

"Yep. Totally. Saw the little wolves and I was like, 'Fenrir lives here.'"

"There are no engravings. Perhaps it was something else. Maybe the book on the altar? You remember it from my description don't you."

"Yep. That was it. I must have imagined the wolves."

"There was no book, Kaede. How did you know?"

Slick old bastard. I sighed. "He spoke to me." *Might as well come clean.*

There was an eruption of noise in the office as everyone but David, Hiroki, and Uncle Tatsuo started yelling at the top of their lungs. The headmaster just stared at me the entire time.

"This is horrible. She must be punished! If she has undone all that we have strived to do for all of these centuries…"

He held up his hand and everyone quieted down. "Has he spoken to you since you left the cave?"

I shook my head.

"Kaede…"

"Honest *kitsune*, Uncle. He hasn't." I held up my hand and made a Vulcan gesture.

"One would assume he has gone back to sleep. Kaede, if you ever go near that cave again…"

"Not gonna happen in this *kitsune's* lifetime. His spiritual energy was…he engulfed me. I was lucky to get out of there alive. And I also promise it wasn't my intent to go there. I was a little upset with Sabine trying to eat me last night, so I went for a walk. I just happened to end up there, I swear."

Everyone looked at Sabine. She started turning red and sputtering. "She…she…"

Uncle Tatsuo closed his eyes and snapped his fingers. A shiver ran down my spine, and judging from everyone else in the room, so did theirs. "Gag order is now in effect on everyone in this room, since Kaede just admitted to her true nature. That should spare us from any other incorrect, yet whimsical, guesses in the future.

Wanting to change the subject, I asked Sabine, "Is your friend okay?" I'd only meant it half teasingly. I really did feel kind of bad for leaving her behind."

"Like you fucking care! What the fuck did you do to her?"

"Got out of the way. She hit the wall *pretty* darn hard. I felt bad for leaving her there, but Fenrir scared the piss out of me. Tell her I'm sorry."

"That is very gracious of you, Kaede," Uncle Tatsuo said with a nod.

"You're taking her side?" Sabine stared at him incredulously.

"If I recall correctly, it was I who said we should tell her what was in the cave to begin with. It was the four guardians who said we should not." He paused to look around the room at the four Laterans. Remy gave him a nod. "Had she known who was enshrined there, she would not have set one paw in there. Had one of you," he paused to stare at Sabine, "Not been so careless with travelling to the cave, she would not have known where it was to begin with. So, yes. I am taking her side. You do not understand the *kitsune* like I do. It was almost as if you did everything in your powers to *lure* her there. Next time maybe you should heed my advice."

I resisted the urge to cheer.

"Everyone may leave now," he said angrily. I turned tail to run. "Not you, Kaede. Sit. Hiroki, you may stay if you wish."

"*Hai.*"

"This is ridiculous. She almost ended the world and she's not even in trouble!"

"Sabine!" Her mother tried to warn her.

Too late. Uncle Tatsuo stood behind his desk, eyes smoldering with fire. His shadow slid up the wall and changed shape, wings fanning out and darkening the room. In an unearthly voice, he growled in his chest. The assistant headmistress stepped in front of her daughter. "Forgive her impudence," she said and bowed her head.

The room brightened as his shadow slid back behind him, returning to the shape of plain old Uncle Tatsuo in his robes. "That is all, Isabella."

She nodded, turned, and ushered her children and David from the room. David didn't even look at me as he left.

As soon as the doors were closed, Uncle Tatsuo waved his hand and they locked behind them. With another wave of his hand, the spiritual power surrounding us coalesced into a shield. He stared at me intently as it settled into place.

"What?"

"Just making sure the connection to Fenrir was severed and he wasn't eavesdropping in his sleep. Did you feel anything when I sealed the room?"

"No? Should I have?"

"Just a precaution. I trust you had the shit scared out of you and all of that was not just an act?"

"No friggin' way. You were right. I wish you had told me what was in there. I remember the story."

"There is more to it. Do you wish to hear it?"

"Is it bad?"

"No. But it might explain everybody's roles a little better."

"Then yes?"

"You remember the three children of Loki?"

"Fenrir, Jormungandr, and Hel?"

"Yes. Very good. Fenrir you met. Unfortunately. What do you remember of Jormundandr?"

151

"The dragon that encircles the world. When he grows large enough, Fenrir wakes and destroys the earth in Ragnarok."

"Yes. And Hel?"

"The god of the underworld."

"Goddess actually."

"My bad," I said with a grin, impressed at how much I had remembered. "But what does that have to do with all of you?"

"What I did not tell you is that each of the children of Loki are the progenitors of their own races…"

"Dragons? You?"

"A descendant, nothing more. As are the rest of the dragons who live in the mountains above the school."

"But you're Japanese?"

He chuckled. "And if I were human, I would be Japanese and look nothing like my Icelandic cousins. Yet we are all dragons."

"True. Let me guess, werewolves are descended from Fenrir?"

"You are right. I assume you know what David is?"

"Yes."

"Yet you did not guess."

"No. We all agreed not to."

"Admirable. Can you guess the descendants of Hel?"

"The big doggies?"

This time his laughter was more relaxed. "Yes. The big doggies. You do not know what they are, do you?"

"Nope."

"Think on it."

"Yeah. I suck at stuff like that. Can you just tell me?"

He sighed but nodded. "Hounds. Hounds of Hel. Hellhounds you would call them."

"No shit."

"I would not lie."

"It's all of them. The Laterans and Sabine's friends?"

"One of them. The other is a wolf like young David."

"Why are they all here? Because of Fenrir?"

"As am I. The school serves two purposes. To train supernatural youth to blend in. That part is factual. The second duty is to keep Ragnarok from becoming a reality."

"What about Jormungandr?"

"Vanished. After the first Ouroboros. The progeny of the Children of Loki managed to subdue Fenrir, but the losses were great. His body and soul split, and one of them sealed beneath the shrine for thousands of years, but he stirs. And is fitful."

"I know. I could feel it."

"What did he say to you?"

"He asked me my name."

Tatsuo frowned and stroked his chin. "Did you give it to him?"

"I tried not to. I told him it was Sabine, but he saw right through that lie and knew my real name."

"He could probably smell it on you."

"He felt angry and comforting at the same time. It was weird."

"There is no greater comfort than death, Kaede."

I shuddered at the morbid thought. "You have all been in the cave. Has he never spoken to any of you?"

"No. We are too akin to him for him to notice. It is why I did not want you to enter the cave. You are also a spiritual messenger. A being created by the gods for the gods. You are lucky he did not use you as a vessel."

"Like an aircraft carrier?"

"No. Like a suit of skin for him to walk around in. He would have devoured you and replaced your consciousness with his."

"Oh. That kind of vessel."

"Kaede-*sama*..."

We both turned and looked at Hiroki. "Yes?"

"Do not go into that cave again…"

"I won't."

"Do you promise?"

"I do. Cross my heart and hope to not…become a skin suit."

Chapter 14

"Very good, Kaede. You're only a couple cents off."

I looked up from the dummy check register to Professor Jones. She was our very human accounting instructor and one of the nicest people I had ever met. It was one of the few classes I enjoyed. I didn't even balk at the idea of filling out a check register. I didn't have the heart to break it to the rest of the class that online banking basically did all of it for you.

"Thank you."

"See if you can figure out where you made a mistake with your debits. Don't go crazy though, it is only a couple of cents. We'll just call that savings," she said and gave me a wink before looking over Hiroki's shoulder. He was practically beaming at me.

My day had started out shitty, but quickly turned around. Uncle Tatsuo had practically let me off the hook with a stern warning. Everything was copasetic between Hiroki and I, Sabine got yelled at, I didn't completely wake up a god, and Hiroki was proud of me. Now if I could just get David to forgive me, everything would be peachy fucking keen.

"Perfect, Hiroki! Excellent work!" Professor Jones patted him on the head and moved away.

He leaned over. "The check for the cleaners was fourteen dollars and twenty-eight cents. Not twenty-six."

I looked at my register. Of course, he was right. "You suck."

"Sometimes. But so do you."

"I do not."

"I was on the couch next to you…"

Heat crept up my cheeks. "You saw?"

"It was a little hard not to notice," he said with a grin.

I sighed. "You're just jealous."

"Perhaps."

I blinked in surprise. "You want to suck David, too?"

It was his turn to blush. "That's…no. I meant…"

I started giggling. "I know. I was kidding."

He chopped me on the top of my head, softly. "You are incorrigible."

"I'm not the one talking about blowjobs."

"No, but you were the one giving them."

I wiggled my eyebrows. "It's almost lunch. We could arrange a little foray into the bathroom. We can pretend I'm the headmistress…" I had meant it as a joke, and I knew he'd say no. Hopefully. I couldn't cheat on David, even with Hiroki.

He chuckled and the bell rang. Thankfully. I'd been too depressed to eat breakfast and my stomach was gnawing on my backbone.

"Food," I practically groaned and salivated on myself.

"Okay, class. Dismissed. I shall see you tomorrow."

I sprang from my seat and headed for the door, not waiting for my babysitter to catch up. First one to the door, I flung it open and winced when it didn't go as far as it should have and stopped with a thud. Hopefully it wasn't anybody important…

"Sorry," I said as I looked around the edge of it at a very irate looking Headmistress Lateran. The stack of papers she had been carrying were ruffled and creased, but still clutched tightly between her hands. I groaned when I realized my life was over.

"Of course, it's you."

156

"I'm really sorry, Headmistress."

"Go. Just…go."

Snapping my mouth shut, I stopped myself from apologizing again and got while the getting was good. Roki slid up next to me, chuckling.

"That wasn't funny. I'm lucky she didn't shorten my tails."

"Yes. It was."

We headed for the dining hall and were almost there when he reached out and grabbed my arm. "Do you wish to find David and eat with him?"

"Probably not. He was *pretty* pissed. Let's just eat and we can sit at one of the larger tables. He can join us or not."

"Are you sure? It might be better to seek him out and apologize."

"Why, Hiroki Nishimura. Are you worried about my relationship?"

He gave me a strange glance. "*Hai*?"

"That's sweet."

"No. It keeps you preoccupied, and my chastity is safer."

I chuckled. He wasn't lying. "Come on. I really need to eat."

We entered and filled our plates, sitting at one of the tables meant for four people, just in case. I was hoping we'd need the extra room. Really, really hoping. My toes were crossed under the table and I kept glancing around nervously as I munched my sandwich.

"Relax," Roki said calmly from across the table.

I took a deep breath and choked on a piece of lettuce, but stopped breathing when David and the twins walked in. His eyes cut across the room and settled on mine. Something passed between us, a feeling. I felt relief, and I hoped he did to. Nausea would have been bad.

Smile. Smile at me, David, I thought at him with all my might.

The corners of his lips started to curl, but then Rome pushed him toward the buffet. I sighed and nibbled my food.

"I thought you were hungry."

"I'll eat. When I know what he's feeling. Either way. I just need to know."

After five minutes of waiting, I had my answer. He sat across the room with Rome and Remy. The sandwich fell from my hand and the tears from my eyes.

"Kaede…"

"It's okay. I'm not feeling that well. I'm going to go lie down."

I got up from my seat and headed toward the door, wiping the tears from my face with the back of my hand. As I was slipping through the door, I face planted into Sabine's chest.

"Watch it, bitch."

I ignored her and went to walk around her when her hand shot out and grabbed my shoulder. "I'm supposed to be having lunch with David, have you seen him? He seemed like he really wanted to talk." I probably would have wished her well if she hadn't started laughing. Her friends, too.

Kill her. Show me you're worthy.

The voice echoed in my head and just goaded me into doing what I already wanted to do. I pulled my hands back and let my foxfire fill them before I hit her with a double open palm hit to the chest. She screeched, crashed into her friends, and then screamed as the fire burned her blazer and blouse. "Fuck you and fuck him. Fuck all of you bitches. And I mean that literally."

I stepped around them as her friends started slapping at the flames and headed to my room, stopping by the Home Economics room to pick up a fresh batch of rice and a new jar. I didn't even bother grabbing a mug. I wasn't going to need it.

158

When I got to my room, I filled the jar with rice and then poured water over it from the pitcher on my dresser. The one that had been magicked to always be full. Holding my hand over it, I sent a little prayer to the *Inari-kami* begging him to give me a reprieve from the pain in my chest. The hurt and sadness.

A rumbling chuckle filled the room. Or my head. It was impossible to tell, but when I lifted the jar to my lips, the dry smell of *sake* wasn't there, but the sweet smell of honey was. Shrugging, I drank.

It burned like *sake* but didn't taste anything like it. Sweet fire glided over my tongue and burned my chest as I gulped it down. When I pulled the jar from my lips, I stared in wonder as the taste of honey filled my mouth. "That isn't *sake*."

Mead. The name filled my head and I nodded in appreciation. After years of drinking the same damn thing, day after day, the reprieve was well earned. I waited for the vomiting that usually accompanied me trying any other liquor, but it never came. I lay back against my headboard and smiled as I sipped my new friend.

The soft, subtle sound of a knock at my door caught me off guard and I gasped. It wasn't Hiroki, he had a key. Chances are it was a professor who had caught me sneaking my way back into the dorms in an effort to skip afternoon classes. Sighing, I got up to face the music. It wasn't as if my life could possibly get any worse.

With a sense of indifference, I turned the knob and stepped back in shock. I'd been expecting a professor, but secretly hoping it would be David, come to tell me he forgave me. But it wasn't. Remy stood in my doorway, an almost worried look on his face. At least it wasn't Rome. I don't think I could have handled that.

"Uh. Hi?"

"Are you okay?"

"Don't beat around the bush much, do you?"

"Not one for mincing words. Want some company or would you prefer to be alone after I have completed my health and safety check?" He gave me a wink.

"Come on in," I said and walked back into the room, leaving him standing in the doorway. I grabbed my jar of fermented honey I had somehow made from rice off the dresser. It was official, the day couldn't possibly get any weirder.

"Is that alcohol?"

"Um. No. It's fruit juice."

"I can smell it from here…"

"You gonna rat me out?"

"No. I was going to ask for a sip. How the hell did you get alcohol into the school?"

"One of my many wonderfully hidden talents," I said and handed the jar over, leaning back on the bed and motioning for him to sit.

He plopped down on the end of mine, instead of Roki's, and I tucked my feet up a little to give him some room. He took a swallow of the mead and his eyes widened. "That's good," he said, handing it back to me.

"So, were you really worried about me or did you come to berate me."

He shrugged. "What's done is done. I'm just happy it didn't go horribly wrong. And for the record, I agreed with Headmaster Tatsuo."

"Great." I didn't really care. The one person I wanted to have stuck up for me was David. I took another drink and passed it back.

He held up his hand and shook his head. "I have guard duty tonight."

"That's kind of boring."

"Well, being here isn't a reward. It's a punishment. And guarding is what the Hounds of Hel do."

"Yeah. I heard about the car accident. Sorry."

His face darkened. Maybe I shouldn't have mentioned knowing about it, but if it was a secret, David should have kept his mouth shut. "Thank you," Remy mumbled and stared at the sea of duvet between us.

"Want to know a secret?"

"What?" He looked up.

"When you fuck up, you don't need to worry about forgetting about it. People will keep reminding you about it over and over and over until the mere thought of the incident pisses you off instead of making you feel bad."

"Speaking from experience?"

"*Years* of it."

"You do seem to attract trouble like Rome attracts blondes."

"You're twins. I'm sure you're not hurting from attractive blondes."

"I prefer my girls with lighter hair," he said with a wink.

"Lighter than blonde?"

"Sometimes."

"You prefer me?" I gulped audibly.

"No way. You're too much trouble," he answered with a smile.

I nodded emphatically. "You have no idea…"

That caused him to break out in a grin. I probably would have denied it if asked, but it was even better than his smile. His smile made him beautiful, but his grin…his grin made him ooze sexiness like an overripe sexmelon. I washed away the drool with another swallow of mead.

"That was quite the show with Sabine you put on."

I frowned, having mostly forgotten about punching her in the chest and setting her on fire. "She okay?"

"Little singed, but I'm sure she deserved it. What did she say to you?"

"That I was basically a piece of shit who fucked up, and she was there to have lunch with David because he hates me now? Or something like that. I have a tendency to drown out unpleasant memories."

"You mean drown, as in drink away?"

"Yeah. Pretty much," I nodded and drank some more. Unpleasant Sabine memories were still swirling around, so I drank some more after that.

Remy reached over and took the jar. "They're only unpleasant because you let them be." He stood and set the jar on the dresser, far from my grasp. "What you should be doing is fun things to make you forget about the unpleasantness. And for the record, David doesn't hate you. He's just hurt, but he'll get over it. He was on his way here when I stopped him, telling him to give you some time. Want me to go send him to you?"

"I don't know," I answered honestly. Giddy as a schoolgirl on the inside, I didn't know how to react.

"I think you do," Remy said and cocked an eyebrow.

"A little."

"You like him. A lot."

I nodded.

"Good. David is good people and has been afraid to get close to girls since Sabine."

"You don't seem to like your sister very much. What about all the blood thicker than water sayings?"

"Sabine is...Sabine. Family is what you make of it, not what you're born into. There is another saying among the hounds. Littermates do not a pack make."

"There is a saying amongst *kitsune*, too. Want to hear it?"

He nodded.

"Hand me my drink."

He sighed, but reached behind him and grabbed it, handing it to me slowly. I took it, upended it, and finished it with a small burp.

He chuckled softly. "What's the saying?"

"That was it. Hand me my drink. *Kitsune love* their booze," I answered with a grin.

"I should get to class. Lunch is about over. Want me to tell David to skip and keep you company?"

"Yes," I said, getting up to walk him out. "Please."

"Will do. Glad you're okay."

Walking up to him, I threw my arms around him, giving him a hug as thanks. "Thanks for caring."

He went rigid in my arms.

"What's wrong? Not a huggy person?" I pulled back, not wanting to offend him.

"No…it's just..."

"What? I stink?"

"No. You smell…really good. *Really* good."

I grinned up at him. "It's my body wash."

"Uh…let's go with that." He pulled away and practically ran to the door.

I made a mental note to hug him more.

Chapter 15

The second knock came, and I practically leapt from the bed and did a somersault. Remy had said he would send David to play hooky with me, but I didn't think he would actually show up. In my excitement, I pulled the door open before fully turning the knob and it ripped out of my hand. I took a deep breath and tried again with a little more success.

David was standing there, a basket hanging from one hand, and a bouquet of hastily ripped flowers in the other. Some of them even had clumps of dirt still attached to their roots. It was the sweetest thing I'd ever seen.

"Hi," he said questioningly, giving a little smile, but I could still see the worry in his eyes. He was afraid I was going to slam the door in his face.

I opted for kissing him instead, reaching up and pulling his face down to mine and refusing to let go with my lips. Unfortunately, even supernatural creatures need oxygen most of the time.

"Woah," he said and gave me a dreamy smile.

I punched him in the arm. "The kiss was for coming back. The punch was for ignoring me at lunch."

He coughed. "Yeah. Sorry about that."

"It's okay, Remy told me you were on your way to see me. But seriously, David… *When* I fuck up, and it will happen from time to time, maybe even minute to minute, be angry. Be pissed. Be whatever, but don't ignore me. I'd rather get yelled at than have you not talk to me."

"I don't think I could ever yell at you."

"I just told you to."

He thought about it for a moment. "Nope. Still couldn't do it. How about I scowl at you and call you a dumb fox?"

"You think I'm a dumb fox?" I pouted.

He lowered himself until he was looking up at my face. "When you don't listen and almost bring about the end of the world? Yep. But I still love you," he lifted his head and kissed the end of my nose.

All nine of my tails burst into being. I lost complete control. The tears started falling down my cheeks and my legs were threatening to give out. I may have even started hyperventilating.

"You're not dumb! You're super smart. A genius fox!" He was starting to panic.

"You...you... You love me?" I stared up at him incredulously.

He stopped for a moment, looking down at the bouquet of flowers and the picnic basket. "Yeah? I thought you kind of knew that?"

"No. I mean I knew you kinda were into me. An affectionate toleration. But...love?"

"Do you not want me to?"

"Yes!"

There was a momentary look of relief on his face and then he lifted an eyebrow. "Wait. Yes. You do want me to, or yes, you don't want me to?"

"That hurt my head. Dumb fox, remember?"

"Kaede," he said and swung his arms around me, flower and picnic basket and all. "I only say that to show you I'm mad at you. I don't think you're dumb."

"Would you say that if I had blown up the world?"

"I wouldn't be here to say it, but yes."

I rubbed my face against his chest. His wonderfully firm, smelling of pine and sexiness, chest.

"Just to clarify, you want me to love you, right?"

"Yes, David. Please love me."

"I think I can do that. Want to have lunch with me?"

"Didn't you eat?"

He pulled back and shook his head. "Do you honestly think I could have eaten after watching you run out of the dining hall like that?"

"I thought you were eating with Sabine?'

"Why would you think...because that's what she said to you when you lit her on fire." He wasn't asking. He figured it out all on his own and sighed in frustration.

"Sorry," I mumbled.

"For thinking she was telling the truth or setting her on fire?"

"I'd never apologize for that. The fire part."

"Kaede, it's you. It will always be you. And it will never be her. Okay?"

"Kay."

"Lunch?"

"Food!"

"Quickest way to a fox's heart."

"Nope. That would be by being the sweetest, handsomest, sexiest wolf on the planet. Care to eat me, Mr. Wolf?" I wiggled my eyebrows at him.

He chuckled and kicked the door closed behind him, setting our food down on the dresser and stuffing the flowers in my empty jar of mead. He was lucky it was empty.

Two steps and he closed the distance between us, grabbing my hips in his now free hands, and pulling me in for another earth-shattering kiss. He walked us backward toward the bed and slid one arm behind me, gently lowering me to the mattress, but never breaking the kiss. I barely had enough sense to dispel my tails as my butt touched the mattress and I finally pulled back from his kiss. "You're not going to make me say it back first?"

"That you love me?"

I nodded, giving him an impish grin.

"I never want you to lie to me. I never want you to feel like you have to. So, only tell me if you mean it."

Reaching up, I covered his cheeks with my hands. "I love you."

"You mean it?"

"Or I wouldn't have said it." I kissed him again gently.

He gave me a dreamy smile and kissed my neck, letting his lips trail over the buttons of my shirt as he moved lower and lower.

"Where you going?"

"You wanted Mr. Wolf to eat you...so that is exactly what he's going to do, Little Red Riding Hood." He grinned at me, settling himself between my legs and slowly pushing my skirt up. With every inch of thigh that he exposed, he planted two kisses, one on each leg. I felt myself grow exponentially wetter with each pass of his lips, too. I was wearing the standard issue, white cotton panties. By the time he reached his destination, I was pretty sure they were going to be translucent in one very large spot.

He stopped lifting the skirt for a moment and just sighed in contentment. "You don't know how long I've been waiting to do this," he said with a grin.

"My...what big teeth you have."

"The better to eat you with, my dear."

I shuddered and spread my legs a little further as he flipped my skirt over my stomach, completely exposing my panties to his hungry eyes. "You smell incredible."

"Shush. You're going to embarrass me."

"I mean it. I've never wanted to taste anything more."

"Less talky, more licky."

He chuckled and touched my clit through the soft material, making a small, gentle circle. I hissed in pleasure as my hips rolled on their own. His finger traced the valley

168

between my lips and swirled in the wetness that had leaked through. Slowly he brought the tip to his lips and he let out a moan of happiness as he sucked it into his mouth.

"Holy hell you taste like honey."

I grinned and made little mewling noises, bucking my hips at him, hoping he'd take the hint.

He slid his fingers behind the front of my panties, grazing my flesh with the back of his fingers, and pulling them away and moving them to the side. I wanted him to attack me, but he just paused to stare.

"What?"

"Even in your most hidden of places, you are absolutely beautiful."

"Huh?"

He smiled at me, leaned down, and kissed me in my most sensitive of places. I hissed in pleasure again, wanting more. "I said," he paused and kissed me again, "that you…" He opened his lips and *really* kissed me, tongue sliding between my lips and dragging across my clit. "Are beautiful." He pulled me apart with two of his fingers and lifted the hood covering my pearl. His lips sealed themselves over it and he sucked gently as his tongue gently teased it.

I saw stars. Thousands of them as his mouth became the center of my existence.

He didn't relent. Every guy who had ever orally administered had used it as a prelude for getting what they wanted. David was an artist who loved to paint. "You're going to make me come," I whispered and ran my fingers through his soft, wavy tresses.

He paused to answer. "That's the whole idea." He attacked me once more and slid a finger inside as he closed his lips back over me and drove every remaining thought from my brain with his tongue. He brought me to the edge, and when he sensed my imminent release, he slowed, letting it slip from me. I growled in frustration and practically grabbed a fistful of his hair.

I felt his chuckle, my legs pressing against the sides of his chest. "Do you want me to finish you?"

"Yes!"

"Do you want to come?"

"Yes...please."

He gently kissed me, not on my clit, but just below. On the juncture of my lips. "I love you," he whispered and gently slid his tongue inside me.

"Oh, fuck. I love you, too."

He pulled his tongue from me and slipped it back inside just as quickly, using both hands to pull me open. His tongue felt a thousand times better than his finger, hard, wet, and delving as far as it could.

"David..."

"Come for me," he answered, swiping his tongue from bottom to top, and mashing against my clit.

I screamed something between his name and a string of obscenities, and my hips thrashed against his mouth. He used his arms to pin my legs down and it made it all that much hotter. A trapped fox in the jaws of a predator. As I lay there panting, he finally released me from his mouth, gave me one last gentle kiss, and rubbed his cheek against me before smiling up at me.

"Woah."

"You look very...relaxed."

"I guess you could call a coma somewhat relaxing." I closed my eyes and let the world spin around us for a moment, smiling.

"You're not in a coma. You wouldn't be able to speak."

"Who said I could? Holy fuck that was amazing. Next time you stop, though, I might squish your head between my thighs like a watermelon. That was mean."

"But it made you come harder."

170

"Maybe, but I'm not entirely convinced that was a good thing. I can't think."

"Don't then." He reached up and ran his fingers through my carefully manicured tuft of white fur, "So soft "

"Do you like it? I was thinking of shaving it off."

"Please don't. Ever. I like it a lot. Not a huge fan of the clean-shaven look. Plus, I like the white…"

"You should see the rest of me," I said and let my ears pop into existence. I wiggled them for effect.

He chuckled. "I'll show you mine if you show me yours."

"I've seen yours," I said with a laugh.

"You know what I meant. I'm actually kind of jealous you can do parts of you. With me it's the whole shebang."

"She bang?" I grinned.

"Only if she wants to."

"She does," I answered and nodded, opening my arms for him to crawl up into.

He stood and slid his pants over his hips without unbuckling the belt or undoing the button. I licked my lips hungrily as he stood out in excitement as he stepped out of his shoes and slid out of the rest of his clothes. I just reached down and slipped my panties off and dropped them on the floor next to me, spreading my legs to let him know how much I wanted him. Needed him.

He crawled back, naked, between my legs and reached out, unbuttoning my shirt from the bottom button, up. "What are you doing?"

"I want to see you naked."

"No, you don't," I said with a little blush and kind of covered my breasts with my elbows.

"Um. Pretty sure I do," he said and stopped what he was doing. "Unless you don't want me to?"

There was no point in lying. "I have little boobs," I said embarrassedly.

171

He chuckled and lifted my elbows away, continuing to unbutton my shirt. "You could have no boobs and it wouldn't change how I feel about you, or how badly I want to see all of you."

"Good. Because you're not getting much more than that…"

"Much more than what?"

"No boobs. Especially lying on my back."

He just shook his head and smiled, pulling my shirt open to expose my plain white bra. "What are you talking about?"

"School issued, *padded* bra." I reached underneath me, unclasping the back, not even remotely wanting to deal with the humiliation of having his face all up in my business while *he* tried to unhook it. For all I knew, he could have been an expert and got it undone faster than I did. Which I *also* didn't want to know. Either way, me undoing it was safest.

With a sigh, I pulled it away from my chest and slid my arms out. Tilting my head, I bared myself to him. And shuddered as he kissed the tip of my nipple, smiling as he licked the other.

"Perfect," was all he said, but I still couldn't look at him. I didn't want to see the disappointment on his face.

"Kaede."

"What?"

"Look at me."

"No."

He reached down and touched my cheek, turning my head to face him. "You're perfect. In every way."

I blushed and started to shake my head, but he wouldn't let me. He stopped me with his lips, kissing me as he slid his cock into me and then crushed me beneath him. My arms wrapped around him as I melted into his kiss and felt the mind-numbing pleasure of him inside me.

"Perfect," he whispered as he rolled me over on top of him, driving him deeper inside me. I pulled back and sat up, giving him a shy smile.

"Fuck, that feels incredible."

"So do you," he answered and cupped my breasts in his hands, giving them a firm squeeze. "I thought you said they were small."

"They are."

"You know the old saying."

"Anything more than a handful is wasteful," I answered and rolled my eyes.

"Nope. I think your breasts were made for my hands. At least that's what it is now, I'm changing it."

Awwww. "Flattery will get you everywhere."

"I'm already where I want to be. No need to go anywhere else."

I blushed and rocked my hips, feeling him slide inside me and smiling as pleasure filled me. Even his eyes shuttered as he whispered my name. Wanting more, I got off my knees and got one foot on the bed, lifting myself up until the tip was just inside my entrance before dropping myself down on him. I did it again., and again, becoming comfortable in the rhythm and feeling him fill me over and over. I couldn't get enough.

"I'm not going to last long."

"Well, there's no such thing as school issue birth control. At least I don't think there is, so warn me."

"Woah. Maybe we should wait? We can get some protection first."

"We'll have it for next time. There's no way I'm stopping." I started to bounce against him, already feeling the beginnings of a second orgasm. "Are you close?"

"Yes."

"So am I."

I began moaning with each thrust. Just as I started to cry out for real, he made my name a warning. Quickly, I pulled him out and jerked him with one hand as I fervently worked my clit with my other. Together, we came.

Hot ropes of his semen landed on my chest and belly as my eyes rolled up into my head and I dropped to the bed between his legs.

"Kaede...stop!"

I opened my eyes and he was practically convulsing as I was still jerking him as a smaller orgasm rolled through me. "Sorry," I said with a grin.

"No, you're not." He laughed. Sitting up, he grabbed my sides and pulled me in for another sweet kiss, not caring in the least that we were smearing his come between our bodies.

Chapter 16

"You are sure you wish me to accompany you?"

I nodded at Hiroki. "We're going into the village. You know damn well you'll be following us anyway, so you might as well be as close as possible and still have fun." I gave him a hug to let him know I wasn't just being practical, I *wanted* him there.

He reached around me with one arm and actually hugged me back for a moment before letting go.

"Come on. We're going to be late."

"Hai," he answered.

Opening the bedroom door, I stopped short when Rome walked out of his room right in front of me. He just nodded, not sighing, not rolling his eyes or giving me a disgusted look. I'd take that as a good sign any day of the week.

"Rome," I said with a small smile.

"Pain in the ass," he acknowledged. At least he smiled a little when he said it.

"Bet your ass. You going, too?" I knew Remy was going, but David hadn't said anything about Rome.

He shook his head. "I have a duty to keep people like you from places they shouldn't be."

"Well, I hope you do a better job than that other girl."

He frowned and cocked an eyebrow at me.

"Kidding! Sheesh."

He nodded and headed toward the stairs.

"Bye to you, too! Have a lovely evening."

He just raised his hand over his head and waved in my general direction.

Hiroki chuckled behind me. "I think you're growing on him."

"Did you just call me a fungus?"

"I was going for parasite, but fungus works, as well."

"You're just jealous cuz he's not into you."

"Was that a butt joke?"

I spun in shock. Roki made a dirty joke and I was totally unprepared for it. "I...I..." I punched him when he started a round of hissing laughter, dark eyes scrunched in mirth.

"Your face..."

"Let's go, Mr. Funnyman."

He laughed all the way down into the common room. David and Remy were waiting on one of the couches. David's face lit up when he saw me and I blushed, giving him a shy smile back. Images of our afternoon tryst threatened to make my panties damp, which would have been mightily uncomfortable wandering the streets of the small Icelandic village.

Are vagicles an actual thing here?

Images of arctic explorers with frozen beards and snotcicles didn't reassure me in the slightest. I shuddered and crossed the room to the boys. "Did you miss me?"

"Every second of every minute," David answered with a grin.

Remy groaned and rolled his eyes.

"Shut up. You know you missed me, too."

"Perhaps," He answered cryptically and got up from the couch, straightening his blazer and nodding at Hiroki.

"So, how are we getting there? Is it a long walk?"

Remy stared at me for a moment and shook his head. "You do know there are cabs outside the school, right?"

"Huh?"

"Cabs. Little yellow cars that take you places? In this case to the village and they only run on the weekends. Unless you have special dispensation from the headmaster… You didn't pay attention at orientation, did you?"

"Yeah. I just forgot," I said with a grin, lying through my little damn teeth.

David patted my head. "She's special."

"You better mean that in a good way."

"Sure. Ready to go?"

"Fine."

We made our way across campus and out the front door of the school, emerging on the lowest level of the platform where we had met on the first day of school.

Ahhh. Memories. "So, what is there to do in this tiny little village?"

Remy and David looked at each other and chuckled. "Figured we'd get some dinner and then figure *something* out," David answered cryptically.

"Why do I feel like there's something you're not telling me?"

"Don't know what you're talking about." He gave me a grin and motioned toward the line of cabs parked along the curb.

Roki got in the front and the three of us squeezed into the back, Remy handing the driver a handful of gold coins.

"Village?"

"Unless there is someplace else you can take us," Remy answered.

"The underworld?"

"We'll pass. The village is fine." He gulped and sat back.

"You're a hellhound. Don't want to visit the motherland?" I grinned at him a little.

"I'm from Italy…"

"Pardon?"

He nodded.

177

"But you don't have an accent?"

He laughed. "Does David? He was born and has lived in Romania for nearly all of his life."

"No. Why is that?" I looked at him.

He looked around me at Remy, saying something in Romanian. Or, at least I assumed it was. It wasn't Italian. Then Remy responded in the same language.

"What?"

"We are trying to figure it out. In fact, none of us have an accent and we all speak English. Why don't you have a Japanese accent?"

"Because I grew up in California."

"Why doesn't Hiroki? Do your parents?"

"No and no. Huh. Never thought about it before."

"None of the instructors, the headmaster. Nobody speaks with an accent. It's just one of those things."

The driver started to chuckle.

Remy looked up, making eye contact in the mirror. "You know why?"

"Because you are not human and did not try to build a tower that reached the heavens…"

"Babylon?" I'd heard the story, again thanks to Uncle Tatsuo.

The driver nodded. "Additionally, the English you are all so fond of speaking is a culmination of *all* languages, bastardizing Latin, French, German. You name it."

"Huh. Learn something new every day. Just wasn't expecting to do it in the back of the cab."

"You should see some of the things people do in the back of cabs," the driver said with another chuckle.

I was officially grossed out and tried very hard not to think about what I might have been sitting on. Thankfully, we were close to the village. We rounded between two mountains and it spread out before us. I whistled as it came into view. "I thought it was a tiny village?"

"It is a village, but none of us ever said the word tiny."

I thought back to every conversation I'd had discussing the village. I'd just *assumed* it was tiny because of the village moniker. I was a horrible person. "What's it called?"

"Oddi."

"That's cute. What does it mean?"

David looked at Remy. "Tongue," Remy answered.

"Okay. Not so cute. Weird name for a village."

"It is where the head of Jormungandr supposedly started... And where the tail was supposed to meet it."

"That makes sense then..." I rolled my eyes.

The cab slowed and pulled over to the side of the main road leading into the village. "Thank you," David said and opened the door, sliding out and offering me a hand. I shivered a little and stood a little closer to David while Remy got out and looked around.

"Where should we go?" David asked him.

"What do you feel like doing?" Remy looked at me.

"Since I've never been here before, I'll leave the planning to you two. I'll just say it's after dinner and I didn't eat much lunch."

"Food first, exploration after. Welcome to Oddi," he said and made a sweeping gesture into the heart of the village.

"Uh...I don't have any Icelandic money. Or American money. Japanese money or any other type either." I lowered my eyes in guilt.

"We have you covered. Both of you." Remy gave Roki a brotherly slap across the shoulder.

"*Arigato gozaimasu*," Roki gave him a little bow.

"You're welcome. Come on. I know a good public house that serves food."

He led the way down the uncrowded street. It curved and opened to the central square and the place was practically bursting with people. "Holy crap."

"Oddi might be a fishing village, but there is a large youth population and they know how to party," David whispered in my ear.

"Why did you wait so long to bring me here?"

He blinked at me in surprise and gave me a little smile. "Want the truth?"

"Always."

"Because it doesn't matter *where* I am with you, I just like being *with* you. And because Icelandic people are ridiculously good looking. I didn't want to bring you here and then have to fight to keep them off you."

"Oh, yeah. Cuz everybody goes for the white-haired, Japanese girls."

David stared at me. Remy and Roki, too.

"What?"

"Nothing," they said in unison and looked at each other.

"She does not know," Hiroki answered, shaking his head.

"Know what?"

"You tell her," he said to David.

"She'll believe you more than me."

"I have been telling her since she was a little girl to no avail."

"Tell me what?"

"How beautiful you are," Remy answered.

"Huh?"

Remy just shook his head and started walking again, weaving his way through the crowd.

"He thinks I'm pretty?" I gawked at David in shock.

He patted me on the head. "Anybody with eyeballs does, sweetie."

I wasn't cold anymore. In fact, I felt a little too warm. Especially in my cheeks. "Thank you." I hugged his arm.

He just kissed the top of my head.

Remy was standing outside a pub called something I had no chance in hell of pronouncing. It hurt my head trying to read it, but warmth, music, and the smell of delicious food wafted from the opening and closing door, beckoning us to go inside.

"Something smells good."

"It's probably the *hákarl*. If you order *anything*, you need to try that. We'll get some as an appetizer."

"Sounds yummers."

One of the waitresses saw our uniforms and pointed to the back. Remy waved us to follow and headed through the curtained-off doorway. It took a moment for my eyes to adjust, the lighting was less than sufficient, but booths lined all four walls and tables filled the room. The occupied ones were filled with students from Aesir Academy. "Why teach us to blend in if everyone separates us anyway?"

David chuckled beside me. "Because us, humans, and booze will probably never mix. This pub has been around longer than the school. They learned that lesson the hard way. In fact, everyone in the village knows we're not human. It's kind of a symbiotic relationship. The students come here and spend money, have a good time, and in return, the isolated village has a steady flow of income."

"Huh." I nodded appreciatively. It was kind of like Yoshida. Not everybody who lived there was supernatural, and every human knew what lived around them.

Remy slid into one of the worn, wooden booths, and Hiroki sat down beside him.

David glanced down at me. "You want the outside or the inside?"

"You sit inside. I'll probably have to pee a lot."

As soon as our butts were in the booth, one of the statuesque blonde waitresses stopped by. Even Hiroki checked her out, as her skirt barely covered her Icelandic ass.

"What can I get for you?" It was the first heavily accented voice I'd heard since I came to Aesir Academy.

"A round of beer and we'll start with some *hákarl*." Remy smiled at her.

"Um, you wouldn't happen to carry *sake* would you?" Her confused look was all the answer I needed. It looked like I was going to be a cheap date tonight. "Water, please."

"Okay." She turned around and headed toward the exit.

"You're not going to drink?" David seemed surprised.

"*Sake* is the only thing I can drink," I answered sadly.

"Oh. I'm sorry. I doubt even the liquor store would carry that."

"It's okay. I can make... Wait. Do you think they have mead? I uh...tried that and it seemed to be okay."

"*Kaede*?" Hiroki made my name a question and cocked an eyebrow. I reached across the floor with my foot and lightly kicked his shin.

"Yeah?"

"Nothing."

Good boy. I turned back to David. "Do you think they have mead?"

"I'm sure they do."

The waitress came back and set my water in front of me, beers in front of the boys, and a tray of something in the middle of the table. "What is that?"

The tray of what looked like fish jerky practically oozed evil.

"*Hákarl*!" The waitress sounded proud and gave me a grin, slapping me heartily on the back. My eyes slowly raised from the tray and stared at Remy. He was grinning from ear to ear and issued me a challenge with his eyes.

"Everybody keeps using that word. What does it mean, *precisely*?"

"Fermented shark." Remy wiggled his eyebrows.

I looked over at Roki. "*Funazushi*?" *Funazushi* was a Japanese delicacy. Fermented carp. My parents were actually quite fond of it, but I'd never been a fan. But, if they thought a little fermented shark was going to turn my stomach, they were sorely mistaken. My parents ate weird shit for breakfast. Literally.

"Do you have mead?" I asked the waitress.

"*Já.*"

"Can I have some, please?"

She nodded and headed back to the bar. "Are you going to try it?" Remy pointed at the shark niblets.

"When I have something to wash it down with."

"Okay."

The waitress returned quickly, setting down the mead in front of me. The subtle sweet smell of honey hit my nose and my mouth started watering. I knew I'd have no trouble keeping it, or the fermented fish, down. The boys were in for a rough night if they thought I was going to go down easy. No pun intended.

The waitress made no motion to leave, and was staring at me rather intently, only shifting her gaze to the dish on the table. I guess she wanted to watch the show, too.

"Fine," I said and grabbed a piece. "How do you eat it?"

"Quickly," she said with a laugh.

I brought the piece to my lips and could smell hair burning as every single follicle in my nasal cavity was instantly scorched by the acidic cloud of rotten evil. I fought hard not to drop the piece and run away, screaming. I had gone fishing with Hiroki as a youngster and brought a cooler full of trout back to the house. Unfortunately, my parents were there upon my return and I might have been a little drunk. They scolded me, and I left the cooler full of fish in the garage. My father discovered it *weeks* later and made me clean it out. The smell was oddly nostalgic, and horrendous, at the same time.

"You want the first bite?" I begged David to save me with my eyes.

"No. I did the trial by rotten shark." He chuckled and shuddered, waving his hands in front of him.

As soon as it touched my tongue, I pressed it against the roof of my mouth instead of chewing it with my teeth. The taste, while quite gross, wasn't half as bad as the smell. "That's not bad," I said and swallowed, sliding the tray over for Hiroki to try.

He grabbed a piece and tossed it into his mouth without experiencing the delectable cloud of fermented horrid nightmare and his eyes widened in surprise as he chewed. "Quite delicious!"

I could have told David I was leaving him for a woman, and he wouldn't have looked more disappointed than at that moment. They both did. They wanted me to gag, and possibly puke. The bastards.

"Want some?" I slid the tray over to them and they both turned slightly green. The waitress started laughing and clapped me on the back.

"Your drink is on me!"

"You're a monster," Remy said incredulously. "Even Rome ran to the bathroom and lost the contents of his stomach."

"Now that, I would have paid to see. But, in all fairness, there is a similar Japanese dish that my parents like. I've eaten it multiple times."

They groaned in disappointment.

I grabbed my mug and brought the mead to my lips. The liquid hit my tongue and evaporated into a cloud of happiness. Or, at least, that's what it felt like. I was so happy to have found a replacement beverage, the giddiness reached my smile as I rocked back and forth.

"Kaede?"

I looked up at Hiroki. "*Já?*"

184

"Your eyes are...glowing."

"Huh?" The giddiness evaporated into a cloud of worry.

Turning my head, I stared at David for confirmation. He nodded. "Yeah. They are. With blue fire? You okay?"

"*Já?*"

"You mean *hai?*" Roki's voice caught my attention. Maybe it was the worry in it.

"Huh? That's what I said?" I took another swallow of mead to curb my worry.

"Maybe it was the *hákarl*," Remy answered thoughtfully.

"Perhaps," Hiroki answered.

"Well, I feel fine."

"Drink in moderation. Let me know if you need to leave," he said, narrowing his eyes for emphasis.

"You worry too much, Hiroki."

"Perhaps."

I went to take another sip, but my mead was empty. Frowning, I picked up my glass of water, in desperate need to quench my thirst. Practically pouring it down my throat, my eyes widened as the familiar taste of honey and the burn of fire slid down my throat. I hadn't added rice as an offering, there was no way I should, or could, have turned it into *sake* or mead. It should have been water, but it wasn't. There was no way in hell I was telling them that, though. They were already worried about me.

"I brought another round," the waitress said as she stepped up to the booth, putting beers and mead down in the center. "Would you like any food?"

"We'll have the lamb," Remy told her.

"Leg?"

"Yes, please."

"We're eating lamb?"

He nodded. "Unless you wish to try the *súrir hrútspungar.*"

"Let me guess. Pickled fish?"

185

He chuckled. "Close. Pickled ram's balls."

"What the fuck? Why would you eat that?" I almost puked just thinking about it. He should have done that instead of the *hákarl*. He would have gotten a better reaction. An explosive one.

"That's what I said." David nodded in agreement.

I was curled up in David's arm, slightly buzzing from the mead when the waitress brought the roasted leg of lamb and another round of drinks.

I grabbed the mug, practically draining it, and frowning. They needed bigger mugs.

"Easy, Kaede," Hiroki cautioned.

The waitress chuckled. "I'll bring you another, sweetie."

"Thank you!" I stuck my tongue out at Roki. "At least *she* likes me."

Remy slid a plate of sliced meat and a few potatoes in front of me. Practically growling, I tore into the food.

"There's silverware." David chuckled.

I raised my head. "I really need to pee. Be right back." I set the meat down and got up too quickly. The room spun a little and I blinked to clear my head.

"Are you all right, Kaede-*sama*?"

"Yeah. Glad we got some real food. Think that shark is still fermenting in my stomach." I turned and headed for the exit, hoping the bathroom was close by.

I found the marked hallway and turned the corner, slamming into Sabine. Blinking rapidly, I briefly wondered why I hadn't seen her in the Aesir Academy room, then I realized it was because she wasn't in the school uniform.

"Sorry," I said, sighed, wished to be anywhere but there, and headed for the bathroom. I never saw the blow, but the pain just before my vision exploded into a field of stars, I felt quite clearly.

Chapter 17

The rumble beneath my cheek woke me from a sound slumber, or maybe it was the cold wetness of the wooden deck of the boat slowly chugging through the water. I'd woken up in worse places, but I wasn't tied up like I was now. My wrists and my ankles were bound. Groaning, I rolled onto my back, ignoring the burning of the ropes.

One of Sabine's cronies was leaning against the side of the boat, staring at me intently. "Sabine, she's awake," she called out toward the front of the vessel.

It was at that moment I truly understood the phrase about being up Shit Creek without a paddle. It took on a whole new meaning. After punching her in the chest and setting her on fire, I'd finally pissed Sabine off enough to dispose of my body in the middle of the ocean.

My head winced with each footstep I heard drawing closer. I could barely see from the pain at the base of my skull. "Oh, hey. How are you, Sabine?"

"Still cracking jokes, I see."

"I try."

Her head appeared in my field of vision, looking down at me with intense hatred in her eyes. "I'd tell you to try harder, but it won't matter shortly."

"Oh, you gonna drop me off at the side of the pier?"

"No. In the middle of the sea. Don't worry, the anchor will make it pretty quick." She grinned, and upside down, it was creepier than usual.

"You're going to kill me? Because you don't like me?" I knew she was a bitch, but an insane bitch? That was a rare combination indeed. I'd secretly been hoping she was just trying to scare me. But when she lifted the anchor off the deck, dropped it over the side of the boat, and flashed an evil smile at me, my hopes were dashed upon the rocks of reality. The rope tied to the anchor quickly pulled on the rope binding my ankles. When there was no more slack, I slowly started to slide across the deck. Sabine walked back over and stepped over me with one leg, squatting down on my chest and stopping me from going overboard.

Thank fuck. And thank fuck she's wearing jeans and not a skirt. Ewww.

"Just wanted to memorize your face before you go. Since I'm the last person who will ever…ever…see it." She traced her fingertip down the front of my school shirt, tearing into the fabric with a claw. Her eyes never left mine, and there was no room for any doubt. Her lights were on, but nobody was home. She was certifiable.

"Stop this, Sabine. You don't want to kill me."

She started laughing and couldn't stop. "Yes, Kaede, I do. I *really* do. Maybe now David will come to his fucking senses. I'll be there to comfort him *sooo* hard when he realizes that you're gone forever."

"No, you won't. He'll fucking kill you once he realizes what you've done!"

"How's he going to know? Are *you* going to tell him?" She cackled maniacally.

"Sabine…" Her friend looked at her worriedly. "We can't kill her! We were just supposed to scare her."

Sabine grinned at me. "Doesn't she look afraid to you, Steph? She looks like she's about to shit her drawers to me."

A light flared in Sabine's eyes and her face relaxed. She smiled at me almost apologetically. "You have my sincere apologies, Kaede. This is how it must be," she whispered and stood, taking the weight off my chest and letting me slide to the edge of the boat. I scrambled to stop myself and managed to wedge my feet under the rail, the weight of the anchor causing the ropes to tear into the flesh of my ankles. I winced in pain, but wasn't going to drown.

"Start the boat," Sabine told her friend in that still calm voice. "Take us to shore."

She looked at her unsurely. "Sabine…"

"Do it, mortal," she said sadly.

Did she just call her mortal?

Sabine, or whomever had taken the helm, leaned back against the rail and stared at me intently. The engine rumbled and the boat surged forward, the anchor nearly ripping my feet from their perch. The faster the boat went, the heavier the weight became. I called my foxfire to my hands, not caring if I burned myself. Gripping the rope in my hands under my back, I let it surge, screaming as it licked my flesh as it burned the ropes.

"Can't have that now, can we?" Sabine stood and held out her hand. A metal rod flew from the other side of the boat and landed in her hand. Without a thought, she plunged it into my shoulder, the pain extinguishing my flames, and the grip of my feet. With a *yank*, my legs pulled up, slamming my ass and back against the side of the boat before I was dragged over. To add injury to insult, my head slammed against the rail as I twisted over it and plunged into the icy black water.

The temperature of the water brought me quickly back to reality and numbed the throbbing pain in my head. My eyes and lungs were already screaming from the frigid cold and lack of air, I hadn't taken a breath before completely submerging. The only sensory input I had was the sound of the boat moving further and further away, muffled as even my ears filled with water.

Water swirled and rushed past me as I sank quickly. Ignoring the pain, I opened my eyes but still saw nothing. The saltwater burned, but nothing compared to my lungs. I was going to die. I couldn't even pop as only blackness was visible whichever way I looked.

Do you wish to live? The voice resonated in my head.

Does a fox shit in the woods? Of course, I do!

Suddenly, light flooded around me, blue hued like my fox fire. I twisted in the water as the eye of a dragon blinked, plunging me into darkness.

Jormungandr... I froze in fear and not from the temperature of the water.

I can smell my brother on you.

A talon reached out and cut the rope between me and the anchor, stopping my descent into the crushing depths. Then the dragon exhaled, and I closed my eyes as I expected to be blasted with his searing breath. Instead, a bubble of air enveloped me and propelled me toward the surface.

Fare thee well, little one.

I looked down and saw him one last time. A giant head resting by his tail...

He's almost encircled the earth...

The bubble and I broke the surface in a spray of water. I coughed and choked as I fought to fill my lungs with air and cough out the seawater I had swallowed. Rolling on my back, I tried to maintain my calm as I floated in the rolling waters. If I wanted *any* chance of survival, I needed to get out of the ropes and out of the water, or I was going to end up a foxburg.

I let my fur envelop me. Its oils keeping some of the chill and water from my skin, but not enough. The ropes were another matter. All *kitsune* and *nogitsune* could call weapons into being. I, however, sucked at it. I had Hiroki, he might have taught me to use a sword, but even *he* got frustrated trying to teach me to call one into being. Floating on my back, arms bound behind me and ankles bound below me, I fervently wished I had practiced more.

"I'm going to die."

No, you're not, a familiar sleepy voice resounded in my mind. *You are mine. Call your sword.*

"I can't!"

You can.

I growled and did as Hiroki had told me so many times. At first, I felt it in my palm, but it slipped away, quickly plunging into the depths. Dispelling it, I tried again. And again. The third time I managed to get my hand around it and there I was, floating in the middle of the ocean, hands tied behind my back, and a katana in my grasp.

"Now what the fuck do I do?"

This time, the voice didn't answer.

Turning my hand, I pointed the blade toward my feet and made damn sure I didn't drop it again. Carefully, I maneuvered the blade between my legs, sharp side down and let it rest on the rope between them. Immediately I started sawing the rope with the sword, head dunking under water with every stroke. Just as I thought I would drown from inhaling too much water, the rope broke free and I started kicking my legs, forcing my head above the rolling waters. A shark fin popped above the surface, not ten feet from my face.

"You have got to be fucking kidding me. I will fucking ferment you, dry you, and eat you!" Taking a large breath, I ducked my head under the surface and let the blade slide through my hands until I felt the hilt between my feet. Grabbing it, I worked the blade between the ropes and kicked until it cut through.

Me and my hands broke through the surface. "Yes!"

I dispelled the blade and called it back to my hand without even thinking about it. Spinning around in the water, I searched for the shark fin in the dimly illuminated water.

"Now what?"

The shark must have lost interest. I didn't see it again as I treaded water for an hour, exhausted. Giving up, I let my tears mix with the seawater around me and started saying goodbyes in my head to everyone that mattered. I even forgave my parents for sending me to fucking Iceland, home of fermented shark and pickled ram's balls.

"I just want to go home…"

You can't. You have things to do, but not where you are. You are my herald, you have power. Walk.

"I'm drowning in the ocean. How?"

You are naught but a babe. Learn. Learn to walk again.

"That's *not* very helpful!" *Think, Kaede. Think. How the hell am I supposed to walk…on water?*

I wasn't going to do it *in* the water. I tried lifting myself up, bracing my hands against the surface. It far from worked and I probably looked like a moron.

Walk…

Before you can walk you need to learn to crawl…

I kicked and propelled myself forward a little, but instead of paddling with my arms, I used them to push myself forward, like the water was a firm surface. It worked a little, but not much.

My father was a celestial messenger to the gods. If he wanted to, he could float in the air and walk through walls. I always assumed it was my *kitsune* half that prevented me from doing it, but maybe it wasn't. Maybe I was just focusing on the wrong half of me. I touched the power inside of me that I always avoided, was always afraid of, and let it loosen a little. I tried it again, and my arms stayed on the surface, pulling my ass along in the water.

A little more power and I was on top, balancing like I was floating on a log and trying fervently not to fall back in. As long as I kept moving, I was fine. After a few minutes of doing it, I crawled on my knees, building speed and *finally* getting up to my feet and lightly running across the surface of the water.

Great. Now which way do I go?

Feel for your friends… You share a bond with your fox and my wolf.

Picturing both, I closed my eyes as I ran, letting my heart guide me. Just like that, I ran and ran. It seemed like forever, but when it felt like my heart and my magic couldn't possibly take any more, I saw the familiar glow of the village.

"Thank fuck." I got my tenth wind and ran as fast as I could, praying the last of my spirit energy wouldn't dwindle to nothing and drop me back into the frigid waters, drowning in sight of the shore.

"You can do it," I chanted with every step.

∞ ∞ ∞

Sunlight, filtering through curtains, finally woke me up. The first thing I noticed was that I had to pee. Horrendously. The second thing I noticed was that I wasn't alone. There were somebodies in my bed. Three of them to be exact. And we were all naked. And morning wood is a real thing.

I lifted my head from the pillow. I was lying on my back and being smothered under a comforter. Remy was on my right, David my left, and Hiroki on top of me with his head resting on my chest. I felt bad and wanted to stuff a pillow under it for some cushion, but more than that, I wanted to run to the bathroom.

"Roki," I whispered his name.

He immediately opened his eyes, lifted his head, and gave me a look of complete and utter relief. "Kaede-*sama*..."

"Talk later. You're lying on my bladder and it's gonna pop."

"My apologies," he crawled off me, dragging the comforter with him and getting up on his knees. He was wide awake, and the rest of him was, too. I stared. Nowhere near his face. "Is that for me?"

"Do not joke at a time like this, Kaede-*sama*. Relieve yourself and then get back in bed. You are not moving today."

I chuckled and extricated my arms from under David and Remy. Remy woke first and pushed me back down on the bed with a massive hand. "You shouldn't be moving."

My arms instinctively covered my breasts. I couldn't help it. But after realizing they had already seen me naked, I gave up and sighed. "I *really* have to pee."

He got up and scooped me from the bed, carrying me to the bathroom door of the room we were in.

"I can pee by myself, you know."

"And I will let you, once I have determined that you successfully made it to said bathroom."

"What happened?"

"We found you on the beach. Tell us the tale of what happened when you are safely back in bed." He set me down on the toilet, putting me directly at eye level with Little Remy. I swear it twitched as I blushed.

"Okay. I made it." I made shooing gestures with my hands. I didn't normally suffer from stage fright, I'd peed in front of Hiroki enough, usually in a dimly lit alley, that it didn't really bother me. *However*, a very naked Remy penis in my face was not conducive to going with the flow.

He chuckled and stepped out of the room, closing the door behind him. Trying to cover the sound, I figured that getting some answers to the billion questions I had seemed like a good plan.

"Where are we?" Always good to start with the basics.

"A hotel very close to the beach where we found you," he answered through the door.

"How did you find me?"

"I did not. Your fox and your wolf did."

So, Fenrir wasn't kidding. Somehow, saying the gods name in my head made it all a little too real. I needed to fess up that he wasn't sleeping. And that I had seen Jormungandr.

Is that what you truly believe? His voice sounded more amused than angry.

It is how the legend goes? Are you telling me that you won't wake up and destroy the world once Jormungandr can reach his own tail?

He chuckled softly in my head. *What fun would it be if I told you?*

I sighed and finished using the toilet, wanting nothing more than to crawl into bed, even if it was with three naked guys. Maybe *because* it was with three naked guys. I just hoped that David wasn't kidding when he said he didn't mind. Plus, this was for truly medicinal purposes.

Or, so I was trying to tell myself. The truth of the matter was that I was almost *afraid* to get back into the bed. Not because of what *could* happen, but because of what it *could* do to David. He was my first serious boyfriend. I loved him, or at least I thought I did. I didn't want to ruin it or hurt him in any way, shape, or form.

Sighing, I washed my hands and rinsed my mouth out with the water from the tap. It was better than nothing and too damn early in the morning for dragon breath. *Sorry, Uncle Tatsuo.*

I dried my face on the scratchy bath towel and opened the door. Rem went to scoop me back up, but I stopped him with a hand to his chiseled, hairless chest. "I can walk a few feet."

"Not worth the risk."

"I'm fine. Seriously…"

"Kaede…you were dead."

"Huh?" I'm not the most articulate of foxes when surprised.

"Not breathing. Almost frozen. Blue lips and skin. We thought you were gone until Hiroki refused to believe it and started giving you CPR."

I peeked around the hellhound at my *nogitsune* sitting at the small table in the corner of the room. His head was in his hands and I could practically feel the waves of relief and worry coming off him. My heart broke.

"Well, I'm telling you, I feel much better. Less dead."

"Fine. But you're not getting out of bed today."

"Are all of you staying with me?"

He chuckled. "I do not think you could pry those two away from you with construction machinery."

"Good. Because I'm exhausted and don't want to be alone. What about you, Remy?"

"I shall stay."

"Because you want to?"

He blushed. I couldn't fucking believe it. I wanted to touch his cheeks just to make sure. "Yes."

I poked him in the chest and gave him a grin. "You *like* me."

"A little. You're amusing when you're not being irritating."

"There's a fine line between amusing and irritating."

"Glad you found one, because the genius and insanity one shall elude you forever."

"Yeah. Not the smartest fox in the den."

"No. But you have heart. Come, return to bed."

"In that order? Or can I return to bed and then come?"

His blush shifted from the pink spectrum to deep crimson. "I see you wish to skate that line again."

"Oh, come on. That was funny!" I grinned at him and climbed up into the bed, snuggling against David. "Hey, handsome."

He kissed me. Not passionately, but with every ounce of love he had for his goofy little girlfriend. I was almost crushed by the weight of it and snuggled against his chest. Remy slid in behind me, encircling me with his warmth.

Something was still missing. I lifted my head and looked at the corner of the room. Hiroki was looking at the three of us and smiling. "You coming?" I turned on my back and held out my arms to him.

"I should not..."

"You should," David said evenly, leaving little room for argument.

Roki sighed and got up, picking the comforter up and crawling onto the bed on his knees, moving forward and spreading it out over us as he lay down, head just below my breasts. I stroked his head and relished in the feeling of being completely protected, safe, and most importantly, warm.

Chapter 18

"Tell him, Kaede." Remy's voice held a measure of anger, a cup of sorry, a teaspoon of regret, and a hefty dollop of hatred.

When the four of us spent the afternoon in bed, I had regaled them with the tale of what had happened and how I ended up on the beach. I'd left *nothing* out, confessing the gods' involvement, but more importantly, I calmly informed Remy of his sister's part in my predicament. I'd felt him stiffen next to me as I told my story. He wasn't shocked, he was pissed. As soon as they deemed me rested enough, he used the hotel phone to call the school and waited until his brother was put on the line. In no uncertain terms, he demanded that Rome meet us at a nearby coffee shop.

And so, there we sat, Rome, Remy, and I. Roki and David were still back at the room. Remy wanted to be alone with his brother when I broke the news to him.

"She doesn't need to. I can smell Sabine on her. As well as the sea and death." Rome's face contorted into a visage of anger. He balled his fist, lifted it high above him and drove it down at the table. Closing my eyes, I turned my head expecting shrapnel that never came. When I finally looked, he had stopped just short of obliterating it, his fist quivering just a fraction of an inch above the table. "Is she that petty? Has she learned *nothing*?"

"Apparently not. She dumped Kaede in the middle of the ocean, tied to an anchor. That is premeditation on her part. You cannot let this go unpunished."

"I know."

"What about your mother? Can't she do something about her?"

"I am alpha. I lead our pack, not my mother. Besides, those two are more alike than I care to admit," Rome said without looking at me, staring at his brother the whole time.

Remy just nodded, but then gave his brother a worried expression. "There is more." He turned and nodded.

"I don't think she was completely in control."

"What?"

I closed my eyes before talking, not wanting to see the crazy look again, the one that Remy gave me when I told him. If Hiroki hadn't been there to tell him that it was not something I would lie about, ever, I'm not even sure if he would have believed me. Even now, I got the feeling of acceptance from him regarding my story. Not so much as he took it as the truth, but more of my perception of the truth. He thought I was mistaken.

"Kaede," Remy cautioned.

"Don't get me wrong, I think she planned on killing me, but I don't think Sabine was driving the car when it actually happened."

"What do you mean?" Rome leaned forward, finally staring at me intently.

I sighed. "One of my abilities is to turn rice and water into *sake*. It's one of the perks of being half celestial messenger. Except, I can't anymore. It turns into mead. Which I had never even heard of. On top of that, Fenrir still speaks to me. And I saw Jormungandr. Down in the ocean. He was almost completely encircling the earth."

"Jormungandr is no more, Tatsuo…"

"Is wrong," I said without a doubt.

Rome looked from me to his brother, who shrugged. *Thanks for backing me up, cheese dick.*

"So, you are saying Jormungandr controlled my sister and made her throw you overboard."

"No. That was Hel."

He blinked and slid his chair back. "You are saying our goddess wished you dead?"

I shrugged. "It wasn't Sabine who kicked me over the edge. Unless your sister is a schizophrenic who calls her best buddies 'mortal' and can make metal rods fly through the air before she stabs me with them, I'd say yes."

"You were stabbed?" Remy asked with more than a bit of shock in his voice.

I nodded, accidentally having left that part out before.

"But you were not wounded. We checked every inch of you…"

"Every inch?" I wiggled my eyebrows.

He sighed in exasperation. "Where were you impaled?"

"My shoulder. But we heal quickly."

"There should have still been a mark."

"I use this vitamin E lotion, it does wonders for scars."

He narrowed his eyes.

"You need to work on your sense of humor."

"For all we know, it was Fenrir," Rome said calmingly to his brother.

"Then why didn't he stop her from dying?"

"Perhaps he did. Maybe she was just really cold and breathing so shallow you did not notice."

Seems like a reasonable explanation to me. Better to think that than I was actually dead. I don't remember any sort of bright light or celestial palaces. Or pits of fire being stirred by horned guys with pointy sticks…

"Either way, this is all speculation." Rome picked up his macchiato and took a sip, shifting his gaze between the two of us. "Kaede, I am glad you are safe. Go nowhere alone."

He gave Remy a meaningful stare. At least I assumed it was meaningful because Remy nodded. He turned his attention back to me. "I have a favor to ask."

Duh duh duuuh. "What?" I tried to keep the skepticism from my voice.

"Tell no one else of what happened. I know you probably wish to see my sister pay for her crimes, but I have my reasons."

I leaned forward. "Let me let you in on a little secret. I don't care."

He nodded. "If that is your wish, we will go to the headmaster."

"No. You're misunderstanding me. I know I can be fucking annoying, and even though she started all this bullshit, I don't care. You get her to leave me alone, and I will leave her alone. Let bygones be bygones."

"Huh?"

It was the first time I'd seen Rome completely confused. I kind of liked it and silently vowed to make it my new goal in life. To keep him in a perpetual state of confusion. It was *infinitely* better than angry.

"You heard me. Let sleeping dogs lie, no pun intended." I held up my hands. "Get her to leave me alone and you can do whatever to her whenever you want. Or not at all."

"Of all the creatures I have ever met, I think you might be the strangest."

"And cutest?" I blinked rapidly and grinned, baring my teeth at him.

A smile finally graced his lips. "Let us not get ahead of ourselves. Classes resume tomorrow. You continue to be your…charming…self. I shall observe our sister. I wish to learn her motives, if there are any ulterior ones, for myself before rendering judgement."

"Rendering judgement. Sounds scary."

Fire flared in his eyes.

"Yep. Scary."

He turned to his brother. "Keep her safe."

"I shall."

Rome got up, threw some cash on the table and left.

"He's so *broody*."

"He has a lot on his shoulders," he answered thoughtfully, staring at his brother's retreating back.

"You love him." I made it a statement, not a question. I could tell.

"I do."

"Roki's the closest I have to a brother, but I kinda get it."

He *finally* looked at me. "I am surprised that you think of him as a brother and not a lover."

I smiled at him over my coffee. "Not for lack of effort on my part. He thinks he is beneath me."

"I think that is where he would rather be…"

I spit my coffee. "If that were true," I said and mopped up the splatters on the table, "then I'd be riding on the Hiroki Highway right now."

"Want my opinion?"

"No. But give it to me anyway."

"After seeing him deal with almost losing you… I think you're full of shit. You might think you want him, but your half-assed attempts at bedding him in the past were nothing but a pretense."

"Exsqueeze me?"

"You heard me."

"But I think you're insane."

"No. You think I'm telling the truth. You know I am. If you wanted to bed someone, there isn't a man, or quite possibly a woman, on this earth who would tell you no."

"You're insane."

"You're certifiable," he answered.

"No duh."

"I think you're afraid of losing him."

"You think I suck in bed?"

"I doubt that. But I know you suck on couches…"

It was my turn to have my cheeks turn a fiery red. "How the hell do you know that? Did David tell you?" I was too embarrassed to be angry. I might spank him later, though.

"Do you think that neither of us could smell it when we came for David that night?"

The fiery blush became a raging inferno. I should have chewed gum or something. "What were we talking about?" *Change the fucking subject.*

"That you are afraid of losing your *kitsune* friend. You do not wish to bed him because you are afraid you will lose him if things do not go well between you."

I sighed. "Fine. You're right." I didn't even bother correcting him about calling Roki a *kitsune*.

"I know."

"Should I tell him?"

"No need. He knows," Remy said with a wink.

"Now I have a question for *you*."

"Yes?"

"If you're Italian, why is your name Remy? Isn't that French?"

He laughed. "Not where I thought you were going with this."

"Answer that one and I may have another for you."

"It is not Remy. Just as Rome's is not Rome."

"Huh?"

"He is Romulus… I am Remus. Rome and Remy are just less of a mouthful."

"Uh…I saw you naked. You're definitely a mouthful." I grinned at my own witty retort.

It was his turn to blush.

∞ ∞ ∞

204

"Shouldn't we be going back to the Academy?" I looked at Remy with more than a bit of concern. I wasn't shy about my body, but the dress he had bought for me was more than a little bit revealing.

"I figured one more day away would be more beneficial to your health than being cooped up in the dorm."

"With your sister," I added.

"Yes."

"And you two are okay with going to a club?"

David and Hiroki nodded. I'll admit, they looked damn good in their jeans and button-down shirts. Even Remy looked stunning. But none of their assets were hanging out.

"You are the one who expressed a desire to dance." Hiroki cocked an eyebrow.

"Yeah, but I didn't think Remy was serious when he asked what I wanted to do."

"Just limit your alcoholic intake. You will be fine. If you start to feel unwell or tired we will leave."

I leaned over and kissed Roki on the cheek. He was so practical sometimes, I just wanted to lock him in a cage. With a hyena. But he was sweet, always. "Fine. Let's go before I change my mind."

Remy smiled and opened the door of our hotel room. Personally, I had a feeling he just wanted to sleep with me in the same bed again. He probably bought the short, revealing dress so I would freeze my little ass off, and he'd have to warm me up again by sleeping naked.

It wasn't a far walk to Jotunheim, the one and only dance club in the village. Because of its geographic isolation, the place was completely *packed*. A line waiting to get in was at least thirty people deep and I was not looking forward to standing outside in my dress for at least an hour.

But then, Remy surprised me and walked right up to the guy behind the velvet rope and whispered something I couldn't hear. Not even with my fox ears. The guy blinked in surprise and opened the rope, letting the four of us inside.

"What did you tell him?" I practically had to shout my question over the blaring techno music filling the club.

"Unlike the pub, this club encourages interaction with supernaturals," he answered.

"Why?"

"Because it is part of its appeal. The whole village knows what the school is. Some of the locals *want* to be closer to us. I found it quite strange, too. But look at the name. You know what Jotunheim is…"

"Land of the giants. Loki's home realm."

He nodded sadly. "It's almost as if they *know*."

"What sleeps beneath them?"

"Yes."

"At least they didn't call it Ragnarok," I mumbled under my breath, but apparently not under enough. Remy nodded with a chuckle.

"Care to dance?" David slid his arm through mine.

"Of course," I answered with a grin.

"Come on," he said and led us out onto the dance floor.

"We'll get a table," Remy called after us.

"Alone at last," David said with a grin.

I nodded and leaned closer, standing on my tiptoes and pulling his face closer. Pausing my dancing, I locked my lips onto his. I missed kissing him. "Mmmm," I said dreamily as I pulled away.

"You're going to make the others jealous."

"So? I'm dating you, not them."

He cocked an eyebrow.

"What?"

"Nothing." He finally started dancing. A creature who could run through the woods at breakneck speed, narrowly dodging trees, and leap over ravines, was horrible at dancing. But I didn't care. I was happier than I had been for a

206

very long time. Getting closer, I put my hands on his hips and managed to at least get him in sync with the music. He even knew he couldn't dance, but did it anyway to make me happy, that much I knew. That and I loved him.

"You're a really good dancer," he said into my ear.

"I majored in it in college."

"They had a big performing arts program?"

"No. I skipped classes to go clubbing."

His laugh was genuine and infectious. "Love you," he said and warmed me with another smile.

"Love you, too." I twirled around, facing away from him and dancing with my back against his chest. It had the desired effect. His hands slid over my hips as he held on for the ride. "Somebody's happy," I called over my shoulder as I felt him harden behind me.

"Not my fault. You have that effect on me."

"I'm glad I do."

"Me, too."

I pushed back a little harder, trapping him between us, grinding against him. "Gosh. We might have to kick the other two out of the room tonight for a little bit."

"Why?"

"Do I need to spell it out for you?" I grinned and grinded harder.

"No. I get that, but why kick them out?" He chuckled, leaning down to bite my ear. I gasped as naughty thoughts and pleasure ran through me.

"You love me. You're into me. The other two…"

"Have it just as bad as I do."

I let it go. It wasn't an argument I wanted to get into. Especially when I was having the time of my life. When the song ended, Remy was standing at the edge of the floor. David gave me a quick kiss, and a gentle lip nibble. "See you at the table. Love you."

"Love you, too," I answered and watched him nod at Remy as he walked by.

"My turn." He strode over to me as the next song started and immediately fell into a groove that *I* found difficult to keep up with. He was better at dancing than I was, maybe even Hiroki.

"Holy shit. Can your brother dance like you?"

He shook his head. "He is more of a Tango and Waltz kind of guy." He winked to let me know he was joking. I hoped.

He put his hands on *my* hips and pulled me closer. "I don't bite."

"Yeah. Pretty sure you do."

"Not in this form. Unless you ask nicely," he said with a wink.

A tingle of pleasure wound its way down my spine. It was rather unexpected. He was hot, but his words shouldn't have given me such a thrill. I needed answers.

"Would you?"

"Bite you? Here in this club, in front of all these people?" He leaned in closer, practically whispering, but I could still hear him over the din of the music. "Take your flesh between my teeth, pressing down until just before the point of piercing you, blurring the line between pleasure and pain. Is that what you want?"

I mewled as the tingle transformed into a torrent. Pain wasn't my thing, and I had never been a fan of biting, but apparently my pussy was. From his words alone, I felt myself become wet and wanting. He had bought me a dress but hadn't purchased me panties. I guess he drew a line at shopping for women's undergarments. If he didn't stop, things were going to get pretty damn uncomfortable.

"You liked that thought, didn't you? I can smell it."

"That's kind of a rude thing to say. Especially since you didn't buy me panties…"

He blinked at me. "That made you wet?"

"Isn't that what you were saying?"

"No. I meant I could smell your desire…" He chuckled. "Right here," he said and let his teeth graze across the skin of my neck, just below my ear.

I practically shuddered in his arms. "Remy…"

"Yes, Kaede?" He kissed the spot after his teeth left it.

"I have a boyfriend…"

"Yes, Kaede?"

"That doesn't deter you?"

"No. In fact, it excites me more."

I turned my head and pressed it against his chest, unable to take anymore. "But I love him. And won't cheat on him," I said with way more conviction than I felt at that moment.

"And he loves you. But I'm not asking you to cheat on him."

"What *are* you asking me?"

"To let me in, too."

"Let you in where?" I looked up and cocked a suspicious eyebrow at him.

He chuckled. "Your heart." He traced the front of my dress with his finger over the heart that was threatening to beat its way out of my chest.

"You want me to love you, too?"

He nodded. "Only if you want to."

"What about David?" I protested.

He smiled. "See. That is the thing about love. It isn't a finite resource. It knows no limits. If you can love him with all of your heart, there would still be room for you to love me, too."

His argument was *very* convincing. He should join the debate team. If the academy had one. "But…"

"I'm not asking you to now. Just think about it. Discuss it with David and Hiroki. I know he loves you, too. Probably the most out of the three of us."

"Wait. *You* love me?"

He nodded without even thinking about it.

"Why? When?"

"I suspect from the first time you were brave enough to verbally berate my brother. I knew in that moment that you were the fox for me."

"You liked that, did you?"

He nodded. "That was one of the bravest things I've ever seen."

"Or dumbest."

"Yes. That, too." Finally, the song ended, and we gave up the pretext of dancing. He took my hand and gave me a gentle tug toward our table. "I wish that song had lasted a little longer."

"You were enjoying teasing me that much?"

"I didn't tease you at all, but that's not the reason."

"What is?"

"To have had the opportunity to find out how you feel about *me.*"

I gripped his hand and stopped moving. He got the hint and froze where he was. "We don't have to be dancing for that to happen."

"I know. But I liked dancing with you."

"And you want to do it more often…"

He nodded.

"I would like that, too. I like you. A lot, Remy."

"More than my brother?"

A bark of laughter escaped me. "Your brother is fun to tease, but I imagine he was angrier at Sabine for trying to steal his opportunity of throwing me overboard."

"Spend more time with him. As I said, once you get to know him…"

"Uh huh. You keep wanting me to take your word on a lot of things…"

He stepped closer to me, leaning down and letting his lips hover just above mine. "Would you rather I prove things to you instead of asking you to trust me?"

Staring at his lips, I wanted to nod. My *kami*, I wanted to nod, but I didn't. I reached out and put my hand on his chest. "I need time."

He smiled and it reached his eyes. "That makes me happy."

"That I'll think about it?"

"Yes. Of course."

"You're not upset?"

"Why the hell would I be?"

"I don't know. Guys are usually like kids on Christmas when it comes to women."

"You've been hanging around the wrong guys."

"Apparently, I have."

His smile got a little bigger. Taking the chance, I leaned over and kissed him on his cheek. "That's for being so fucking sweet."

"I bet you taste sweeter."

I blushed, a million dirty images flashing through my one-track brain.

He rolled his eyes and pointed at my neck. "Was talking about there again," he explained patiently.

"Yeah. I figured that out. Eventually."

He leaned over and kissed *my* cheek. "That's for being so ridiculously irresistible."

Chapter 19

"David, he wants to be my boyfriend, too!" I gave him a shocked look and he just laughed. I was sore, and tired, just a tad bit tipsy, but it had been one of the best nights of my life.

"He can hear you, you know." He pointed at Remy walking next to Hiroki on our way back to the hotel.

"What's he got, dog ears?" I snickered at my own joke.

"Yes, he does," Remy answered from up ahead.

"And a sexy butt," I said a little louder. He shook it for me.

"I was talking about Hiroki!" I called back.

Hiroki ignored me. The bastard.

"And how do you feel about that?" David asked curiously.

"Hiroki's butt?"

"No. Remy as a boyfriend."

"How the hell should I know? You're the first serious relationship I've ever had."

He slowed his pace, stopping me with him. "Go ahead, we'll catch up," he said softly into the night air. Remy and Hiroki both waved over their shoulders. Then he turned to face me. "About having Remy as a boyfriend. What are you thinking?"

The giddiness of the few drinks I'd had left me in a fit of fear. "It scares the fuck out of me."

"What? Why?"

My breathing quickened as I shifted from foot to foot. "Because."

David reached over and put his hands on my shoulders, steadying me. "Talk to me, Kaede. Why are you afraid? Is it of Remy? Because I was telling you the truth when I told you I would have no trouble laying my life on the line to protect you. No matter what..."

I violently shook my head, making myself a little dizzy. "No! I'm not afraid of him. Or you. Or any of you, honestly. I trust all of you and know you wouldn't hurt me on purpose."

"Then what are you afraid of exactly?"

"I'm..." I paused, sucking in some air and pursing my lips. "I'm not good enough."

"What did you just say?"

"I suck as a human being. A *kitsune*. Whatever. I don't deserve *you*. Why the hell would I deserve your best friend, too? Can't we just keep it simple? You and me."

"You really think that?"

I nodded in embarrassment. "It's the truth."

"No, Kaede. It's not. The truth couldn't be further from what you're thinking right now. You. Are. Amazing." He wrapped his arms around me and pressed his face against mine. "Why do you think that?"

"Because... Because it's what everybody has always told me."

He pulled back. "Who? Your parents?"

"My parents are disappointed in me, but they're not assholes. Most of the time. No. The few guys I've...slept...with." I trailed off in a mumble, not really wanting to talk about it.

"Let me get this straight. You're judging your self-worth based off the opinion of guys who only wanted one thing from you?"

"Maybe."

He kissed my forehead. "I know you're smarter than that, Kaede."

"Not usually, no."

"Well, you are. And funny. And beautiful. And perfect. Just be you. Everything else will fall into place."

"Unless the world gets eaten by the evil god sleeping beneath us."

A strange look passed over David's face.

"What?"

He shook his head. "Nothing."

"You don't think he's evil."

"Do you?" He tilted his head.

"No. Angry, yes. Evil, no."

He nodded and shrugged.

"Come on. Let's go back to the hotel, I'm literally freezing my butt off here."

"We can't have that." He reached down and slid his hands up my legs, under my dress, palming my ass in his hands. His extraordinarily warm hands. Times like that, I was glad he was a werewolf.

"Mmm." I nuzzled his neck.

"Come on. This will be even better in a warm bed."

"With four of us?" I cocked an eyebrow at him.

"We have two rooms. We all just slept in there to keep you warm."

"And you were going to tell me this when?" I playfully punched him in the arm.

"When you started to panic."

"Men." I stomped off slowly, waiting for him to catch up.

"You're telling me you didn't like waking up in the middle of a man blanket?"

"It had its finer points."

"Well, invite whomever or no one to join us tonight. It is up to you."

"If I do, it will be just to sleep. I kind of like the megasnuggles."

"I could tell."

"How?"

"You were smiling in your sleep."

We made it to the front door and David pulled it open, letting me get into the warm lobby. Thankfully, our room was on the first floor and we didn't need to deal with the stairs since the hotel didn't have an elevator. He went to stick the key in when the door opened from the inside and Hiroki motioned us in.

"Were you two warming up the bed?" I grinned at him and got an eyeroll back.

"Why, did you want to watch?"

I nodded back at him, wiggling my eyebrows. "I'd even hold the video camera."

"I bet."

"Might even pay to see it happen," I said with a laugh, turning toward my boyfriend. He was staring at us incredulous. "What?"

"Seeing guys being…intimate? That would excite you?"

I blushed in response. "Yeah. I think it's kind of hot. Does that bother you?"

He shook his head. "No! It's just…just when I thought you couldn't be any more perfect, you surprise me."

"Don't tell me you're bisexual?" It was my turn to be shocked.

"No! I've never. Let's just say the thought doesn't disgust me."

Remy stepped out of the bathroom, drying his hands. "What about you?" I grinned at him.

"Like guys?"

I nodded.

He shook his head. "Sorry to disappoint you."

"I'm not."

"Uh huh. You should see the look on your face."

"Oh, don't get me wrong. I'd totally watch you make out with another guy. But to each his own."

"What about you? Ever had sex with a girl?"

"Once. But we were both really drunk."

"Now *that* I would pay to see," David said in awe.

"Most guys would. Not gonna happen, though," I answered with a wink.

"We should probably get to sleep. We need to be back at school tomorrow." Remy sounded a little disappointed, but maybe that was just me.

"Maybe we should go back tonight. We do have class in the morning." As much as I wanted to be in the middle of a puppy pile, the thought of getting up extra early to get a cab back to school to get ready was mighty unappealing.

Remy sighed. "We can't."

"Huh?"

"It is why we did not go back today."

"Why?"

He motioned for me to sit. "When we found you, we called for a cab. The driver refused to take you back to the academy."

"Am I in trouble?"

Remy shook his head. "No. But you were technically dead."

"So?"

"Where do Charons ferry the dead?"

"To the underworld…"

He nodded.

"But I'm not dead now."

"No. But the smell of it is still on you."

I sniffed my armpits. I didn't smell dead. "How do you know?"

"What am I, Kaede?"

"A hellhound."

He nodded. "Guardian of the underworld. Trust me, I know. I'm hoping it is gone by the morning and we can get you back. Otherwise we're going to have a *long* walk."

I narrowed my eyes in suspicion, but Roki was standing behind him, nodding. "Okay. But no funny business."

"What do you mean?"

"Sex. We can all sleep in here. I won't make you go in the other room if you want to stay, but no…you know."

He chuckled. "Furthest thing from my mind."

"You have a dick. I doubt it."

He just smiled and started unbuttoning his shirt. I meant to go to the bathroom, but I couldn't. My eyes wouldn't let me while they were glued to his chest as the shirt slowly opened.

"Do you need help getting undressed?" David's voice broke through my fascination.

"No. I need to pee. I'll get undressed in the bathroom."

"Okay," he said softly.

Practically running, I closed the bathroom door and put my back against it, giving my head a moment to clear. Finally, I slipped the dress over my head and used the toilet before washing up at the sink. I didn't have any of my toiletries and made do with what the hotel had left for us.

When I stepped back into the bedroom, David and Remy were in the bed and Roki was waiting patiently for me, holding the blanket. I guessed he planned on keeping my legs warm again. I think he might have been taking one for the team to keep the situations from getting out of hand. Damn it.

Remy smiled and motioned for me to get into my spot between them. "Awww, but I wanna see you spoon David."

"I cannot protect you if you are not between us," he answered smoothly.

"Fine, fine. You just don't wanna be the little spoon." Instead of climbing up from the foot of the bed, I crawled over Remy, straddling him for a moment to tease him. His eyes were feasting upon my flesh as I slowly dragged myself over him, chuckling as the desire in his eyes became quite apparent.

"Little tease," he said with a chuckle. At least he was a good sport. Not that I trusted him completely, but enough.

Rolling off him, I landed on my back between them. Hiroki crawled up over my legs and brought the blanket up over us before curling up over my hip and putting his arm over my thighs. I sighed contentedly. Going back to school and sleeping alone was going to suck.

David rolled on his side, sliding his arm over my chest just under my breasts, burying his face in my neck and kissing me softly. Remy turned and kissed the top of my head and put his hand on my stomach just above Roki's head. Lifting the blanket, I checked on him to make sure he was comfortable. David's cock was practically in his face and he grinned at me. I couldn't help it, I busted out laughing.

"You can sleep up here with the big kids if you want."

"I am fine."

"Okay. Night, Roki."

"Night, Kaede-*sama*."

∞ ∞ ∞

Waking up in a bed full of naked guys is completely different from falling asleep in a bed full of naked guys. I couldn't lie still and kept fidgeting. Finally, it got to the point where David rubbed my bare chest just below my neck. It wasn't sexual in nature, just meant to be calming and he whispered, "Relax. We won't do anything to you while you're sleeping. I swear to you."

That kind of hurt my feelings. I twisted my neck to look over at him. "I know you won't. I wasn't even worried about that. If I didn't trust everybody in this bed, I wouldn't be here."

"Oh. Sorry. Just seemed like you were worried."

"No. I'm...anxious?"

"For tomorrow?"

"No."

"Then what?"

"I'm lying in a bed full of naked men. What the fuck do you think I'm anxious about?"

He chuckled, Remy chuckled, and even Roki gave a short bark of laughter from under the covers. It was a good thing it was almost completely dark in the room or they would have seen the furious blush on my cheeks.

"Would touching us help?"

"Huh?"

"We each have a hand on you. Yours are balled tightly beside you trying oh so hard not to touch us. Is that what is bothering you?" Remy wasn't teasing, merely being observant. Too observant.

"I don't know. Maybe?"

"I do not mind, if you wish."

"I bet you don't." I sighed and lifted my hands, unclenching my fists, unsure as to where to put them that wouldn't be completely awkward, I settled for their hips, draping a hand over each of them.

Guys feel different from girls. Most of the time. Their skin just feels thicker, rougher, or at least it did to me. The skin on their hips, however, was a completely different story. Soft and smooth, I had intended to just rest my hands on them. Almost instantly, I found myself letting my fingers glide over their hips in fascination.

Remy was the first to squirm. "That tickles."

"Oops. Sorry."

"No, you're not."

220

"Nope, not in the slightest. If I had known you were ticklish, I would have taken you prisoner long ago."

"I think you already might have," David said with a little chuckle.

"Pardon?"

"He's already your prisoner."

"Shut up, David," Remy warned.

"What does he mean?" I asked Remy.

"Nothing."

David's chuckles turned into a snicker. "Somebody start talking," I said levelly and rapidly traced my fingers along their sides.

"You captured his heart," David said through fits of laughter.

I stopped moving, unable to. Completely losing all ability to even *think* about moving. "What?"

"David..." Remy made his name a warning.

"Fine. I'll shut up."

"I won't," I said and turned my head to Remy. "What did he mean?"

He sighed. "Let's just say I'm a little more than infatuated with you."

"Like in a good way?"

"Of course," he answered confused.

"Oh. Okay then. I'm good with that," I said with a grin, hoping he could see my teeth in the darkened room.

He kissed the top of my head again and I smiled, wiggling back onto the pillow, letting my fingers glide over his soft skin some more. When his cock throbbed against my thigh, I realized how much he was enjoying the intimate contact, too.

David's hand resumed its circular motion over my breastbone, dipping a little lower with each pass. When the bottom of his hand grazed my nipples, I let out a little sigh.

David's mouth gently kissed my neck. Remy's grazed my face. I didn't know which way to lean, so I tilted my head back, letting them explore the softness of my skin with their lips. David kissed his way to my ear. "Touch him if you want."

"I am."

"You know what I mean…"

Oh. Oooh. "I don't know if I can."

"I'm not telling you to. I'm telling you that I am completely fine with it if you do."

Somehow, that made my heart flutter, and I turned my head, touching my lips to his. The hand on Remy's hip slipped between us, and I let my fingers run the length of his hardness. When they reached the tip, I gripped him, pushing back and stroking him.

His lips and his teeth found my shoulder, grazing, kissing, loving. "Kaede," he practically moaned my name. It was driving me insane and I wanted more.

I lifted my hand from David's hip and ran my fingers through Hiroki's slick hair before grabbing the cock beside him. David breathed heavier into my mouth as I stroked the both of them.

"May I kiss you?" Remy's breath against my skin sent a shiver down my stomach and settled on my clit. I gasped from the sheer need in his voice. Pulling away from David, I looked in *his* eyes, not for permission, but to see how he felt about it. There was only love. I grazed his lips one more time before turning my head and letting Remy devour my mouth.

And he did. His lips pressed against mine, his tongue slipped into my mouth, and he drank from my soul. There were good kissers, there were expert kissers, there were gods, and then there was Remy. I loved David, there wasn't a doubt in my heart, but Remy ignited something in me that I had never experienced before. Need. His kisses were like heroin. The first one was free, but I would be craving them every moment of every day, for the rest of my life.

He pulled away and I almost cried, until he grazed my chin with his teeth. My back arched and David found my nipple with his mouth. I picked up my pace with my hands, wanting to give them as much pleasure as they were giving me.

And then Roki's tongue slipped between the lips of my pussy.

No. Fucking. Way. I paused a minute to make sure I was *really* feeling what I thought I was feeling. *Nope. That's not a finger. No, oh, my kami. Oooh. No. That is definitely not a finger.* I wanted to scream with joy, happiness, and just because his tongue was inside my pussy. I also kind of wanted to slap him in the head. Not to stop, no way in hell was I going for the clitoris interruptus, but because it took being in a bed with two other naked guys for him to realize he wanted me.

My head snapped toward David as my breathing quickened. He held my nipple gently between his teeth and was flicking his tongue across the tip when he saw my eyes widen and a moan escape my lips. Letting go, he lifted the cover, saw Hiroki and smiled.

"How does it feel?"

"I'm on fire. From everywhere."

"It's about time," he said and grinned happily for me as he pulled the cover from us and threw it to the ground behind him, exposing all our nakedness and play. I groaned at the sight of my hands wrapped around their flesh as Hiroki was suckling my clit.

I felt brazen, a little slutty, but most of all I felt loved. Then my first orgasm hit, starting in my toes. They curled as my legs spasmed and I let go of David's cock to press Hiroki's head into my pussy, practically grinding myself against his face as waves of pleasure washed through me and

223

then battered me against the shore. I closed my eyes as I let out a primal scream. Remy, not wanting to wake the people in the surrounding buildings, smothered my scream with a kiss.

When I finally came down, Remy pulled away. "I'm jealous. I wanted to do that."

"Get eaten by Roki?"

He shook his head and smiled, knowing I was joking. He was learning. "No. I wanted to taste you."

"Give me a few minutes and you can get your wish." I chuckled and ran my fingers through Roki's hair again. His head was still moving, and David let out a grunt of pleasure. I turned to look and found his eyes were wide open, staring at me in pleasure and...something else. "He's..."

I looked down at Hiroki. He had turned to face David, and had his lips firmly planted on the end of his cock, suckling it much like he had my clit. The only difference was he had one hand around the base of it and was stroking it in time with the movements of his head. My pussy leaked even more. It was pretty fucking hot watching him suck my boyfriend's dick. I was jealous.

I turned to Remy and wormed my way down to the foot of the bed until I was back to back with Hiroki, our naked asses touching. Looking over my shoulder, I whispered, "That's fucking hot," as I got a firm grip on Remy's shaft and took him in my mouth.

His hands immediately shot to my hair, not to force himself further in, but to hold on for the ride I was about to give him.

"Race you," Hiroki said with a chuckle.

"No fair. You had a head start." I took Remy in as far as I could go. He could have gone a *lot* farther, but I wasn't that talented. I liked my oxygen. But, as I pulled away, I undulated my tongue against the underside of him and his hips bucked in pleasure as he let out a little hiss of air.

"Fuuuck," he whispered as I went back down on him.

I listened to their breathing. David sounded way closer than Remy. It was time to cheat. Using my other hand, I lifted his leg, cupping his balls in my hand and gently rolling them. Quickly pulling away, I pulled them into my mouth for a moment, letting my tongue continue where my hand left off. As I worked, I gathered some saliva and moistened my finger, then slid it between his legs and lightly ran over his hole.

"Kaede," he warned. Of course, I didn't listen. I let go of his balls and plunged his shaft into my mouth at the exact moment I let the tip of my finger slip inside him. "Holy fuck," he grunted as he started practically fucking my mouth, unable to stop. Wrapping my tongue around him, I let him go as I doubled my efforts with my finger. "Little. Minx." Whatever else he was trying to say became lost as he grunted at the pleasure assaulting him.

I pulled away. "Want me to stop?"

"Don't you fucking dare." Even with his cock free from my ministrations, his hips still rocked against my finger. He was enjoying it more than he cared to admit. He deserved a reward. I took him back into my mouth and started humming as I sucked.

"I'm going to come."

"Where. Where do you want to come, Remy?"

His brain tried to process my question. "Face. Let me come on your face.

I took him back in my mouth, sucked him hard on just the tip of his cock, assaulted him with my tongue just under the tip as I fingered his ass. He didn't stand a chance. I felt him tense in my mouth as his balls started to spasm. "I'm coming!"

I pulled him from my mouth and rubbed his cock against my lips and face. He erupted with a force I hadn't been expecting and the first spurt shot up and over me. David's startled shout told me where it landed. I chuckled as I let him unload the rest of it around my mouth and neck.

"Fuck, fuck, fuck, fuuuck," he grunted with each ejaculation.

I turned to smirk at Roki in triumph, but he was too busy swallowing his prize. David eyes were practically rolled up inside his head and he had a dreamy smile on his face.

"Want a kiss?" I'd said it to see the horrified look on his face, but he surprised me when he nodded. Then I noticed the cum from Remy's first shot splattered across his cheek.

I gave Remy's cock one final squeeze and crawled back up the bed, licking Remy's come from my boyfriend's face and kissing him with all the love, admiration, lust, and happiness I had. It took a while to show him just how much there was. I fell asleep in his arms again.

Chapter 20

Needless to say, we were late for school. The Charon's cab didn't even pull up until midafternoon. I don't think any of us gave a shit, either. Remy planned on filling in the headmaster as to everything that had transpired over the weekend anyway.

"Go. Don't worry about classes. I'll catch up with you guys later." Remy stopped to give me a kiss before heading to the administration building.

"Guess you're his girlfriend now, too," David said, giving me a wink. "Go have a shower and a nap if you want. I'll see you at dinner?"

"Of course," I answered him with a grin.

"Take care of her?" He looked up at Roki.

"Every day."

He nodded and headed toward his room. Unfortunately, it was at the opposite end of the hall from ours and on the first floor.

"Come. Let us get you cleaned up."

"Oh. We're gonna have a talk first, you and I." I poked him in the chest, and he blushed.

"*Hai.*"

I headed for the main entrance to Breckenridge Hall and popped up the stairs, skidding to a stop as Rome exited his room. He blinked in surprise. "Aren't you supposed to be in class?"

"Aren't you."

"Yes."

"Guess we're both a couple of delinquents then."

He opened his mouth to deliver what I'm sure was a witty retort when he stopped and looked at the torn, battered, school uniform I was wearing. My magical abilities didn't include tailoring. "I'm glad you're safe," he said and gently touched my shoulder in a completely uncharacteristic gesture.

Hiroki finally made it to the top of the landing. "Me, too." I answered. Hiroki stood behind me and put a comforting hand on my back.

Rome narrowed his eyes. "Where's Remy?"

"He's heading to the headmaster's office now if you want to catch up."

He sighed. "I will. Thank you," he said with more respect than I thought him capable of. He turned to leave but stopped. He glared down at me, but not in anger. "I'm sorry," he said simply and left us standing there, both of our mouths agape, shocking us twice within minutes.

When he was out of earshot, even for a dog, I whispered over my shoulder. "Did that just happen?"

"*Hai.*"

Shaking my head, I unlocked the door to our room and slipped inside, holding it for Hiroki.

"I am in need of a shower."

"Me, too. Everybody's in class. Wash my back?"

"I do not think they would take too kindly to a man being in the women's restroom."

I sighed. "Pweez?"

He sighed and rolled his eyes before he nodded.

I squealed and grabbed my shower things, including a couple of towels. Stripping, I put on my bathrobe and waited for him to get ready.

"Hurry up, old man."

228

"I am coming."

Not yet, you aren't...

As if he could hear my thoughts, he turned and narrowed his eyes at me.

"What?" I tried my best to look innocent. It was *really* hard.

"Nothing," he said suspiciously, putting on his robe and grabbing his shampoo, soap, body wash, shaving cream, aftershave, body lotion combination bottle. Being a guy seemed so much easier. And less messy.

This time he led the way out the door and toward the bathroom. I noticed he glanced nervously around the closer we got. There was no way we were going to get caught. "Relax, Roki."

"Easy for you to say. Let us use the men's bathroom."

"Ew. No way. You know what guys do in showers?"

"Probably the same things girls do," he said and cocked his eyebrow at me.

"Well, yeah. But we don't shoot stuff everywhere."

"You did last night..."

Wait. "What?"

He chuckled. "You must have been overly excited..."

"No way? I squirted?"

"*Hai.*"

"Sorry?"

"Do not be. I enjoyed it."

"Ew."

"That was not what I thought at the time."

We entered the bathroom and headed for the showers. I opened the stall. There would be enough room for the both of us. Barely. I started the water and turned back around. "So. What brought that on?"

"I imagine it was the overstimulation of your senses while I orally administered pleasure upon your clitoris."

"I'm not talking about *that*. Well, that. But that. You've refused every opportunity in the past. What made last night so special?"

He shrugged. "I do not know."

"Yes, you do. Spill it. Was it because you were in bed with two guys? Finally got excited enough to do me?" I hadn't meant it to sound snarky and I winced when I realized it did.

He sighed and put his hands on my shoulders, pulling me in for a hug. "No. It was almost losing you, Kaede. I realized just how very special you are to me and how much I do love you."

"You love me?" I sniffed and scuffed the tile with my foot.

"You know I do. I always have. I just did not realize how very much."

I smiled and looked up at him. "You loooove me. Hiroki loves Kaede." I grinned.

He laughed. "I do."

"I do, too." I hugged him, smiling with my face pressed against his chest. "But you stink." I pulled away and pulled off my bathrobe, getting into the shower and standing under the water. I rinsed my hair and felt it get slick with shampoo. Hiroki stepped closer and began working it into my hair and I sighed contentedly as I leaned back against him, letting him massage my scalp with his magic fingers.

"I missed this."

"I missed washing your hair. Rinse. It has been quite a long time. Right around the time you stopped keeping your hands to yourself, I believe…"

I stuck my tongue out at him and put my head back under, letting it wash away the suds, sputtering water as it rolled over my lips.

"Please stop spitting on me."

"It's just water."

He flicked my nipple.

"Hey!"

I smiled as he laughed. "Your mother is going to kill me if she finds out."

"She won't. If she does, we'll elope." I grinned without looking at him. Until he kissed me. I wrapped my arms around him, pulling him under the water with me.

He pulled away. "Conditioner?"

"Yes. Please."

I squeezed the water from my hair as he poured it on his hand, using his fingers to drag it through my white strands, only slightly darkened from the water.

He reached around me, rinsing his hands, and then put some body wash onto my shower scrunchy. I leaned my head forward, barely missing the spray as he started on my back. I groaned in pleasure. Someone rubbing your head, and someone washing your back were two of the greatest feelings in the world. To get them both, minutes apart…heaven.

"Mmmm. Thank you, Roki."

"My pleasure."

"Nope. Pretty sure it's mine."

I gasped when he went lower, running the scrunchy over the cheeks of my ass. Apparently, this was a full-service Kaede wash…

He squatted down, working his way down my legs and back up, letting his fingers run through the cleft of my ass, cleaning everything. I gasped as unexpected pleasure shivered through me.

"Turn."

Without question, I did. Standing in front of him as he started on my shoulders, gently washed my breasts, and then my stomach. When he used his bare hand to wash my lady parts, I was panting with pleasure. "Hiroki?"

"*Hai?*"

"Don't stop."

He slowly slid his fingers over me, not stopping, just as I asked. He leaned over and finished washing me with his other hand and then dropped the scrunchy. Still diddling my clit, he backed me up against the wall and kissed me, the spray running over both of us. Reaching down, I slid my hand over his cock. He reached down and hooked an arm under my leg, lifting it and stepping closer.

"You never came last night."

"No," he grunted and locked his lips onto mine. He grabbed my other leg and held me in the air as he pressed himself inside me.

I pulled my lips from his. "I'm not too heavy?"

"You weigh nothing, but the weight of you on my heart is immeasurable."

I couldn't help the grin his words caused before I smashed my lips back onto his, kissing him with all the want and desire that had been building up within me over the years.

Luckily, he wasn't much taller than me. Sex standing up wasn't impossible and I gasped as he slid every inch of him up into me, lifting me in the process and pinning me against the cold wet tile as he began fucking me with everything he had.

I shuddered against him, pressing my forehead against his as I rode his cock in the shower of Aesir Academy. The last place in the world I thought we would ever fuck for the first time.

"Roki, I'm going to come."

"As am I."

"Will you come inside me?"

"Is it safe?'

"Yes," I lied, but I wanted him to finish inside me. I needed him to.

He buried his head in my neck and quickened his pace. "So close," he whispered.

"I'm coming, Roki…"

Impaled on him, I did. I slammed myself against him, bouncing as my breath left me. He grunted and nearly crushed me against the wall as I felt him spasm inside me, unloading his pent-up passion from the night before.

"I love you," I whispered as I held on to him and cried.

"Are you okay?" He pulled away and let me slide down him, getting my feet on the ground.

The tears fell harder as he pulled free from me. And I felt empty.

"Kaede!" He was starting to panic and my cries turned to laughter. "What is wrong?"

"I'm happy, you jerk. Why the hell did we wait so long?"

He sighed in relief. "Because I am stupid."

I nodded in agreement, still crying and laughing as I kissed him again and again. "I'm happy. So happy. Let's get you clean."

He nodded and we finished our shower. I had just shut the water off and wiped the water off my face when Roki covered my mouth with his hand and pushed us against the wall away from the stall door. He made a shushing motion with his free hand and pulled the other from my mouth.

Footsteps entered the bathroom and then the sound of sobbing echoed off the tiled walls.

"She's alive! I'm dead!"

Sabine.

"You should have taken her head. Just when you think the fox is in your trap, it will gnaw off its own foot for freedom."

The other voice was still Sabine's, but utterly devoid of emotion. It was the same voice I had heard come from her mouth on the boat. The goddess, Hel.

I peeked over the shower door and around the corner. Without a sound, I ducked back. I hadn't seen Sabine, but I saw her reflection in the mirror.

"What am I going to do?"

"What you should have done in the first place. Kill her."

"But my brothers will stop me."

"You do not understand, Child. You do not have a choice. If she does not die, Fenrir will continue to wake and bring destruction upon this world. Is that not worth your life?"

"You want me to die?"

"No. But it may be necessary to vanquish his herald."

"Why me?"

"Because you are my progeny. You will do as I ask."

"But my brothers…"

"Both have feelings for the girl. They are useless to me now."

The sound of a punch and broken glass falling echoed through the bathroom. She had broken the mirror, but not her future.

"Fine. Next time I can get her alone, I'll finish the job."

"I know you will. I love you, my child."

"I love you, too." She said it, but it didn't sound very convincing. Not even to me.

Her footsteps echoed as she practically ran from the bathroom.

"Well, fuck a duck."

Hiroki coughed and covered his mouth. "Foxes are more fun," he whispered.

Staring at him, mouth agape, every rational thought left my brain. He made a funny. "Did you just…"

"*Hai.*" He snickered.

"I am so fucking proud of you right now."

He grinned and blushed, but then his face got serious. "What should we do?"

234

"Tell Remy. She's their sister. Hel is their…god? Ancestor? Grandmother? I don't know, but it's their mess."

"*Hai.*"

"Come on. Let's get dressed."

I threw on my bathrobe and stuffed as many toiletries into the oversized pockets as I could, jamming the rest into Roki's. Peeking out of the bathroom to make sure the coast was clear, I padded down the hallway as quickly and quietly as I could manage.

"Now you are trying for stealth?"

I gave Roki a nasty glare over my shoulder. "What do you mean try? I am a ninja."

"Ninjas don't wear bathrobes."

"They do when they take a bath."

"Ninjas do not bathe. They frighten the dirt away."

"Shut up, Roki." Slipping the key in the lock, I twisted it open and let us into the room. "Let's get dressed and go see Uncle."

"I thought you wished to tell the twins first?"

"I'm hoping to catch them there," I said and let the door close. It stopped when a hand slipped inside, catching it before it clicked. Calling my katana, I stepped into my stance just as Remy's head peeked in the door.

"Oh, thank *kami.*"

"You were expecting someone else?" He stepped into the room. "Is it okay if I come in? I heard you mention us."

"You were just the man I wanted to see," I released my sword back into nothingness and leapt at him, catching him and kissing him. He went tense under my onslaught.

I pulled away, absolutely horrified. "I'm sorry? Should I not have kissed you?" My heart broke a little. To spend a weekend with someone, to do all the things we'd done, only to have him shy away from a kiss… I slowly slid down from his chest, putting my feet on the floor and backing up.

Remy tilted his head and narrowed his eyes. "Fox…"

"What?"

"You are under a gross misconception."

"I kind of realized that when you didn't kiss me back."

"You wanted me to?"

It was my turn to tilt my head and narrow my eyes. "I had your cock in my mouth. I didn't think you would mind a kiss." I was starting to get a little pissed. Especially at his surprised look and then hearty laugh. "Are you fucking kidding me right now?"

He was having trouble breathing, waving his hands in front of me. I debated my logic of letting my sword fade away. He was uncircumcised. I could have remedied that for him.

"Fox…"

"Dog."

That shut him up. "As I was *trying* to tell you…I am not Remy."

"Rome?" Icy fear seized my chest.

He nodded.

I wanted to throw up. "No." I covered my mouth with my hand. I had my tongue in his mouth. I coughed and resisted the urge to spit. "Sorry."

"Seeing you squirm like this made it worth it. Although, I am absolutely horrified that you kissed me after having my brother's junk in your mouth."

"Hahaha. Indirect kiss!" It was worth it to see him turn green.

"Do you have any mouthwash?'

"No, but I can conjure up some booze. Want some?"

He cocked an eyebrow at me, and the expression was so like his brother, I almost gasped. I'd *never* had trouble telling them apart since the moment I'd met them. Why I had mistaken him for Remy, was beyond me. *Maybe you were just hoping it was him.*

"What kind of booze."

"Well, it used to be *sake* but now it's mead. Where's Remy?"

"Still speaking to the headmaster. He sent me to make sure you were safe."

He's worried about me. I grinned a little.

"Your sister was just in the bathroom talking to herself in the mirror. She still wants to kill me. So does Hel."

He sighed and sat down at my desk. "I'll have that drink now."

Chapter 21

"She's gone."

I sighed at Remy as he sat down at our table, not that I was surprised. After I recapped the events of the bathroom scenario to Rome, he had stormed off in a fit of rage, heading back to the headmaster's office and to find his sister. That had blossomed to a search of the entire school by faculty, staff, and a few of the students. Steph and her other friend were under observation until she was found.

Hiroki and I had just sat down for dinner. David had been sent to guard the temple. I didn't see the point, the only person stupid enough to go there was me and I'd been there, done that, wasn't going to fucking do it again, ever. It's not like Sabine wanted to free Fenrir, she and her goddess were going to great lengths to make sure that didn't happen. Namely, by killing me.

"Well, judging by her conversation with herself, she couldn't have gone far. She was under strict orders to put me out of my misery."

Remy sighed and kissed my cheek. "Sorry, Kaede. We'll find her and keep you safe. Even if it means disobeying Hel."

There was a crack of thunder outside the school and I squeaked as I jumped in my chair.

"Easy, Kaede. Thor is the least of our worries."

I groaned, not even wanting to think about it. I was a messenger *of* the gods. To be targeted by one…made for a jumpy fox.

You accept it.

Fenrir's voice caught me off guard. He'd been silent since I made it back to land. I'd assumed he'd gone back to sleep. *Accept what?*

Your role as messenger. You have fought against what you are since the day of your birth.

A chill ran up my spine. *Yes. I have. My father always accepted his role, but it always seemed too much responsibility for a silly little fox like me. Having fun was more important.*

And now?

I am what I am. It doesn't look like I can hide from it. I'm sorry, Fenrir. I belong to the Inari-kami.

The echoing rumble of laughter resonating with the thunder was my first warning. The searing pain in my head was my second.

"Kaede…" The worry in Remy's voice was the last. He and Roki were sliding their chairs away from the table.

"What?"

"Your skin…"

I looked down at my arms, fearing a rash. It looked normal to me. "What about it?"

The girl at the table next to us gasped. Remy turned to her. "Mirror?"

She shook her head, but the other girl seated at her table pulled one out of her blazer jacket. With a shaking hand, she passed it to Remy, who opened it and held it up in front of me.

My eyes had bleached. That was the first thing I noticed. They were no longer blue. They'd turned an unearthly shade of ice gray. The blue of my eyes had drained to my cheeks as two runes appeared from the corner of my mouth, swept up to the corners of my eyes and then swept back down under my ears, disappearing around my neck. A neck that held a ghostly tattoo of a chain in the same hue of blue.

"What the ever-loving fuck?"

You have accepted what you are. I have claimed you as my fylgjur.

"Fenrir is talking to you right now, isn't he?" Remy reached out with his other hand, gently touching mine and gasping as he made contact.

"Do not touch her, hound of my sister," I said, unwillingly. My voice echoed in the dining hall, causing the students to start leaving through the door. Even the girl who surrendered the mirror, stood and hastily walked away.

"Look into her heart. She knows I don't mean her any harm."

He speaks the truth, yet his sister has already attempted to take your life.

Yeah. She's a crazy bitch.

Much like my sister.

Yeah. Family sucks sometimes.

He chuckled in my head. *So young and yet so wise.*

I chuckled, hopefully in *his* head. *Far from it. Which makes me wonder, why me?*

You have the blood of gods coursing through your veins. You are a true herald. You will prepare the world for my return and you will free me from these cursed dwarven chains...

The stories played themselves back through my mind. The binding of Fenrir. The gods and goddesses of Aesir binding him to prevent Ragnarok. It was upon the third binding, using chains forged by the dwarves, that they were successful. Mostly. One of the gods, Tyr, had lost a hand to the jaws of the giant wolf.

Fenrir chuckled at the memory. I wasn't sure if it was my memory or his as our experiences blended into a larger whole.

"You can't." I started speaking aloud.

What can I not?

"Start Ragnarok. Why do you want to destroy the world?"

You share my memories, as I share yours, little fox. Tell me, what is Ragnarok...

I opened my mouth to spit out how he wanted to swallow the earth and the sun, but something stopped me. The same thing forced me to delve into all the memories floating through my brain that weren't mine. Playing through his binding again, I saw the fear on the gods' faces. He was the son of Loki. Loki, not born of the tribe of Aesir, but of their frost giant foes. Born to bring about the destruction of...them. Seated upon *Yggdrasil* were nine worlds. Ragnarok signaled the destruction of Asgard, not Midgard, the realms of humans. The gods weren't trying to stop him from eating the world, they were trying to stop him from destroying Asgard.

"Oh."

Learn for yourself what will transpire. You shall free me one way or another, little fox. You are mine.

And just like that, he was gone, and I was alone in my own head. I sucked in a breath of air and frantically shook in my seat. Hiroki and Remy swarmed me, controlling the convulsions as the world shifted back into focus.

"We are so fucked."

∞ ∞ ∞

Uncle Tatsuo set the steaming mug of tea down in front of me. "Maybe it is time to contact your parents." He said and sat down on the ancient wood in front of me.

I picked up the mug and took a small sip, wincing at the heat and the flavor. Uncle didn't put sugar in his tea, nor did he apparently put it in mine. I looked at the contents, wishing fervently it was *sake* and wincing when it turned gold.

Beggars can't be choosers, I thought as I downed the cup that had transformed into mead.

"Accepting his gifts only binds you more tightly to him."

I nodded. "I know, but the tea wasn't cutting it."

"I do have some *sake*..." He stood, took my cup, and walked over to the ornate wooden cupboard behind the desk. He pulled out a clay jar and poured its contents straight into my teacup. He walked over and handed it to me, patting me on the head before sitting down.

It changed as soon as it touched my lips, a fact that didn't go unnoticed by the headmaster. "Yes. Maybe your father can help you break the bond and return you to the *Inari-kami*."

"I'm Japanese. American. Why me?"

"Why me?" He motioned to the school. "I am as firmly entrenched into this as you, yet I am also Japanese."

"But you're a dragon."

"Which seems to be the fact that you are missing, as well."

I thought about it for a moment. "It's what we are, not who we are that matters."

"Precisely," he said and beamed. "You are a celestial messenger, and I am a dragon. It does not matter where we came from."

I rubbed my eyes and drank my mead. "How do we stop him?"

He crossed his arms and pushed himself back on the desk a little farther, letting his legs dangle over the edge. "I do not know. For now, we will keep you safe and we will keep you far away from him. I'm of half a mind to send you back home..."

"That would solve everything wouldn't it?" Fear gripped my chest. As much as I didn't want to go to Aesir Academy, it was growing on me. More so, certain people were growing on me. To return to California…to go back to my old life of being alone… The thought wasn't nearly as appealing as it would have been a little over a month ago. Or even a week ago. Sure, the near-death experiences were a bummer, but I was still breathing. When my head wasn't being invaded by a god.

"It might. I'm more afraid of what it would do to you. Fenrir has bound you to him," he said and motioned to the runic tattoos on my face and the chain tattoo around my neck. "To tear you from him might mean the end of you. I think it safer to bring your father here to inspect what has been done."

"He's going to kill me."

"He loves you more than you could possibly know."

"Uh huh."

Tatsuo sighed. "Kaede…you were on a path of self-destruction. No matter what they said, did, or punished you with, you would not change your path. Did you know that the both of them stayed up every night until Hiroki brought you home? Do you know when the last time they slept at night was?"

I did a quick calculation… "Woah."

"Yes."

"Why didn't they tell me. More importantly, why the fuck didn't they show me?"

"It is not their way. They wish to guide, not rule your life."

"Kinda felt that way?"

"Were you imprisoned? No. They let you do as you wished."

"With supervision!"

"Hiroki was never your jailor. He was your friend, your confidant. Your brother. Although, that title has been replaced with lover, I see."

I blushed furiously. "You knew?"

"Eyes of the dragon," he said with a chuckle, squinting at me. "And I see he is not the only one…"

My blush went thermonuclear. I was *seeing* red. "Uncle Tatsuo…"

He held up his hand. "In my youth, I had the pleasure of six wives at one time. I am not judging you."

I decided to shut my mouth. Not talking about it seemed a much better option. "So, what's the plan?"

"To make one. That is the first part. I shall send for your father."

As much as I didn't want him to, I found myself nodding. If he could free me from Fenrir, this nightmare would be over. "After that?"

"That will be decided after we see how the first part goes."

"You are very wise." I rolled my eyes, wanting things to go back to normal.

"In the meantime, do not go anywhere by yourself. Hel wants you dead and probably to drag your soul to Hel to keep you away from Fenrir forever."

"I still don't see why he needs me."

"To break the chain. He chose you for a reason. We just do not know what it is. Yet."

"I hate waiting."

"So much like your mother, it is uncanny."

I narrowed my eyes at him. "My mother? Mrs. Primandproper?"

He laughed. "One day, when you're older, I'm sure you will hear some of the tales of her youth… Then again, maybe not. You do not need any inspiration."

I had a *very* hard time picturing what he could possibly be talking about. My mother put the pro in proper. I fell asleep watching her make tea. The woman added twenty-eight steps to everything and looked like she was trying to figure out a way to add twenty more just to make it more fun. It drove me crazy.

"So, do I have your permission to skip class and hide out in my room? For safety reasons?"

"Silly fox. The expression about safety in numbers is there for a reason."

"Why is that?"

"Because it is true."

"How did I know you were going to say that? Can I at least go down to the village tonight and buy some makeup?"

"Your beauty needs no enhancement."

"I meant to cover the blue marks on my face."

"That is the mark of a god. I do not think Cover Girl will easy, breezy, beautiful that off your face."

Chapter 22

I woke up screaming in fear. Something was wrong, I just didn't know what. Hiroki was by my side in a flash. "Shhhh, Kaede. It's just a dream."

"Roki?"

"You haven't woken from a nightmare in years."

I groaned, trying to shake off the feeling. "I didn't miss that. I wonder why now?"

"You're usually too drunk to stir from a nightmare. What was it about?" He leaned me back on the bed and stroked my hair like he used to when I was a kit.

"I don't know. Just a panicked feeling in my sleep."

"Relax. Go back to sleep."

"What time is it?"

There was a pause while he checked the clock. "It's four in the morning."

Nodding, I closed my eyes and snuggled back into my pillow. I smiled at the gentle kiss on my forehead and nearly banged my head against his as I sat back up. Someone was pounding on the door to our room.

"Sorry," I muttered and slid out of the bed. I undid the deadbolt and pulled the door open. "Remy? What's wrong."

"Rome," he corrected me. I was still having trouble telling them apart. "David is…missing."

"What do you mean?" It was a stupid question, I know, but it was all my brain came up with.

"Remy went to relieve him at the temple...and David wasn't there."

"Well, he wouldn't have just wandered off."

"Precisely." He shifted uncomfortably.

"You think he ran away," I said deadpan, recognizing the look on his face.

"I do. Remy does not."

"Where would he have gone?"

"Sabine..."

My heart stopped beating as pain seized it. "No," I whispered.

"I am going to have to agree with your brother," Hiroki said behind me. "He loves Kaede. There is no way he would have left to be with your sister..."

"That is what Remy said. Maybe he was jealous of Remy?"

"No. He was the one who talked me into also seeing your brother. Hell, he wanted me to date Roki, too. Even you."

"Me?" He chuckled.

I let it go, too worried about David to verbally spar with Rome. Then another thought settled in my head. "What if he didn't leave?"

"What?"

"What if your sister took him? She seemed to be having trouble letting go."

Instead of outright denying it, he stopped to actually *think* about it. I was kind of shocked. Usually, when people accused family members of things, the gut reaction was to deny. That wasn't true of the Laterans. They might have their faults, but blind family loyalty wasn't one of them. His action forced me to raise my opinion of him a little higher. If he kept it up, I was going to have to quit teasing him. One day a week. Maybe.

"Are her friends still under guard?"

"Yes," Rom answered, cocking an eyebrow in question.

"Let them go. We can't find her, but you know, sure as shit, they'll probably make a bee line for her if they can."

He nodded in thought. "Smart little fox."

"Thanks. I have my moments. When I'm sober."

"It's probably safer for all of us that those times are few and far between."

"I know right?" I stepped up to him. "In all seriousness, we need to find David. I have a bad feeling about this."

He nodded. "As do I."

"Thank you for telling me."

"You're welcome. Go back to sleep. I'll let you know if we find him. Or anything."

"Thanks, Rome."

Without another word, he was out the door and I settled my back against it once it was closed. The fear in the pit of my stomach threatened to chew its way out the front.

"You are not going to take his advice. I can tell. Where are we going?"

"To fucking look for David, that's where."

"As I figured."

"You don't think we should?"

"I think we should follow your plan to let Sabine's friends lead us to her. Stumbling around blindly in the dark will not be useful."

"So, we should follow Rome is what you're saying?"

"*Hai.* But I would suggest not getting caught. He will be…angry with you."

"Angri*er*."

"*Hai.*"

∞ ∞ ∞

249

"Is that him?" I tried to peek between the branches of the row of hedges across the way from the administration building, and ended up with a stick in the eye.

"Shhh. Yes," Hiroki answered.

"Let's follow him," I said and went to move, but Roki stopped me with a hand on my arm, motioning for silence.

Looking back toward Rome, I froze. He was staring directly in our direction, tilting his head and listening. He was going to be tough to follow with his damn dog ears.

Crouched behind the bushes, motionless, in the pitch dark was not how I wanted to spend fifty-seven seconds of my life. I knew because I counted until he turned and started walking back toward our dorm.

We kept to the shadows, farther back than I would have liked, but it paid off. He made it all the way to the dorm without turning back around. "He's going to the back entrance," I whispered. "Head for the dining hall. We can watch for them to come out from there."

"*Hai.*"

We set up camp behind one of the large columns that surrounded the hall. Hiding behind one, we waited. And waited. Then waited some more. "We should have brought some playing cards…"

Hiroki just nodded and blew into his hands. The sun would be up soon, but the pre-dawn morning was way colder than the night air.

"Think they'd notice if we started a fire?"

"Probably," A voice said behind us. A familiar voice. Rome's deep chuckle echoed around us.

I stood up straight and turned around slowly. "About time you got here. We've been waiting for like an hour."

"Uh huh. Go back to bed, Kaede. They're not the brightest of girls, but they're not stupid enough to run straight to Sabine."

"Then why are you here watching?"

250

"I heard you moving around in the bushes by the headmaster's office. I was waiting to see what kind of stupid situation you were going to get yourself into."

"You mean *if*, right?"

"No. When. I got tired of waiting."

"Shhh," Roki whispered and pointed. Two blonde heads bopped out the back door and jogged down the stone steps, heading straight for the woods.

"You were saying?" I elbowed Rome in the ribs.

"Wow. They really are that stupid." He stared after them, shaking his head.

"My plan worked. Muhahaha. That makes me kind of brilliant, doesn't it?" I grinned at him.

"No. It just means that you put yourself in their shoes. You think like them." He rolled his eyes and patted me on the head.

"Did you just call me stupid?"

"I would never. I was saying when the situation calls for it, you do not struggle to think like an idiot."

"Oh. Thank you."

"You're welcome."

Hiroki's hissing laughter ruined our bonding moment. "Maybe we should follow them?"

"Their hearing is as good as mine. Give them a head start. I can track them."

"GPS?"

"Nose."

"We need James Bond and get Toucan Sam." I sighed and leaned back against the column.

"Who?"

"Toucan Sam? Froot Loops? Follow your nose?"

"The cereal bird?"

"Yes."

"Are you saying I have a big nose?"

I sighed and shook my head. "Nevermind."

And he calls me stupid.

"Can you guys communicate with telepathy or something?"

"What? No. Why?"

I stared thoughtfully in the direction the girls had gone. "How do they know where to find Sabine?"

He reached into his pocket and pulled out a phone. "There's these wonderful technological devices call smart phones…"

"Why didn't you use it to track her?"

"Because she has her location services off. I even tried texting and calling. She didn't answer either."

"But she answers Tweedle-slut and Tweedle-ho?"

"They are her…handmaidens, I guess you would call them. *La ancella.*"

Not gonna lie, the Italian was kind of sexy. Even from Rome's lips… I'd have to get Remy to talk Italian to me later. *I wonder what Romanian sounds like…*

"We should go. They are far enough ahead." He took off toward the woods and as soon as he was close enough, he leaped into the air and landed on all four paws of a *giant* black dog. He looked back over his shoulder at us and *huffed.*

"That is a big dog." Roki shuddered next to me.

"Yeah. Maybe we should change, too."

"*Hai.* Hopefully he does not try to eat us." He shifted into his fox form and scurried after Rome.

I shrugged. "When in Rome… Oh, my *kami*, that sounds dirty…" I chuckled and shifted, still laughing through my fox lips as I took off after them.

I started to panic when we followed the same trail that lead to the Temple of Fenrir. Even Rome turned and gave me a worried puppy look. He growled and carried on. I could feel the tension leave him as he followed the scent up another mountain path before the clearing. This one was very overgrown and hardly used. I hadn't even seen it the last time I'd come this way and almost destroyed the world.

You have come.

Shit, I thought to myself and not at him. Or at least I hoped. *No. One of the hellhounds took my wolf friend. We are trying to get him back. Going the totally opposite direction from you. Sorry. I'll try and stop by on my way back.*

His laughter resonated in my head. *You cannot lie to me, little fox. Find your friend. It is not time for me to wake. Yet.*

I didn't like the "yet" he threw onto the end of his thought. Not even a little bit. *Dun dun duuun.*

Lost in thought, my head nearly collided with Rome's leg. Thankfully he was much taller than me in his hellhound form. That would have sucked. I crawled under him and *yipped* from under his chin.

His head was almost as big as I was, and it was a little intimidating as he looked down at me. He growled low in his chest and looked back up.

"Where are they?" I managed to form the words with my fox mouth. I could talk, but it wasn't easy and I kind of sounded like a snake instead of a fox. Making sibilant sounds with sharp incisors sucked.

He just growled and crept forward. Either he wasn't in the mood to chat or hellhounds couldn't talk. I was betting on the latter. There was no way he could have gone that long without insulting me without a reason.

Without warning, he dropped to the ground and blended in with the foliage. The sun hadn't crested the horizon yet, but once it did, he was going to stick out like a sore thumb. Kind of like I was with my white fur, but at least I could hide behind him. I wanted to see what was going on. I shifted back to demi-human, snagged a leaf and slapped it against my arm, turning my skin, clothes, and hair variations of black and gray. The ultimate nighttime camouflage. Unfortunately, my spells only lasted a short while.

Picking my way along his side, I stopped next to his cheek, absentmindedly rubbing his jowls as I looked to see what had stopped him. We were on the edge of a clearing. On the opposite side was a tiny cottage. "Did you know that was there?"

He shook his doggy head.

"I'm going to go take a look."

He growled.

"I'll be fine."

He snorted.

"Seriously. I can be quiet."

That was the first time I ever heard a dog laugh.

I flipped him off and hugged the edge of the clearing as I headed toward the house. Roki nipped my heel and leapt into the foliage. I did the same, just as the front door opened and one of Sabine's friends stepped out and lit up a cigarette.

Tsk Tsk. That's against school rules. I think?

The other one walked outside, a frustrated look on her face. "Where the hell is she?"

My heart broke. If they didn't know where Sabine was...

Do you wish to know?

Until the day I died, which I fervently hoped would be *many* years in the future, I would never get used to a god's voice just popping into my head whenever it wanted. *You know where David is?*

I can smell all my children.

Tell me, please...

Little fox, nothing is for free. Even for my herald. You wish to find him?

Yes!

Come grace me with your presence.

I can't. I am forbidden and there's no way I'm going to overpower a hellhound.

254

Bring him with you.

He wouldn't let me come even if I begged.

You are a fox. He is a hound. It is in his blood to chase you...

You want me to run? My mouth opened in shock.

Prove your worth. If you make it to me, I will protect you. Let me see a hunt, even if it is in my dreams.

You swear you can find him?

I have no reason to lie.

You won't wake up?

You have my word.

Without even pretending to hide anymore, I stood and walked to the middle of the clearing, ignoring the shouts of the assholes on the porch. I made eye contact with the hellhound lying on the forest floor.

"I'm sorry," I said and shifted, taking off at full speed toward the far side of the clearing.

Roki tackled me from behind. "What are you doing!" His speech in fox form was much better than mine. He'd had longer to practice.

"Back off, Hiroki!" I snarled as we tumbled through some underbrush. When we stopped, I popped thirty-feet away. Rome's howl echoed all around us as he crashed into the forest.

Fuck. Thanks, Roki. I took off running again, popping whenever visible distance opened up in the patchy forest.

Good. You have the lead.

Distracting... I sent a mental sigh at the slumbering god.

Weaving through the trees, I made it back to the trail leading to the clearing and the cave entrance. Just a few more moments, and I'd be safe. Or so I thought until the six-hundred-pound hellhound crashed from the bushes and took a swipe at me with its enormous paw. Rome wasn't fucking around. He was out for my ass, and *not* in the fun way.

255

I ducked, flattening myself and popping on top of him, springing from his shoulders and focusing on a spot as far away as I could safely pop to. His paw swiped my hindquarters, knocking me into a tree with enough impact to blast the air from my lungs. I saw stars as I slid down the tree and crumpled to the ground in a heap. He growled in anger as he closed the distance between us.

I opened my eyes, popped behind him, and then back down the trail, going in the wrong direction but putting some distance between us.

Shifting into my demi-form, I called my blade.

"You have to let me pass," I said tiredly.

He shifted back, not even looking winded. "There's no way, Kaede. You're not getting any closer to that cave."

"He promised to help me find David."

"And you believe him? He's a god. The son of the original trickster, himself. He's using you to wake up."

"I believe him."

"You're a fool."

"Fuck you, Romeo." I took off running, blade leading the way and screaming as I charged.

He shook his head and shifted back, stomping his paws and crouching to spring. When I was close enough, he leaped into the air, intending to squish me beneath his massive weight, playing for keeps.

I grinned and launched my sword at his exposed underbelly, shifted, and popped to the spot he had launched himself from. Without looking back, I popped four more times consecutively and then ran as fast as I could, closing the last thirty feet between me and the entrance to the cave, slamming into Remy's chest as he stood there, blocking the way.

"No! That's cheating!" He pushed me from the mouth of the cave.

I didn't fall to the ground, he didn't shove me that hard, but I knew from looking at his face he wasn't happy to see me. "You can't be *here, Kaede!*"

"Fenrir," I called over him. "I made it!"

Yes. You did. I shall honor our agreement.

The runes on my face flared, briefly illuminating the ground in front of me blue. The chain started to burn and twist, not choking, but more than a little unpleasant. The howling of a hundred wolves filled the night air, causing each of us to stop in our tracks and shiver in the cascade of the lupine symphony. Crashing could be heard all around us as they converged on the clearing. Even the girls walked into the clearing, one looking confused and the other shifting into a werewolf to come stand beside me, standing on two legs and snarling at Remy.

"*Kaede...*"

"You need to let me pass, Remy. He won't awaken, I swear on my life."

"But can you swear on every life in this world? I know you love him, Kaede, but come on! Do you think he'd want you to risk everything?"

"I trust him, Remy. Just as I trust you." I slowly walked toward him, the different packs of wolves following behind me.

With a sigh, he stepped aside just as Rome started crashing through the wolves, not caring if he injured them or not. The werewolf beside me turned to intercept the threat.

"Stop him, Remy."

"I can step aside, but I will not fight my brother. I love you, but don't put me in that position."

I nodded. He was right and was being more than fair. I turned and called my sword again.

You do not wish to kill him.

No, I answered honestly.

Use the chain to bind him.

257

There was only one chain I could think of. I reached up and touched the tattoo around my neck. It flared to life again, becoming real beneath my fingers. I wrapped them around it and pulled, dragging it from my skin and flinging it at the charging hellhound.

It shot from my fingers, snaking around Rome's legs, tripping him and felling him. As soon as he stopped plowing the earth with his face, the ghostly blue chain enveloped his legs completely, and wormed its way around his muzzle. Helplessly, he looked at me as I shot him an apologetic look.

Thank you, Fenrir.

The chains that bind me are yours to command. And when the time comes, when you are ready, you will command them to release me. You will set me upon my enemies, and I shall spare the world that is precious to you.

As long as Midgard remains unharmed, I will help you.

That is all I can ask. The one you call Sabine has taken my wolf with her. She means to lure you to Helheim.

"How do I find her?"

How does one get to the underworld?

"Oh, come on. There's no secret door here in the back or something? There's *always* a secret door in the abandoned temple!"

Little fox, my body is imprisoned in the underworld. This temple was built to house my spirit in the mortal realm. They would not link them together...

"Good point. So, find the underworld, find the boyfriend."

Yes.

"You make it sound so easy."

If you have help...it might be. A word of caution. Should you see my sister...

"Give her a message?" I was his herald after all.

Run.

"Oh. Good plan. Thanks."

His mental chuckle caressed my cheek and left me standing there staring at the twins and Hiroki. They were looking at me like I lost my damn mind. I might have. That would probably be a better option than being hijacked by a Norse god and planning a trip to hell to save my boyfriend from his psychotic sister. "Sabine dragged him to hell," I told them earnestly.

"To…hell?" Rome growled at me as he dusted himself off. While conversing with Fenrir, the chains had released him. "You are certifiably insane."

"True story, bro, but I'm telling you the truth. Just like I've been getting visits from Fenrir, your sister has been acting as host for Hel. Hel wants me dead, and to do that…your sister abducted David and is waiting for me in Helheim. How the hell do I get to hell? The underworld. Helheim. Whatever."

Rome looked at Remy. Remy looked at Hiroki. Hiroki looked like he wanted to put me to bed with a cold washrag on my head.

"I'm not kidding!"

"How do you know all this?" Remy put his hands on his hips.

"Uh, hello? Did you not just hear me talking to Fenrir?"

"Kaede-*sama*…we saw you talking to yourself."

I narrowed my eyes at Hiroki, wanting to smack the worried look off his face, but if I thought about it, what they witnessed probably looked like me losing my marbles. Or Sabine in a bathroom. Whatever.

"Fine. Screw all of you. I'll find a way all by myself. And rescue him. All by myself. And kick your sister's ass…all by myself. Okay? Come on, Hiroki. You're coming with me."

I turned around and stomped out of the temple, blinking in the bright morning sun. "How the hell is it morning already?"

The wolves were gone and there weren't any bodies, thankfully. Sabine's pets were standing there looking very uncomfortable. "What?"

"We're sorry," the hellhound named Steph said, then turned around and walked away. The werewolf, whose name I *still* didn't know, knelt on the ground.

I sighed. "Thank you," I said to her. She did help me when it mattered. "You can go."

She shook her head.

"Seriously. Go. Go to class or something. Get an edumacation. Do something with your life other than the lackey of evil bitches."

"I will. I guess I'm the lackey of a good bitch now."

"Pardon?" I wasn't ruffled at being called a bitch. Or that she called me good. It was the lackey part I had a problem with. I already had one of those. Or used to. Guess he was more of a boyfriend now. The thought made me smile, but I shook my head and walked over to the American werewolf in Iceland.

"You seriously think I could trust you?" I felt bad for saying it, but it was the truth. "You'd toss me to Sabine the first chance you got, even if you didn't want to."

"No. I...uh... I couldn't."

"Sure, you could. That's what former lackeys of evil bitches do. My new master treats me nice and gives me puddings, but my old master...she used to beat me so good. It's a whole psychological bullshit thing I just came up with, but I wouldn't put it past you."

She sighed and shook her head. "You don't understand, I *can't*!" She snarled and lifted her head, exposing her neck. Standing above her as she knelt on the ground, I missed the ghostly gray tattoo of a chain encircling her neck. Hesitantly, I reached out and touched it, pulling my hand back as it writhed beneath my fingers.

"Oh."

"Yeah, oh. Fenrir literally just made me your bitch," she said with a little chuckle that didn't reach her eyes. I knew how she felt.

Reaching out my hand, she took it and I helped her to her feet.

"Thanks for your help earlier. Were all the wolves okay?"

"Yes," Rome answered behind me. "I would not have hurt them on purpose."

I was still pissed at him, but I said, "Thank you."

He nodded.

"Kaede," Remy continued.

"I meant what I said. It's fine if you don't believe me or not want to help. I have Hiroki and…" I looked at my new forced friend, not knowing her name. She blinked in surprise.

"Meagan."

She winced in pain as I saw double. *She is your Geri. You will address her as such. As punishment, she has lost who and what she was.*

"Geri," she said again, shaking her head.

Ouch. That's gotta hurt. I wasn't talking about having Fenrir in her head, either. "As I was saying," I continued to Remy, "Hiroki, Geri, and I got this."

I started heading back to school.

"If you think that I'm not going to help you get our friend back, you're wrong. And for the record, I *do* believe you. I just don't want you to be right. Or put yourself in danger. But, I'm your boyfriend, too. Of course I'll help."

"You are?" I stopped in my tracks.

"What? Helping you?"

"No. The other part. The boyfriend part."

"I am? Aren't I?"

It was really hard, but I managed not to grin from ear to ear. "Maybe. I'll consider it. Maybe. Yes. Okay. You is." I might have grinned. "Can we go save the other one now?"

"Yes."

"No." Rome answered.

"No?" We said in unison.

"Not until we arm ourselves, inform Tatsuo and my mother, and come up with a plan to get to the underworld."

"Your sister knows the way and you don't?"

"My sister is a Priestess of Hel. I am but the head of the family. Her ties to Helheim are greater than mine, but I still command the family. Just as my mother can expel me from school."

Made sense in a roundabout, dysfunctional sort of way. "I'm good with that. Maybe Uncle Tatsuo or your mother will know the way."

"I already know," Hiroki said quietly.

We all turned to stare at him incredulously. "Care to share? Cuz sharing is caring."

"We take a cab…"

"Charon," Rome, Remy, and I said in unison…

Chapter 23

Four in the back, one in the front wasn't as kinky as it sounded when you were talking about cab seats. Rome and Remy were on the outside seats in the back, Roki in the middle, and I was kind of halfway draped between Hiroki and Remy. Geri was in the front, happily ignoring the rest of us. She might be mine, but she wasn't exactly thrilled about it.

I sighed and leaned back against my boys, ready for the cab ride from hell. No, that would be the return trip. I was ready for the cab ride *to* hell.

Sitting there, winding through the mountains, I played back in my head everything Uncle Tatsuo had told us. Headmistress Lateran was nowhere to be found, but he didn't seem overly concerned for her well-being. It was us he was worried about. Especially me. "Kaede...if anything happens to *you*."

"It won't be the end of the world! Literally!"

He hadn't appreciated my joke.

He had reminded me exactly what my mother would do to him should anything horrific happen to me. I'd tried to make the argument for having a fucking dragon go with us, but the look he gave me was enough to quell that idea. Guess he wasn't too worried about pissing off my mother. He'd even come up with some sort of bullshit excuse about tipping the scales of blah, blah, blah if he even put one claw

263

inside the boundaries of the underworld. Sounded like a bucket of dragon shit to me, but I wasn't about to argue with someone with teeth longer than me.

Sighing, I put my head against Remy's shoulder and stared at the immaculate ceiling inside the cab. That was the first giveaway that it wasn't a human cab. There was no gum stuck to it. "You smell good," I told Remy without looking up at him.

He didn't respond.

I have this thing about being ignored, especially by my boyfriend. I don't like it. Especially since I hadn't done anything wrong. Lately. Being my usual charming, and playful, self, I reached over and pinched his nipple.

"Ow! What the hell is wrong with you?"

"Rome?" I looked up at his face and then around Roki. Remy was sitting there waving at me, trying *very* hard not to laugh. "Oops. Why didn't you tell me you weren't you?"

"In what fucking world does that sentence make sense?"

"The under? I don't know. I thought you were Remy. Why didn't you tell me to get the hell off you when I draped myself across you like you were my therapist's couch?"

"You have a therapist?"

"Several."

"Find better ones."

"Tried."

He chuckled and looked back out the window, watching the mountains pass us by. "We should be there soon," he said ominously. Almost sounding worried.

"Ima go lay on your brother. He likes it when I pinch his nipples."

"You do that."

"I will."

"Good."

"Fine," I said and turned around, squishing Roki's giblets as I moved across his lap. He shot me a dirty look.

264

"It's not that far to Hell. You could have stayed where you were. I was enjoying watching my brother being so uncomfortable," Remy whispered.

"I can hear you, Rem."

"I know," he whispered again. "Just admit it. You liked having the fox on your lap."

Rome turned and shot him a look of pure disgust. *But* the corner of his mouth twitched, almost like he was battling a…smile? Surely, I was mistaken.

"It's cold. She's warm. And she doesn't smell unpleasant."

"Awww. You're so sweet," I said and put my feet on his lap, leaning against Remy and grinning.

Rome turned and looked out the window, ignoring my using him as a footrest. I snuggled up against Remy's shoulder, enjoying his warmth and giving Roki a sad smile. I was worried about David and felt a little guilty about playing games with Rome. Rome and Remy had assured me that he was safe, that in some deep, sick, twisted way, Sabine truly cared for David. She was just using him as bait. I just hoped they were right.

"Something is worrying me," Rome said and didn't turn to look at us. The fear in my stomach welled to twice its original size.

"What?" I wanted to reach over and turn his head to see his face, but I would have had to use my foot. He might not appreciate that.

"Why is Tatsuo letting you go to the underwold?"

"What do you mean, brother?" Remy shifted beneath me.

Rome turned to look at *him*. It made me a little jealous. "I'll be honest…"

"Need a drink first?" I grinned at him. His eyes flickered to me for a moment, but he resisted the urge to plink me in the forehead for being a snot.

"I took you to his office to tell him of your plan so he could talk you out of it."

My eyes narrowed in anger. "You'd leave your friend in the hands of your psychopathic sister in *hell*? What the hell is wrong with you?"

"I did not say that. I said I wanted him to talk *you* out of going. I would still have made the journey to rescue him. I'm also sure Remy would have gone with me."

"You're worried about me?" I stared in disbelief.

"No." He shifted in his seat uncomfortably. "I'm worried about you being physically in the same realm as Fenrir."

"Uh huh. Promise not to let the doggy off his leash while we're there."

"That's not what I'm afraid of."

"What?"

"His body lies in Helheim, his Consciousness, even sleeping, lies in the temple of Midgard. I'm worried about him following you to Helheim."

"Oh."

"Yes."

"Should I wait in the car?"

"You would?"

"No. But thanks for playing."

He sighed and nodded. "I didn't think so."

"If Uncle Tatsuo isn't worried, you shouldn't be, either."

"That's what I'm afraid of," he answered cryptically and turned back toward the window. "We're here," he said and sat up rigidly.

I leaned forward to look out his window. We were over a fucking volcano. "Um…" The cab turned and we were plummeting sideways, heading straight for the base of it. I managed not to scream. Barely. "Tell me we're not going inside. Tell me we're not going inside."

"We're going inside," Rome answered.

266

"I told you not to fucking tell me that!" I punched him in the arm. He laughed. I should have pinched his nipple. Apparently, they were sensitive.

I looked out the windshield, over the seat and fought not to turn green and puke on Rome. We were going *really* fast and weren't showing any signs of slowing. Even when we were about to slam into the base of it. By the time I saw the cave, I was already hyperventilating. And I might have peed a little. *Sorry, Roki.*

The cave curved downward and we splashed down onto a river. The cab miraculously floated on the surface as everything around us flared brightly with blue flames, not unlike my fox fire. "The River Styx," I whispered breathlessly.

The Charon driving turned and nodded over his shoulder, his face taking on an unearthly skeletal visage. It would probably be impolite to tell him to keep his eyes on the river and wear a hoodie, so I kept my mouth shut.

I leaned over Remy and looked out his window. The river was pitch black, only illuminated by the fires skimming its surface. Oily, black hands reached out to glide their greasy fingers along the side of the cab, some of them had nails long enough to make me shudder from the noise it made as they scratched the metal.

"You okay?" Remy gently touched my cheek.

"Yeah. I just *really* want to go swimming right now, but I didn't bring my bathing suit. So, I'm kinda bummed."

"We could go skinny dipping later…"

I grinned at him and wiggled my eyebrows. "Tell you what, when we get David back and everyone home safely, I'll take you up on that. But it has to be a hot spring or no go."

"Deal!" He sealed it with a kiss.

The thought, and the kiss, sent a shiver down my spine that caressed my nether regions… I might have peed a little. Okay, it wasn't pee. *Sorry, Roki.*

Sighing, I leaned back against Remy and sat quietly for the remainder of the short journey through the Tunnel of Crud. I sat back up when we slowed and drifted toward a dock of skull encrusted stone.

"Land of the Dead," the Charon said with a crackly voice and the two passenger side doors opened. Geri practically leaped from her seat, not that I blamed her. She was the one sitting next to Skeletor. Rome stepped out and held out a hand for me. I assumed it was for me. Unless he was all about the Roki, which I would have been fine with, too, as long as I got to watch. Grabbing his hand, he pulled me from the cab, not letting go as Remy and Roki got out on their own.

"I'm okay," I told Rome, staring at my hand in his. He coughed and let go.

We'd done it. We made it to Hell in one piece. Now we just needed to figure out *where* in the hell we needed to go.

"Let's go," Rome said quietly, almost whispering.

"Where?" I finally voiced my concerns.

"To find Sabine?"

"Do you have a map?"

"No. Something better," he said and shifted, sniffing the air around us.

"Ahh. The Bitch Tracker 9000. Glad you brought yours."

He huffed and started walking up the stone steps, his paws barely fitting on the shallow ledges and taking three of them at a time.

"Want a ride?" Remy's voice slid silkily into my ear.

"Here? Now? Shouldn't we find David first?"

He chuckled and shifted too, holding a leg out for me to step on. He was such a gentlehound.

"Why, thank you, kind sir." I scrambled up his back and put my leg over his fur covered muscle, settling myself behind his head and putting my hands on either side to steady myself. "You coming, Roki? Geri?"

"I shall run."

"Suit yourself. Can't believe you're passing up an opportunity to have a hot guy between your legs, but if you're uncomfortable with it…"

"Kaede-*sama*?"

"Yes, Roki-*kun*?"

"Shut up."

That was the first time in my life he had ever told me to shut up. He'd asked for me to stop talking, of course. Everybody I knew had at one point or another. But for the words "shut" and "up" to be used consecutively with such commanding intent… I kind of liked it. "You know that's not gonna happen. But that was kind of hot. Say it again."

He chuckled, rolled his eyes, and shook his head.

I looked down at Geri. She had watched our exchange with a curious look on her face. "Want a ride?"

She bowed politely before shaking her head. "I will run with your friend."

Remy took off after Rome, the jerking motion catching me off guard. I'd never even ridden a horse, let alone a dog. The experience was…yeah. Kind of frightening, but the motions beneath me were… Let's just say why I finally understood the whole bareback movement popular among women riders. By the time we stopped, I was leaning against his head, smiling lazily and tracing circles through his fur.

"Why are we stopping?"

Rome shifted back, hastily making shushing noises with his hand and lips. I slid down off Remy's back and crept over to the now crouching and hiding behind a rock, Rome. He was peering around it and I looked over his shoulder. Skeletal guards were blocking a passage through the rock. I thought somebody had left them to rot, but their heads were moving, looking for intruders with empty eye sockets.

"What are we going to do?"

"I don't know. If we fight them, we might alert an army."

"Aren't you a hellhound? Can't you just tell them to bugger off or something?"

"Hellhounds are guardians. We keep people from going where they shouldn't."

"Bang up job, too," I mumbled under my breath. The look he gave me was unpleasant, and yet pleasant at the same time. He was angry, but he was kind of hotter when he was angry. "Well it's not like there's another hole through the giant stone wall that seems to be in the way of the direction we need to go. Don't doggies like bones?"

"Not when they're moving. And dusty."

"Fine. Watch this."

I reached into my blazer jacket and plucked one of the leaves I kept there for such emergencies. Turning myself invisible, I quickly headed for the corpse corps. Each spell I cast on myself lasted for a certain amount of time, depending on the intricacy of the magic. Invisibility lasted for only a few moments, otherwise it would have been first and foremost in my repertoire. School would have been *way* more fun if I could turn invisible all the time. But I probably would have been expelled by the end of the first day.

As quickly as I could, I ran to the one in the center, picked up a rock and bashed it in the side of its skull. The others immediately went on alert. I hoped the one in the center would think one of the others had done it and started a Three Stooges comedy routine, but they didn't. They spread out and started looking for intruders.

I threw another large rock off to the side behind a formation of stalagmites. My plan worked, and all but two of them went to investigate. But then my spell ran out of juice and I popped back into existence before they disappeared.

"Fuck."

The two standing closest to the fissure passage pulled their swords and charged me. I squeaked and called my katana, narrowly missing blocking both of their slashing attacks.

"Great plan," Rome said snidely and shifted behind me, batting one of the skeletons away while I managed to remove the skull of the other with my sword. The remaining dozen or so, rushed back, swords drawn.

Remy barreled through them like bowling pins. With swords. A couple of them got some nasty slashes in mid-charge, but he brushed it off as he and his brother began a coordinated attack that left me breathless. Roki was right behind them, separating skulls from neckbones with his katana. Until the day I died, or even after that, I would never tire of watching his swordplay. I was good, he was exponentially better. He had to be, since he lacked most of the combat magics because of his *nogitsune* lineage.

Even Geri had shifted and was tearing them apart, limb from limb. When the last one had been reduced to two-hundred-and-six individual pieces, we all turned nervously to the gaping hole through the wall. Nothing came through, no horns of alarm were blaring, and we sighed in relief we hadn't been discovered.

I looked down at the pile of bones at Remy's feet. "Ikea skeleton!"

Rome smacked me in the back of the head. "Don't help!"

"Hey. I distracted some of them momentarily for a little bit while you got in position to decimate them with your mighty paws!"

He shook his head, his eyes never leaving me as he fought not to scream in frustration. "Gah!" He stomped off, throwing his hands up in the air and shaking his fists.

"I think he likes you," Remy said with a chuckle as he passed by me to follow his brother through the fissure.

"You guys are going for the same hole? Kinky!" I grinned at Roki and headed after them.

Slamming into one of their backs, I rubbed my nose and stepped around them. "Give a girl some warning when you stop…"

Exiting through the hole, I'd stepped out onto a wide mesa, overlooking the City of the Dead. Hellheim. The underworld.

The brownish stone beside us muted into mottled grays and blacks the closer it got to the walled fortress of a thousand spires. The cavern above it had to have been over a thousand feet high and green lights twinkled among the murderous stalactites above. No movement could be seen behind the obsidian walls surrounding the city, but purple, blue, and black flames twinkled everywhere we looked. It was beautiful. It was scary. It was the most impressive thing I'd ever seen. And I'd seen Remy, David, and Hiroki naked in the same bed.

"That's really far away. And how the hell are we going to find her once we get there? And did anybody bring any food? I'm like *really* hungry. And I have to pee."

All four of them turned and stared at me.

"What?"

"You're like a little fucking kid sometimes."

"That makes you a perv. I see how you look at me."

"Like I want to strangle you?"

"Uh, that's not really my kink. But you can call me names and spank me if you want." I grinned at him.

Remy coughed as his brother turned crimson red and then shifted to the ultraviolet spectrum. "Seriously? Can you not take *anything* seriously?"

I glanced down just below his belt, cocked an eyebrow, and looked back up at him. "Nerp."

"Nerp? What the hell is a nerp?"

"Do not get her started," Hiroki stepped behind me and covered my mouth with his hand. I licked it like Stitch licking a window, but he held fast, and I was getting saliva all over my face. It's much less fun when it's your own.

Rome calmed down and shook his head. "Sabine is in that direction." He pointed at the city. "I won't know where exactly until we get in there. Do we go, or do we go back?"

"Gmof," I muttered behind Roki's hand.

"You are sure?"

I nodded. It was easier than talking. Less messy, too.

"All right. Let's go."

Roki let go of my face and we started marching toward the city. "Seriously though. Does anybody have like a Snickers Bar or something?"

"Shut up!"

"Cuz Rome needs a snickers bar. He's an asshole when he's hungry."

Chapter 24

Getting into the city was easier than getting into the cavern. There were guards, but not outside the wall. They were inside, almost like their job wasn't to keep people out, but *in*. It was a city of the dead, that was probably the case. We'd just need to figure out if getting home was going to be a problem later. If we survived.

"Where is everybody?" One of the twins kept looking around suspiciously. It was pissing me off how much trouble I was having telling them apart. If I didn't identify one and keep my eyes on him, or if Rome wasn't telling me I was stupid and yelling at me, I had to ask who was who. Their hair, their clothes, their stance…all identical. *Maybe I should just kiss them and then gauge their reaction. That could be fun.*

But whichever one asked where everyone was, was right. The giant empty city was more than a little creepy. "I don't know. Maybe it's bingo night at the First Church of Hel?"

"That's Tuesdays. It's only Monday," Remy answered. It had to be Remy. Rome didn't have a sense of humor. I bounced and walked over to him, clinging to his arm to keep them straight.

"Can I help you?"

"Rome?'

He nodded.

I sighed. "When did you get a sense of humor?"

"They were in the gumball machine by the front gate. You didn't buy one?"

"I used my quarters at the laundromat."

"Should have told me. I would have bought you one. Hel knows you could use one." He grinned at his insult. I, personally, gave it a seven out of ten, but I was proud of him. Subtle, with just a hint of witticism.

"I buy in bulk off eBay. Gumball senses of humor lose their flavor after eighteen seconds. Then you have to spit it out."

His face fell and I felt kind of bad.

"So, which way do we go, George?"

He looked at me still clinging to his arm and I let go. At least he didn't shift while I was holding him. That might have been kind of awkward. Rome shifted and sniffed. Remy came up to me and offered me his arm. "Is this what you wanted?"

"Yes. Why can't I tell you two apart anymore?" I shot him a worried glance.

He just smiled.

"What?"

"Tell you later."

"Let us go," Hiroki said and motioned to the retreating backside of big, black, and fuzzy Rome.

Remy and I followed behind him, arm in arm, Geri off to our right, and Hiroki followed behind us, guarding our rear. Or looking at them. I shook mine just in case it was the latter. Having multiple boyfriends was a lot more fun than I thought it would be.

"Focus, Kaede."

Guess he was staring at my ass. Just to tease him, I shifted into my demi form, letting my tails lift the back of my skirt as they fanned out behind me. My ears began flicking around and I stopped cold, Remy jerking me forward with my unexpected stop.

"What is it?"

I let go of his arm, sounds assaulting me from all directions. Rome stopped and looked back at me over his big doggy shoulder, unconcerned about the cacophony surrounding us. "Do you not hear that?" I asked him.

He shifted back. "Hear what?"

"Roki?"

He let his ears and tails out, flicking around as they listened. "I hear nothing, Kaede-*sama*..."

How they could *not* hear it was beyond me. Moaning, chains shuffling, feet dragging... It was the soundtrack of a zombie movie and I was about to piss my panties. They were *close*, too. "They're here," I whispered.

"Kaede, shift your eyes..."

I looked at Hiroki, shaking my head in fear. I didn't want to. It was bad enough that I could *hear* them. I didn't want to see what was around us.

"What's going on?" Rome sounded worried for me.

"Kaede is half inari fox as well as *kitsune*. She is a celestial messenger."

"We knew that," Remy said, nodding. "What does that mean for us right now?"

"She can see the celestial. The dead souls of this realm."

"They're all around us?"

I nodded in panic. "It's why the city seemed empty. It *is* a city of the dead. We just couldn't see them."

"We're hellhounds. The progeny of Hel, herself. Why wouldn't we be able to?"

"How the fuck should I know? What do we do?" I was failing to keep the panic out of my voice. Without realizing, I'd backed Remy and I up against one of the walls of the building.

"Shift your eyes, Kaede-*sama*. We need to know."

Remy tightened his grip on my arm and nodded at me encouragingly. I let my essence touch my eyes and almost

277

shit myself. We were surrounded by the souls of the dead. "I see dead people," I whispered.

"How many?" Rome asked like it fucking mattered.

"Uh…all of them? We're surrounded."

"Can we hurt them? Can they hurt us?" Geri was making circles, staring in every direction and waiting for one of them to touch her.

"I don't *know*!"

One of them got close enough to Rome to reach out and touch his arm. He shrieked in pain and stepped away from the haggard soul.

"Yes! They can!" I nodded for emphasis.

Rome just sighed and shook his head, still holding his hand over the smoking wound in his arm. "How do we fight what we can't see?"

"Charge through them, swinging like madmen," Remy answered. "We take the lead and plow the way, track our sister, and get the hell out of here."

"Good plan." I squeezed his arm.

He nodded and looked at Geri and Hiroki. "Keep her safe." Then he shifted and stood by his brother as he did the same. They growled and started swiping souls in front of them. I sighed in disappointment. Their paws swished through them like smoke and they rematerialized a few feet away. They couldn't hurt them.

"Not gonna work! They're just moving out of the way!"

We were officially fucked.

Even Fenrir, who normally imparted words of wisdom during such moments of oh fuckery, was eerily silent. His body might be in hell, but his soul wasn't. I guessed he had difficulty with long distance calls. Probably didn't want to pay the fees. He should have opted for the interdimensional plan. It saved you a *ton* of money in the long run.

"Try your celestial fire, Kaede-sama…"

I couldn't exactly blast it out of my hand like a flame thrower. I could either do little floaty balls or call it to my hand, and I sure as shit wasn't touching them damn things. Either way it wouldn't be very effective against the horde of souls surrounding us.

"Katana!"

"Huh?"

Hiroki sighed and almost stomped his foot in frustration. "Use...your...sword."

"Oh. Why didn't you say that first?"

He did stomp his foot.

I called my katana and my celestial fire and let it slide up the blade. "Here goes nothing," I said and poured all the power I had into it. It flared a brilliant blue, leaving trails of fox fire in its wake like a light saber. I even made, "Jooo Jooo, Karaaaaak," noises as I swung the blade at the spirits surrounding us.

Wherever the blade touched, they dissipated into black smoke, but they shrieked and didn't reappear. It was working.

"What happens when you kill a soul in hell? Does it go to heaven or just kind of cease to exist?"

"How the hell should we know?" That was Rome. Definitely Rome.

"Well, it's working but I kinda feel bad."

"Just keep swinging!"

Using my blade, I stepped in front of the twins. They must have shifted back to make themselves smaller targets. I wasn't a very good shield.

"Which way?"

"Straight, go between the two largest spires and head for the highest building in the back. The one that looks like a temple. She's there. So is David. They're close enough to scent."

"Roger, Roger."

"Who's Roger?"

"You are," I answered and kept swinging, cutting a swath for us. The souls weren't stupid enough to not know that my swing was lethal, either. They started backing away and after a few more insta-kills, they fled the area. Thank the fucking fucks. My arms were sore, and I was sweating.

"You did it," Remy said and patted the top of my head. I lowered my sword but didn't feel comfortable enough to dispel it or the fire. Plus, it made a good torch and was kind of cool looking. I wondered if the school would let me run around the halls with it to show off.

We huddled together until we cleared the streets of Lower Detroit and made it to the stone steps leading up to the temple. Once we were there, I ran up the first couple, eager to get to David, but Remy stopped me with a hand on my shoulder.

"Go slow. We don't know what we're walking into. Whatever it is, it's most likely a trap."

I sighed and nodded, realizing the truth behind Remy's words. I dispelled my blade, leaned up on my tiptoes, and kissed him. I'd only meant it to be a peck, but my nerves got the best of me and I wrapped my arms around him, and it turned into something much, much hotter. Pulling away, I gave him a small smile and giggled at the confused look on his face. Then panic set in. I looked around him on the stairs and his twin was laughing his ass off.

"Rome?" I looked up again, afraid of what I would see.

He was turning red and struggling to form words. I kissed the wrong one again. "Oh, come on. Wear a fucking bell or something!" I turned around and took another step, waiting for them to follow me. At least I lightened the mood. Even Geri was chuckling as we traversed the multitude of steps.

At least, with everybody behind me, not one of them could see the blush that had crept up to *my* cheeks.

Finally, we reached the landing and I peeked over the ledge before fully exposing myself to whatever was waiting for us. There was no sign of Sabine. David, however, was lying unconscious–or so I hoped–on a stone altar in the middle of the open temple. The roof was supported by columns on all sides, leaving no room for anybody, or anything, to hide.

"David!" I ran into the temple.

As soon as my foot touched the first stone tile, the columns flared to life and shimmering walls of spectral purple flames coalesced, blocking anyone else from entering.

Sabine's high-pitched laughter echoed off the flame walls as if they were stone. Rome had been right. It was a trap and I walked into it like a stupid ass fox. Hopefully I wouldn't have to gnaw my leg off to get out of it.

I spun around in circles, calling my sword and flame back into existence, looking for the source of the laughter. She was nowhere to be seen.

"Show yourself, Sabine."

An arm slipped out of nothingness and sliced open my arm at the shoulder. My blazer took the brunt of the damage, but I could feel the sting of the slice and the blue blazer turned purple as my blood seeped into it. As quickly as it had attacked, the arm was gone, safely tucked into whatever pocket it had sprung from.

My fox ears twitched around the room, listening for the slightest of movements. The muffled shouts and yells from outside the walls urged me to be careful and let me know I wasn't alone. That I had people with me who cared about me, loved me, and were worried about me. It didn't do me much good cut off from them, but it gave me courage.

"So, this is how we're gonna play it? You're gonna rely on *sneak* attacks? Come out and fight me like a woman, you Amazonian coward."

"You're not worth my time. Plus, I like seeing you squirm like the rodent you are."

"Foxes aren't rodents, you hellish bitch. And you can't say you aren't a hellish bitch, because you're literally a female dog from hell. So, suck it, Sabina the Teenage Bitch."

"My name is Sabine!"

Her blade sliced across the material of my back and I ignored the pain, swinging my blade around me and nicking the tip of her dagger just as she pulled it back into nothingness. At least I hit a nerve with my verbal dig.

"David. Wake up!"

"He won't. Not until I release him from his slumber."

"Why did you take him? Had to resort to kidnapping to get a date with my boyfriend?"

"He's not your fucking boyfriend!"

"Oh, yeah he is. I had sooo much fun with him. He does this trick with his tongue… Oh. I probably shouldn't tell you this. You might get upset."

I took a chance and spun around, driving my sword down, but she didn't attack. I knew I'd pissed her off though, she was remaining eerily silent. It was time to up my game.

"Your brother, too. Holy shit, does he know how to make a Lady feel good…"

I had used the spin and strike. She would be expecting it again. This time, I fainted and sliced upward just as the dagger and hand were emerging, I'd gone for the hand, but she realized my feint. I hit the blade squarely this time, but she managed not to drop it. She screeched as the fire singed the hair on her knuckles, though. I chuckled.

"Yeah. You should have seen us. David, Remy, and Hiroki…all naked, sweaty, and sexy. Next time I'll take a video when it's just David and me. I'll play it for you in your little corner of Hell."

The shouts warned me of her attack. Instead of slicing, she was aiming for my heart, straight behind me. I rolled forward and came up, throwing my sword at the hand. She pulled it back, but my katana followed her through the hole. The handle and half the blade clattered to the ground before dissipating into nothingness.

She thought I was disarmed.

Big mistake.

She opened another portal to deliver the final blow, but she never got the chance. As soon as I saw the opening, I called my blade and fire and jammed them through the hole where her hand and dagger were just emerging. My blade pushed hers away and slid deeper into the hole, making a slick, wet, squelching sound as it slid home into her chest. I heard her gurgle from the opening.

The portal didn't close, it tore wider as it ripped through the fabric of reality and she flopped forward, slapping loudly against the ground in front of me. She didn't move, or even twitch. I hadn't meant to kill her, and I panicked as I reached down and grabbed her wrist, dragging her from the other space.

As soon as she was free, I rolled her over and the rip in space vanished with a *pop*. The front of her shirt was soaked in blood, but luckily, she was right-handed. My blade pierced her chest on the opposite side of her heart. My flames had even cauterized the wound. She wasn't dead, but she wouldn't be waking up anytime soon, either.

The walls fell and everyone rushed into the room. The twins converged on their sister, checking that she was still breathing. I was worried they would hate me–Rome even more than he already did–when they both looked up and nodded, knowing I had little choice. I gave them a sad smile before running over to David.

He was warm to the touch and breathing normally. I cried out in happiness as I leaned down and kissed him. When my lips touched his, they started moving and he kissed me back. "Kaede?"

"You better not be surprised it was me kissing you, Sleeping Beauty."

"Where am I? How did I get here? Why are you bleeding?"

"Long story. For later. Let's get the *hell* out of here," I said, chuckling at my own joke.

Helping him up, I slipped under his shoulder and walked him to the others. "Geri, help him."

"Yes, Kaede." She slipped under his other arm and he blinked in surprise seeing Sabine's buddy helping me.

"Long story," I said again to quell his confusion. "Let's get out of here."

The temple began to rumble, feeling like an earthquake had spawned beneath it. The sound of the ground tearing prodded everyone to run. One of the twins scooped his sister up and led the way.

"What in the hell?"

"Exactly." Hiroki nodded and grabbed my hand, dragging me behind David and Geri.

Please don't let me have woken Fenrir. Please don't let me have woken Fenrir.

"It's Hel," the other twin said from the ledge of the temple, looking down at the ground below. One giant paw had sprung from the ground and the other was trying to tear its way out. They weren't wolf paws. They were the paws of a hellhound. The largest hellhound I could have possible imagined. It had torn a quarter of the city apart as it tried to free itself from beneath.

"Is there another way out?" I asked, but the only person who might have known the answer was passed out in her brother's arms.

"Maybe," the other twin said and pulled a box from his blazer jacket. "A little insurance for a safe retreat, your uncle said." He opened the box and reached inside, pulling out a flute carved in the likeness of a dragon. He put it to his lips, dropping the box, and blowing a pure tone that echoed through the entire cavern.

"What do we do now?" I asked after he finished playing the dragon whistle.

"We wait? He didn't say what it did, just to blow it if we needed it."

For the first time in my fucking life, I refrained from making a joke. I was too scared to be funny. Hel had ripped open the earth enough to fit her big ugly doggy head through and I didn't want to end up god puppy chow.

I doubted the whistle would work. We were in a cavern, kami knows how deep, below an active volcano. There was no way Uncle Tatsuo would be flying in to save our asses from the jaws of doom.

"Look," the twin holding Sabine said, nodding at Hel.

With a resigned sigh, I looked over the ledge. I expected her to be ready to pounce, but she howled in rage as serpentine coils wrapped themselves around her, pulling her back into the earth.

"Jormungandr?"

They both shook their heads. "Fafnir," they answered reverently.

The story flooded into my brain. Fafnir was the son of a dwarf king that had been turned into a dragon when he donned a cursed ring... Made sense why there was a dragon underground in the pits of Helheim.

"Let's get the fuck out of here," I said deadpan and headed for the stairs, wanting nothing more than to get back to school. Even I saw the irony in that.

Epilogue

"Come on in," I said and held the door open, too tired for words.

Remy walked in, smiling at me, and I could almost feel the love pouring off him in waves. "You were amazing."

I blushed. I couldn't believe we had actually done it. Thanks to Uncle Tatsuo. He had beamed and pumped his fist as we sat in his office, regaling him with our tale. He simply nodded when we had told him about Hel emerging from the ground, almost as if he had been expecting it. That had been the reason he had sent along the Flute of Fafnir.

Of the twins' mother, there was still no trace. But Uncle Tatsuo seemed to still not be worried about her absence. I chalked it up to him sending her somewhere and not wanting to tell us about it. Not that I liked her or anything, but the twins were worried, and *that* bothered me. Especially with their sister locked up in the school dungeon, a dungeon I didn't even know existed. I might have been a little more well behaved if I had. Good deterrent. "Go to class, don't be an asshole, or we'll throw you in the dungeon." Way better than detention.

David was resting comfortably in the infirmary wing. He had woken up but was still suffering side effects from whatever spell Sabine had him under for so long. The nurse, whatever she was, seemed to think he would be fine but wanted to keep him under observation. I was a little disappointed. I wanted my David spoons. And forks.

Thankfully my wounds were quick to heal and I was more than ready for him to be released. Once I got a good night's sleep.

Geri's roommate, Steph, would be having detention from now until the end of the school year, but she wasn't going to be expelled or thrown in the dungeon. She counted herself lucky, apologized again to me, almost earnestly, and swore not to have anything to do with Sabine again until the day she died. She also would be on guard duty for a *very* long time. They'd even contracted another couple of hellhounds, not wanting to rely on the students since Fenrir was much more coherent than he'd been in the history of forever. I thought it was a damn fine idea, especially since it freed one of my boyfriends up at night.

"You wish to be alone?"

I sighed and kind of wanted to throttle Hiroki. Sometimes, he was just *too* damn considerate. "Hiroki, I never want you to feel like you have to run off. You're a part of me, too."

He nodded and relaxed on his bed. I was too tired to get frisky, anyway.

"Sit," I told Remy, motioning to my bed.

He plopped down, just as tired as I was, and leaned back against the headboard. I crawled back against him, leaning back against his chest and sighing comfortably, wishing my bathrobe was a little thinner. The heat from his chest was almost overwhelming and I was still a little damp from the shower.

"You smell amazing," he said into my ear.

I smiled, leaned back, and kissed his chin.

We might have been tired, but not too exhausted to kiss. His hand cupped my cheek and tilted me toward him. I rolled on my side and let him devour my mouth with his. I couldn't help myself, with the excitement of everything coming to a temporary close, I was giddy and happy.

There was a knock at the door. *Of fucking course, there is.*

"I shall get it." Hiroki got up from his bed and answered it. A moment later, he was back into the room with Rome.

Embarrassed, I rolled back over and made sure I was covered with my robe. Didn't need *him* seeing my drooling Kaede bits. The kiss was hot. "Hey, Rome. How you feeling?"

He blinked at me in confusion and looked up at his brother questioningly. I felt him shrug beneath me.

"Remy?"

Faux-Rome nodded.

I turned around behind me and Rome had a startled look on his face. "I thought you knew it was me?"

"You asshole!" I pinched his nipple.

"Kaede… I swear to you upon my very soul, I thought you knew it was me! I would never impersonate my brother to get closer to you."

"Wait. So, kissing me. You thought I was into you, too?"

"You're not?"

Oh, boy. "Rome…"

He blushed but didn't get angry. "I'm sorry."

"Rome…"

"Please, Kaede. Don't make this any more embarrassing than it already is. I don't think I can take it. I am *truly* sorry."

"Rome!"

"Kaede!"

"Rome!" I was done playing and locked both of his nipples between the thumb and forefinger of each of my hands.

He stared at me blankly.

"It's okay."

"Could you let go of my nipples now?"

Remy was sitting on Roki's bed, next to him. They had parked their butts to watch the Kaede and Rome Show. They

289

were both wiping their eyes. They both seemed to have trouble breathing.

"Well, I need to get going." Rome almost gently pushed me away from him and stood up, heading for the door. His retreat just caused Roki and Remy to laugh harder.

"Laugh it up, Jerky Boys," I said after narrowing my eyes at the pair.

"Jerky boys? As in dried meat?" Remy looked so confused.

"No. As in…" I made a male masturbatory gesture with my hand. "You can use lotion, so your meat doesn't get dried out, but you ain't getting nothing from me tonight!" I lurched off the bed to stop Rome from running away. He had already made it through the door and I shot out behind him, grabbing a fistful of blazer in my hand.

The door clicked shut behind me and we were alone in the hallway. I didn't know what to say to him. "Are you okay?"

"I'm fine."

Closing my eyes, I shook my head and let my forehead press against his chest. I couldn't look him in the eye. "I didn't know."

"I know. We're twins. It's not your fault."

"That's not what I'm talking about. I didn't know you were into me. You caught me completely off guard."

"And you don't like me…"

"Want the truth?"

"No. It's okay, little fox. I understand… I wasn't exactly nice to you."

Hearing the hurt in his voice, I finally did lift my head. "I wasn't exactly nice to you either. You tripped my asshole sensors the first time I met you. But don't run away mad. It's not that I don't *like* you, and I mean that in a purely I don't want to stab you in the face with a rubber dick kind of way. We went from enemies to frenemies. Somewhere along the lines we finally became friends, and I was actually *really* happy about that. With that said, I wouldn't be *opposed* to becoming...something more."

"You wouldn't?"

"Why would I? You're hot, when you're not scowling at me in frustration. You're nice, when you're not being mean to me. You're sweet, when you're not being a sourpuss–"

"I get it!"

"Do you? I know the Rome under all that crusty exterior and grumpy interior, is someone I could definitely see myself kinda falling in love with. One day. Not, *today*. Maybe next week, maybe next year. Maybe before we graduate. Maybe before global warming floods the planet and we all drown–"

It was hard to continue when he leaned down and silenced me with a soft kiss. "You talk way too damn much, little fox."

"And you don't talk enough, you dumb dog."

"Fair enough. So, friends for now and we'll work on things before we go any further?"

"That's a good plan. I like this plan." I stood on my tiptoes and grinned at him. "We'll call *that* plan 29-D!"

"I thought 29-D was you fall madly in love with me."

"Silly dog. That's 29-E. We have to get through the D first..."

He smiled at me, turned and headed for the stairs. I was grateful that I had run after him and we'd gotten through our little misunderstanding. He was learning. Never rush a *kitsune*. We did things at our own pace, in our own time. Leaning against the door to my bedroom, I smiled at his retreating back. There were also things I needed to learn. Like which Lateran brother was which. That was causing way too many embarrassing, make Kaede blush moments.

I fucking hate being embarrassed, I thought as the door to my bedroom opened and I fell inside.

About the Author

A late comer to the writing game, Jacquelyn had always been a fan of romance novels and lately become addicted to the reverse harem category. I mean seriously, who wouldn't? Sitting alone one night she flipped open her laptop and said, "I'm going to give this a whirl." And thus, the Lovin' the Coven series was given life. She has designs on other series as well, but only time shall tell.

As for her, she is five-foot-something, with graying hair, wicked eyes, an eager smile, and an annoying laugh. She lives at home with her dog, a cat, and that is about all she is comfortable sharing.

Other Works

Lovin' the Coven Series
(Reverse Harem- 7 book series)

First Moon
Second Blood
Third Charm
Fourth Rite
Fifth Essence
Sixth Sense
Seventh Seal

The Fox and the Hounds
(Reverse Harem – trilogy)

A Tail of Woah
A Tail of Two Kitties
The Tell Tail Heart